TAKING CHARGE

by

PETE & SHEILA THOMPSON

TOMSUN

PRESS

LLC

Taking Charge
Copyright © 2026 by Pete & Sheila Thompson.
All rights reserved.
Fonts from Adobe
"The Leader of the Luddites" (1812) is a work in the public domain. The original text is reproduced from public domain sources.

Our talented niece, Hannah Wilson, designed the cover of our book. We thank her, our editor, P. J. Hoover, and all of our pre-readers for their assistance and candid feedback.

For more information, contact
Tomsun Press LLC
tomsunpress@thompso.net
psthompson.com

ISBN: 979-8-9942750-1-6 (trade paperback)
ISBN: 979-8-9942750-2-3 (hardcover)
ISBN: 979-8-9942750-0-9 (ebook)

First edition: March 2026

This book is dedicated to our children. May
you remain curious, keep learning, and find
the courage to follow your passions.

TABLE OF CONTENTS

*Between intention and action
lies a shadow
where doubt and consequence take root.*

—Inspired by T.S. Eliot's The Hollow Men

PROLOGUE

Two Years Ago

The first time the alarm clock sounded, her hand reached out and slapped the snooze button immediately. The second time it went off, she threw her pillow at it, pulled the covers over her head and rolled over. But the pillow didn't smother Sia singing "Unstoppable", the teenage girl's morning wake up tune. She begrudgingly rolled out of bed and stepped into the shower to get ready for her babysitting job.

By the time she made it out the door she was running late. She quickly pulled her long blonde hair into a low ponytail, secured her bike helmet, then sped off, anxiously peddling toward her babysitting job. The music blasting on her AirPods kept her focused on chasing the beat of the song, making her legs spin faster and faster. She had promised that she would be on time to watch the kids because Mrs. Hensley had an important meeting that morning. So, she raced her bike down the street, barely slowing down when she approached the four-way intersection in the residential neighborhood.

Her peripheral vision darkened as a car entered the intersection at the same time. The car did not swerve or alter the direction of its path. There was no warning sound of screeching brakes. No horn blasted in alert. The only noise was the violent impact of metal-on-metal followed by a sickening thud as her body flew onto the car's hood then hit the pavement forcefully.

A man walking his dog witnessed the accident and instinctively dropped the leash and ran to the teenager's side. Her body lay perfectly still on the hard asphalt– twisted awkwardly in a silent, broken heap; but she had a pulse. Blood seeped from under her helmet, turning her blonde ponytail a sickening crimson. The dog walker frantically dialed 911 on his cell phone as he stood up to investigate the car to check on the driver. A man in business attire, clearly en route to work, sat rigid behind the wheel with wide eyes, a pale face, and his mouth hanging slack in shock. His hands gripped his phone in front of him as he had been in the middle of sending a text at the time of the accident.

The self-driving car had failed to detect the girl on the bike in time.

The man's text was never sent.

The girl's life was forever altered.

An hour later Tess's phone vibrated in the pocket of her spa robe hanging on the back of the door, interrupting her state of relaxation.

"Damn it," she swore silently, mad at herself for not keeping her phone in the locker with her purse and clothes.

Desperate to relish every moment of her much-needed massage, Tess ignored the incessant vibration. She'd just completed her master's thesis after burning the candle at both ends for months and was celebrating with a relaxing spa treatment. The lights in the treatment room were dimmed, soothing music played on the speakers, and the table was warm and cozy underneath Tess as the masseuse methodically kneaded the tension out of her back. Tess drifted off to sleep when the sound of her phone vibrated yet again. Indignantly, she ignored her phone and focused on the last ten minutes of her deep-tissue treatment.

When Tess finally exited the treatment room and shuffled in her slippers back to the women's locker room to get changed, she grabbed her phone out of the pocket of her spa robe. Her world turned upside down. She could barely figure out what her father was saying in his voicemail because his voice was so thick with tears and his broken words incomprehensible. But she heard the words *sister, hospital,* and *critical condition.* Her relaxed back stiffened and her jaw clenched as tears spilled from her eyes. Tess couldn't believe she had ignored those calls earlier. It was stupid and selfish. Shaking with anxiety, she threw on her clothes and collected her belongings. She raced down the hall to the reception area, slapped more than enough cash onto the counter, and bolted out the door, praying she'd make it to the hospital in time.

ONE

TIME TICKS BY

Present Day, Santa Cruz, California

"Six more minutes for this set," Shep yelled out over the booming music and the sound of weights slamming onto the ground in the gym where three members were doing power clean lifts.

Are you kidding me? Mariana thought, checking her heart rate as she hopped up and down, attempting to complete as many box jumps as she could. *I'm never going to hit my number.* She clenched her teeth and forced her legs to move faster, pushing herself to get close to her personal record.

Tess, drenched with sweat, pulled the handle in unison with her legs as fast as she could on the rowing machine. She bit down on her lower lip and grunted as her muscles screamed at her in fatigue.

The six minutes until they could change stations ticked by–slowly.

Ben Shepman, known to everyone as Shep, walked around to the different CrossFit stations, encouraging everyone to keep pushing themselves and adjusting their form to avoid injury. He was the head instructor and owner of the gym.

Thirty minutes later, the class finally ended. The sore, fatigued muscles of all the participants contradicted their adrenaline high from the extreme workout. Mariana and Tess sat on floor mats to stretch as their shaky, wired bodies normalized after the intense physical activity.

"That was brutal," Tess said. "I never thought the class was going to end."

Mariana leaned over her legs and grabbed her toes. "You aren't kidding! I'm wiped out. I just hope I have the energy for my meeting this morning with Raj and the new potential client."

"Why does he want a software engineer at a sales meeting anyway?"

"We're trying to land a deal to place multiple electric-vehicle charging stations at convenience stores nationwide, and with Joel out on family leave, he asked me to sit in on the meeting. I guess the client has a lot of technical questions about how the software updates remotely." Joel was the head of engineering and Mariana's boss. When he went on leave, Raj Anand, the CEO of Cell-Spot, appointed Mariana to temporarily lead the team.

"Well, we better shower and get going so we aren't late."

The two retreated to the women's locker room to get ready for work. When Mariana changed into her work attire, she looked dramatically different. She had walked into Shep's Gym that morning in her athletic tights and tank top with her long black hair swept up in a messy ponytail and walked out of the locker room as a beautiful force to be reckoned with. Her silk blouse gently hugged her figure, softening her athletic shoulders and highlighting her hazel-green eyes. Her black pencil skirt revealed her long, muscular legs that didn't require stockings because her golden-brown skin was silky smooth. The outfit was complete with patent leather heels that added three more inches to her already five-foot-eight height. She didn't normally dress formally for work, but she had been specifically told to wear professional attire for the client meeting.

"I'll be right there," she told Tess, who was heading out the door to the parking lot. "I want to ask Shep a question." Tess and Mariana were college roommates at UCLA. After graduating, Mariana went to work for Cell-Spot in Mountain View, California, while Tess attended UC Berkeley to get her Master of Engineering degree. Even though they were relatively close in proximity, they didn't see each other very often over the course of those two years. Recently, the two of them spent a significant amount of time together, working at the same company and sharing an apartment.

"Take your time," Tess replied. "I'm not the one who

has a meeting with our CEO, *Mr. Uptight*, at the office this morning."

Mariana laughed and strolled by Shep's office, popping in to thank him for the workout and to catch one more glimpse of the man who occupied her dreams every night. At six-foot-three with a body chiseled to perfection, wavy brown hair highlighted naturally from the sun, and striking blue eyes, Shep's physical presence captured the attention of many inside and outside the gym. More captivating though was his ability to make everyone feel empowered to be their best. He was a hard trainer and expected his clients to strive for constant improvement. His intoxicating nature motivated people, and his gym made everyone feel welcome.

Shep looked up from his cluttered desk and did a double take, practically choking on his protein drink when he saw Mariana.

"Wow, you clean up nicely," he managed to say without spitting up his drink. "Are you off to something special today?"

Mariana's eyes lit up from his reaction, and with a slow smile, she nodded. "Yep. Meeting with a new potential client at work. Thanks for the great workout today. I was wondering if tomorrow morning we could meet a few minutes before class to talk about how I can keep seeing improvements in my workouts. I feel like I've hit a plateau."

"Absolutely," responded Shep.

"Great. I'll see you tomorrow morning," said Mariana.

"Yeah...catch you later," Shep replied as he watched

her walk out the door.

Mariana crossed the parking lot and carefully climbed into Tess's beat-up old Chevy SUV.

"When are you going to get a new car?" Mariana complained to Tess. "If this thing breaks down on the way to my meeting, I'll never get over it."

Tess laughed, rubbed her dashboard, and replied, "Scout has been great to me over the years. I can't afford a new car, and I have no intention of trading him in. He still has many more miles left, so don't offend him. Anyway," Tess continued as she drove out of the parking lot, "did you talk to your heartthrob on the way out? When are you going to get the nerve to just ask him out?"

Mariana groaned, "Ugh–I wish I could. I just don't want to mess up our friendship, and I certainly don't want to make it awkward. What if he says no, or we go out and it's a huge flop?"

"I doubt that will happen. I've caught him checking you out on the sly."

"Well, I'm not willing to cross that line. Anyway, I don't have time to date anyone. I'm slammed at work."

Tess took the on-ramp to Highway 17, leaving Santa Cruz to begin their daily commute over the winding mountain road. Within minutes, she brought the car to a full stop.

"Oh, you've got to be kidding me," moaned Mariana. "Why is traffic so bad this morning? I cannot be late, or Raj will kill me."

TWO

THE FIRST TEST

One Year Ago, Europe

Two men sat in a mountain chalet deep in the Swiss Alps, at a private retreat overlooking a picturesque view of the snow-capped mountains. They were alone in the room in front of a vast picture-window highlighting the panoramic view of the frosty white mountainside glistening in the sun. A roaring fire in the corner created a warm ambiance and cast dancing shadows on the walls. It had been a while since they last met in person, so they began their conversation by enjoying a glass of the finest Balvenie 40-year-old scotch.

One of the men, dressed in an expensive tailored suit, clearly the leader, took another sip of his scotch. He smiled politely at the other man, known to him as *the specialist*, then spoke with a strong Spanish accent–an accent the specialist had learned to revere as well as dread. "The test was extremely successful. We now have confidence that we can manipulate these types of industrial control systems. Our partners in various countries have proven helpful in keeping our group's involvement unknown and in shifting the blame to suspected governments. We are ready to proceed with the next stage of the program as soon as you get us access."

The specialist put his glass down, nodded approvingly, and responded, "Thank you. The team did exceptional work. I have read the news articles. They report it exactly as you prescribed and make it clear it resulted from an enemy government action." He then paused to regain his composure. "We are working on gaining access to the new target company. It is difficult to assign a precise timeline, and it may be several months. As soon as I have confirmation, I'll let you know, and we'll proceed."

"Hmm," said the leader. "We may have a good access point. I'll have one of my American contacts reach out to you to discuss the possibility."

"Great," said the specialist. "If the first stage is successful, then we'll move to a full-scale implementation. At that point, I will need your help with other aspects of the program. We must be ready to influence the press and government agencies. Timing will be critical."

The leader contemplated the next set of actions while admiring the beautiful natural mountain landscape. He crossed his legs and clasped his hands together. After a few drawn-out moments, he turned back to the specialist. "Tell me more about what steps are required."

The specialist leaned forward in his chair, stared straight at him to convey confidence, and described the challenges that lay ahead. He went through all the details and tried to explain the technical aspects in simple terms. He knew the leader came across as a gentleman but was nothing of the sort. If the leader lost confidence in him, he would never be seen again. The leader first hired him for a project several years before. Since then, the specialist had completed various assignments, but this current project was the biggest and riskiest by far. He admired the leader. Although he had a Jekyll and Hyde personality, he was also well-educated and articulate, and relished in providing context and historical examples to prove his point.

The leader had been watching the specialist with a mix of curiosity and skepticism. He considered all the sequential steps the specialist laid out and determined that the risk was manageable. However, to reinforce his power and to instill motivational fear in the other man, the leader's face hardened, and his eyes turned cold as he stoically commented, "We have a lot riding on this operation. It cannot fail. We're putting faith in you to succeed. Don't let us down and keep me updated on progress along the way. No surprises will be tolerated." The specialist nodded, acknowledging the implicit threat and significance of his responsibility in this operation.

With no contextual transition, the leader changed the subject. "Tell me, what do you think is man's nature?"

The specialist gazed at him for a few seconds, unsure how to respond and tried to figure out what he should say. Finally, he reacted, "Well, I haven't really thought much about it. I guess I would say it is innocent initially and therefore inherently good. However, we are all influenced by external experiences as we grow up, and this can change our nature and make us more negative and cynical about society."

The leader gave a dismissive nod and said, "Your belief aligns with the great French philosopher Jean-Jacques Rousseau, who lived in the 1700s and greatly influenced the French Revolution. He believed people are naturally good but corrupted by society to become evil and unhappy. I have given this much thought over the years. Philosophers have debated this topic for thousands of years. In ancient Greece, Socrates, Plato, and Aristotle spent years observing people and forming opinions on this matter. Socrates, unlike you, did not believe that people are born innocent with a blank slate. He thought that the soul of man lived across different people, and each new person had to recollect what had been learned previously. If they did this and invested in educating themselves, they would truly know what is right versus wrong and would take actions that are inherently good."

The specialist, trying to stay focused on the conversation, nodded to show his attention. The leader continued, "China developed its own philosophy around man's nature from the early teachings of Confucius. Confucius's two famous disciples, Mencius and Xunzi, believed that people must cultivate and influence human nature, but they differed on the starting point. Mencius believed people started as inherently good, and Xunzi believed the opposite."

Not wanting to say the wrong thing, the specialist chose to turn the tables. "What do *you* believe is man's nature?"

The leader stared intently at the specialist with a supercilious expression, paused for several seconds, and then spoke in a calming voice. "I am most aligned with the 17th-century English philosopher Thomas Hobbes. He believed people to be inherently selfish. They have a relentless desire for power, and fear is a motivating factor. Hobbes demonstrated how people participate in acts of kindness, but it is a mask for their self-interest. People need the rule of law and strong leadership. They need a governor to regulate these negative tendencies and to keep the balance. Hobbes called this leadership the Leviathan." He hesitated deliberately before completing his commentary. "This is why we are here today."

After letting his words hang in the air momentarily, the leader's pursed lips softened, transforming his arrogant demeanor to charming host. He poured them both another drink and switched the subject to discuss less profound topics. The meeting ended shortly thereafter, and the two exited the building and disappeared back the way they had come.

The next day the specialist's phone rang. After checking the incoming number, he picked it up and said hello.

"I heard you need an entry point to gain access to the target company," said the American contact.

"Yes."

"A former student of mine might be perfect. She was on my research team at UCLA years ago and later interned at my company when she was in graduate school. She's currently working at the target company as a software engineer."

"Excellent," said the specialist. "Tell me more..."

BREAKING NEWS

Hackers Remotely Shut Down Central Heating Units Across Apartments in Ukraine and The Czech Republic

CyberWatch
March 14, 2024

For several days in the heart of winter, citizens in Ukraine and the Czech Republic were without heating in sub-zero temperatures. Authorities have recently disclosed that this resulted from a successful cyberattack via the internet to remotely access commercial building centralized heating, ventilation, and air conditioning systems (HVAC) in almost a thousand apartment units. By manipulating the actual temperature settings with erroneous readings, hackers were able to trick the systems into not turning on despite the extreme cold. The attack targeted established industrial control systems, called Modbus, that are supposed to be resilient to attacks. Authorities have charged no one and are being careful not to point the finger directly at Russia, even though the IP addresses on the devices originated from Moscow. Authorities are checking other industrial control systems across Ukraine and the Czech Republic for similar vulnerabilities, and caution that this type of cyberattack could be implemented against any industrial control system that uses Modbus.

THREE

TIME WILL TELL

Present Day, Santa Cruz, California

Traffic eventually eased, and Tess pulled into the CellSpot parking lot at exactly 8:50AM. Mariana was getting more anxious about the meeting and took a deep breath to calm her nerves. As they hustled into the office, Tess witnessed Mariana's shoulders creep up with tension, and her increased pace made her walk awkwardly in her high heels. "Good luck in your meeting," Tess said. "Just relax and picture Shep naked sitting in front of you."

Mariana pursed her lips. "If I do that, I won't be able to concentrate!"

"That's what all the speech experts suggest. Regardless, you know all your material and you'll be amazing.

Just be yourself."

"Well, thank goodness we made it here just in time."

At 8:59AM Mariana walked into the boardroom. Everyone was already in attendance and seated. They were in the middle of small talk introductions, but the room grew quiet as Mariana strode in and found an empty seat at the farthest end of the table away from the CEO and team of clients, hoping she wouldn't have to say much during the meeting.

"Now that we're all here, let's get started," announced Raj. "Let me begin by saying that we're excited you're considering putting CellSpot chargers into all your convenience stores. This will be a game changer for the electric vehicle industry and will make it very easy for drivers to find a place to charge their cars no matter where they are. Our latest software release enables much faster charging, so people won't have to wait long either. We believe we are the perfect partner to meet your needs and look forward to finalizing the agreement. I've brought representatives from each function of the company to this meeting so we can make sure to answer all your questions."

One executive raised his hand and asked, "Will you please explain how you can ensure long lines don't become an issue?"

Tim, Product Lead for CellSpot, spoke up. "We have several methods for handling congestion. One, of course, is reducing the time it takes for the car's battery to recharge. We have cut the time in half already and plan to continue to reduce the charging time. Two, our software knows how many people are already charging or waiting to charge at any location. We also know the number of electric cars in the vicinity that will most likely require a charge in the immediate future. We use all this data to intelligently route cars to the most logical location and balance the navigation across the demand to reduce the load on any one location. Like how your car navigation system works and reroutes you when there is an accident, CellSpot has the same capability for navigation to charging stations and given the ubiquity of our software in cars and in charging stations, we have the most intelligent and real-time system available on the market."

"Great," another executive said. "Please describe how the charging station and car communicate during charging."

Tim nodded, "Yes, we can explain that. Mariana is here, and she does the development for our communications between charging stations and cars, so I will ask her to walk everyone through this."

Mariana glanced up and started fumbling around with her computer. She realized no slides were being used for this presentation, so she just had to explain verbally. She took a deep breath and started in. "Thanks, Tim. It's a little more complicated than how traditional gas stations work. Let me explain the difference. With gas, the consumer simply inserts a credit card, and that tells the system who is buying the gas and which payment method to use. There is a physical sensor in the gas gauge which then tells the gas nozzle when the tank is full and turns off the gas line. With electric cars, more communication is required. You might think it's just like plugging in your iPhone to charge it at night. However, in this case, when you plug in the nozzle into the electric car, not only does the electric current begin to charge the car battery, but also a data connection is established between the car and the charging station. The technology for this is called Power Line Communication. It has been around for a very long time and is used in many industries. The data travels over the electric current and communicates several fields between the car and charging station and remotely back to the central office as needed. Industries use this technology for things like payment authorization, car-specific information, software upgrades, and most importantly, it tells the charger when the battery has reached full capacity and should turn off. This is extremely important because manufacturers make electric car batteries from lithium-ion, and you can't overcharge them, or the batteries can heat too much and potentially explode or start a fire. Our software is constantly monitoring the charge strength and managing it appropriately–"

Another client executive cut Mariana off by asking, "I get that, but how much of a concern is cybersecurity? Could someone break into the software and change the settings or get private information about the owners of the car?"

Mariana shook her head. "No. Our software employs all the latest cybersecurity technology," she said. "We take security seriously and have made certain there are no vulnerabilities. Additionally, Power Line Communication uses industry standards that have existed for decades and are used extensively in many industrial environments, where testing has made them robust against attacks. I feel confident that our software won't be hacked, and if someone tried, we would immediately know about it and shut it down."

"What about these lithium batteries?" the executive continued. "Can we ensure that overheating won't occur and cause potential fires or explosions?"

Mariana responded with a calm smile. "Yes, this issue should never arise. We continuously monitor the charge and temperature and automatically turn it off when it hits a certain level. The user can't override this." There was a brief pause in the room, and then the questions shifted to pricing, revenue sharing, and legal matters.

Relief flowed through Mariana. The client seemed satisfied with the answers as they nodded in agreement. *Good sign*, she thought when the meeting ended and the client promised to get back to them by the end of the week.

After the meeting, Mariana started walking back to her cube when Raj caught up to her and stopped her mid-stride. The CEO was a tall, slender man with strong, chiseled features, dark hair and eyes that could either light up invitingly or darken with disapproval. Everyone liked Raj when he was in a good mood, but if you got on his bad side or he was having a rough day, it was best to stay out of his way.

"Great job today, Mariana. You were very credible

and confident with your answers, and I know the client appreciated how you described the complexity in simple terms and assured them that their concerns were unfounded." Raj pumped his fist in the air. "This is going to be another incredible year for us." Then he stormed down the hallway to his next meeting.

Tess eyed the exchange between Raj and Mariana from across the room, and once Raj walked away, she quickly hurried over. "Well, that looked like it went well."

"Yeah. I think we landed them," Mariana said with a smile. "I was so nervous because Tim called me out to answer a bunch of their questions, but they seemed to like my answers. I need to respond to some emails, but after that, do you want to go get lunch and I can fill you in more?"

"Sounds great. Let's go to Pacific Catch. I'm craving their ahi poke."

"Actually, that's perfect," replied Mariana. "I need to zip into Target to pick up some plastic bins and cleaning supplies. It's around the corner from the restaurant. I promised myself that I would finally organize my messy closet this weekend."

"I know. These long hours have been such a grind lately," Tess said. "I'll definitely help with the cleaning this weekend. But I'm also going apartment hunting. I really appreciate you letting me crash with you this past year, but I'm sure you're ready to have your space back to yourself."

"It's fine. Honestly. My lease will be up in a few months. Maybe we should look at bigger apartments and move in together officially. I've really enjoyed having you around, and you know Drake loves having you there as well."

"Ha. You know I adore Drake. It's so cool you named your cat after our old training grounds at UCLA. I miss running around that track. Anyway, thank you. I would really love to keep living with you," Tess said as she reached out and gave Mariana a quick hug.

An hour later, Tess and Mariana could finally take a break and grab some lunch. They discussed the meeting that took place that morning, some of the current software issues they were dealing with, the demands their boss placed on them while he was out on family leave, and their "to do" list that appeared to be growing significantly faster than they could manage.

"Ugh, let's stop talking about work," Mariana said. "I'm so drained! Tell me something fun...Are you still talking to that guy online? How's your family doing? Is your sister responding to her new therapy? What about your upcoming triathlon? How's the training going?"

Tess laughed, "Okay, okay. Slow down, girlfriend! Yes, I'm still talking to Keith online. My family is doing well. Addie is not really responding to her new physical therapy regimen, but she just started, and the doc said it will take some time. And my triathlon training is going well. It's not for another three months, so I still have a lot of time to prepare. I do need to start interval training and work on my transition time between events."

"Well, it'd help if you got rid of that archaic watch you wear," interjected Mariana, pointing to Tess's wrist.

"Get yourself a smartwatch. Do you realize that you can download training apps to help you out? They can really help you improve performance."

Tess looked down at her old-fashioned analog watch. She ran her fingers across the inside clasp that formed together like a square knot, with one side of the band being leather and the other side steel. "The professor I did research with at UCLA gave it to me. He's the one who quit teaching to become the CEO of an environmental engineering firm and later hired me as an intern. Anyway, he gave me this watch after Addie's accident. He wanted me to remember how simple things were when we were younger. He believes we need to slow down time. He was mortified to hear that Addie was struck by a car on autopilot." Then she scoffed, "I haven't told him I'm working for CellSpot. He would be so disappointed in me if he knew."

"Wouldn't he be proud of the fact that you're working to ensure the safety of others, so this doesn't happen again?"

"Yeah, maybe...but I think he'd rather stop the advancement of AI altogether. He thinks we've opened Pandora's Box and unless we put a lid on it, our world is going to spin out of control."

Tess looked down at her watch, contemplating her situation with a sense of dread. She knew she was out of sync with the slow, continuous movement of the mechanical hands, but was unsure how to change her path.

FOUR

IT HAPPENED AGAIN

Santa Cruz, California

Tess was bending over picking up a sandy, sticky candy wrapper and a squashed beer can discarded by disrespectful beachgoers when her phone rang. She shoved the items in her trash bag, then yanked the rubber glove off her hand so she could retrieve the call. It was her mom.

"Hey, Mom. What's up?"

"Oh my God, Tess. Have you seen the news? It happened again!"

"No. I've been volunteering for Save Our Shores all morning. What happened?"

"A self-driving car caused another major accident," her mom responded, then proceeded to read the story to Tess. "Highway surveillance footage shows a vehicle changing lanes then abruptly braking in the far-left lane of the San Francisco Bay Bridge, resulting in a nine-vehicle crash. The crash injured 12 people, including an infant and a 4-year-old child, and blocked traffic on the bridge for over an hour. The driver told police he had been using the car's self-driving feature and when the car changed lanes, something must have triggered it to malfunction."

"You've got to be kidding me," Tess interjected. "I hope everyone's okay."

"It only says that the injured were taken to the hospital for assessment. Dear Lord, when is this going to end? Why haven't they pulled all these cars off the road?"

Tess sighed deeply. "It's not that simple, Mom. They argue they are still in testing phases under regulatory supervision, and it's believed that over time autonomous vehicles will be much safer than human drivers by eliminating human error."

"Testing at the expense of others," her mom barked into the phone. "While they continue to produce these modes of destruction, I'm pushing your sister in a wheelchair to her next physical therapy appointment!"

Tess didn't respond. She knew no words could negate the reality of her sister's situation. A tear silently rolled down her cheek. She finally spoke up. "I gotta go, Mom. I need to catch up with the other volunteers. I'll call you later when I get home." Then before she ended the call she added, "Give Addie a hug for me. I love you, Mom."

The weight of what her mom told her made Tess's

knees buckle. She plopped on the sand and sat in silence, staring out at the ocean, consumed by her thoughts. *What am I doing? How can I work for a company that enables the very thing that ruined my sister's life? I didn't go to school for this. CellSpot isn't an environmental firm striving to save our planet. UGH! As soon as I make enough money to pay off her medical bills, I'm looking for a new job. I can't do this anymore.*

Tess turned her attention to her phone to text Keith–the one person she knew who felt the same way. Sharing her feelings with him was therapeutic, even though it was only through online conversations. They'd met on an internet forum for environmental engineers and learned that they had a lot in common–both strong advocates for protecting the environment, similar educational backgrounds, dedicated to work, and avid athletes. Their friendship quickly grew, and they ended up connecting online frequently. They had yet to meet in person because Keith was working for a company based in New York and traveled a lot. He was currently on a research project in Iceland, but that didn't stop him from texting with her.

FIVE

KEITH

Santa Cruz, California

After a long day at the office, Tess and Mariana spent the evening in their apartment working on their laptops. Another deadline was coming up to complete the latest software release for the charging station platform. Mariana was busy on her laptop sitting at the kitchen table, while Tess sat on the couch with Drake nudging his way in, fighting for lap space with her computer.

Tess looked up and noticed that Mariana was in deep concentration as she typed away on her laptop. Tess, on the other hand, was having trouble focusing. She finally completed a new software check-in and was about to start a full test to make sure it didn't have any bugs or cause issues with other new software components, but her mind wasn't focused on that. Instead, she kept thinking about Keith. She really appreciated their friendship. She wondered if it would ever develop to the next step. Of course, she'd never met him in person. She barely knew what he looked like because they'd only seen each other's profile pictures on their web forum, but it didn't matter. The connection they clearly had made with all the back-and-forth texting was apparent. She found it odd that he preferred texting over FaceTime, but she tried to respect his privacy and recognized that not everyone was comfortable being live on camera. Just then, she heard a *ping* and saw that she had a new text message notification on her laptop from Keith. He texted that he was back from his trip to Iceland and that he had attached a photo. Tess double-clicked on the image to make it larger so she could see it in more detail on her Mac.

Her blood pressure increased and adrenaline rushed throughout her body as she saved the image to her Photos app. Keith was standing in front of a beautiful landscape of the countryside. Right behind him was a flowing river with a waterfall in the background. The ground was a mix of greens and browns with what looked like mossy grass. Far behind was the outline of a huge mountain with a pointy top and horizontal rock striations going up the entire mountainside. It looked like someone had placed a large witch's hat on the vast meadow. The sky was blue with dramatic clouds looking like they were disappearing into the back of the photo. It was almost too perfect. But Tess didn't care about the landscape. She only wanted to zoom in on Keith–thirty years old, around six feet tall with long, wavy dark hair, and wearing black glasses. He had a big smile on his face, scruffy from his travels and working outside on the project. He appeared to be in great shape–lean, yet muscular with strong facial features. He was wearing a black Patagonia jacket with jeans and hiking boots, and his hand was raised as if he was in the process of waving to the camera. Tess's heart skipped a beat. *Damn, he is tall, dark and handsome*, she thought to herself.

She blurted out to Mariana, "Keith sent me a full picture of himself, and OMG is he sexy!"

Mariana looked up from across the room with a huge smile on her face. Noticing that the cat was anchoring Tess to the couch, Mariana said, "That's awesome. Send me the photo so I can see it as well on my laptop."

"Well, what do you think?" asked Tess, watching every aspect of Mariana's facial expressions as she scrutinized the photo.

"He looks like a model," quipped Mariana as the smile on her face got even bigger. She glanced over at Tess, knowing that Tess was hanging on her every word. "He's really hot. I think you should send a picture of yourself back to him."

Tess's face grew pale and panic set in her eyes. "Ugh, no pressure. I hope he likes what he sees..." Once the picture was sent, she tried to focus on work again.

Later that night, when Tess and Mariana were finally getting ready to power down their laptops, Keith sent her another text.

Keith: Hey Tess. I just woke up again. Can't sleep—jet lag is killing me. I liked the picture you sent. Was that after the last triathlon you did?

Tess: Yes :) How was your Iceland project?

Keith: Great! I was working at one of their hydropower plants. Iceland's electricity grid is fully produced from renewable resources. We analyzed their plans to become completely carbon neutral and fossil-fuel-free

Tess: I've heard they have an aggressive timeline. The environmental firm I was working at during grad school focused on geothermal energy. I loved that job but the only position they offered was in Oregon and I couldn't leave my sister

Keith: Well you landed a great job at CellSpot

Tess: The pay is great but there's still the whole self-driving car thing

Keith: But you'll prevent more accidents in the future, right?

Tess: I thought I'd be able to make a difference, but we only focus on the charging units, not the components tied to autonomous driving

Keith: I see why this is weighing on you then

Tess: And then there's the whole battery issue. The production and disposal of them will cause huge environmental hazards

Keith: Are you thinking of quitting?

Tess: Maybe. I need to secure another job first...can't afford to walk away from this income right now

Keith: I hear you. Let's talk more later. I'm beat

Tess: Hope you can sleep the rest of the night

Keith: Thanks

Mariana watched Tess madly typing away as she cleared the kitchen table and packed up her work bag for the next day. Tess's facial expression changed from delighted to frustrated, and Mariana was curious what was going on.

"Was that Keith again?" Mariana asked.

Tess nodded. "Yeah."

"Everything okay? You look upset."

Tess didn't want to admit that she was getting worked up about CellSpot again. Complaining seemed impertinent when Mariana was the one who helped her get the job in the first place. So, Tess politely smiled and said, "No, everything is fine. I just wish Keith and I could meet in person. We connect on so many levels–it stinks that we live so far apart."

Mariana was about to respond, but Tess made herself appear busy powering down her laptop and collecting her items. Then she hurried down the hall to get ready for bed.

"Goodnight," Mariana yelled after her.

"Goodnight."

SIX

COLLISION COURSE

Multiple Locations

"Hello everyone! This is an exciting day for all of us!" announced Raj Anand, the CEO of Cell-Spot, as he addressed the employees in the company auditorium. "I called this all-hands meeting to celebrate our ongoing success. Ten years ago, we started this company believing that electric vehicles would become ubiquitous and require a similar infrastructure to gasoline stations. We wanted to create the next generation of gas stations, providing electric charging and allowing people to drive anywhere they want using electric vehicles. It hasn't been easy, but that vision is finally coming together. We now have tens of thousands of charging stations, and our software continues to be best-in-class, driving the standards for all electric vehicle charging and interoperability with all types of vehicles. We continue to expand our footprint domestically and internationally. Our charging stations are by far the quickest and simplest for consumer and commercial vehicles to use, and we're making tremendous progress driving energy savings for companies and governments across the electric grids. This past week, we rolled out a new software release to all our charging stations and partners. The upgrade rolled out smoothly and efficiently, and we've already received great reviews from users and the industry. Thanks to all of you for staying focused and striving for greatness with this latest release! It's a testament to the amazing people we have in this company. *You* are the reason we continue to lead this industry!"

The audience began clapping, so Raj waited for the noise to die down before he continued. "Not only are all the engineering teams doing fantastic work, but so are our sales and marketing teams. We're very close to signing several new contracts with the largest commercial fleets of electric vehicles in the world. Closing these deals will cement our leadership position in the industry and allow us to be the dominant player driving the future of electric vehicle charging. It's paramount that we continue to perform well during the sales process and demonstrate the reason we should be chosen for each of these deals. Just look at our stock price. We've tripled it over the past year, and I'm confident we can do that again by closing these new deals!"

Raj paused for dramatic effect and let everyone do

the math in their heads of what would happen to their individual wealth if the stock price continued its staggering climb. "We all want the same thing. We need to be extra diligent and make sure that nothing goes wrong over the coming weeks and months. Thank you again, and here's to another stellar year for CellSpot!"

Everyone started clapping again. Raj waved to the crowd and to the camera for all the folks watching remotely via livestream. He flashed his charming smile that had been on the covers of almost every business magazine over the last year. He then walked off the stage and into the backroom, letting another executive take over the rest of the meeting by showing a product demonstration of the latest software release.

When the all-hands meeting ended, Raj gestured to his executive team, then slipped out the side door before anyone could approach him. He really needed a moment alone to breathe. While he felt confident that the company was about to scale to a whole new level, he was also anxious for this to become a reality. Everything was riding on CellSpot's success. *Everything*. Raj felt confident about the company's imminent expansion, yet he also felt a sense of urgency for it to materialize. Raj had allowed CellSpot to overextend dramatically this past year with capital purchases and hardware inventory. The last couple of years they had also been confidentially working on Project Hover, a brand-new type of charging solution, and the investment was extremely large, requiring significant debt to fund. Raj knew he was balancing the company on a very thin tightrope and was nervous it would all come crashing down. If they didn't land these new contracts soon, the loan payments would come due, and he would be hard-pressed to keep his investors on board. This could cause their stock price to tank, and he'd be forced out of the company. Raj would do anything to not have this happen.

At the same time on the other side of the globe, another meeting was taking place–this one more secretive. As usual, the meeting was set up through the appropriate secure channels using only the agreed-upon communication protocols. Physical presence was mandatory–nothing over the phone, nothing in writing. Only the shared symbol, a date and a time had been received by each participant as an invite. Fifteen of them made the journey and were assembled in the customary meeting space. This location was not on any map–unknown to the world at large. A secret chamber known only to this organization and well off the beaten track. As it was underground, it was considerably cooler and only dimly lit. Given the unusual environment, the temperature in the facility stayed at an almost constant fifty-seven degrees. The air was well-ventilated, but eerily quiet.

They were seated at a large, round table made from walnut. Dark and rich in tone. Clearly handmade with exquisite details. The chairs were also handmade with the finest upholstery. Each chair was crafted differently with unique carvings and shapes for the arms and legs.

At close glance, it was apparent that square nails had been used to assemble the chairs and table, like how artisans would have done it centuries past. In stark contrast to the furniture, there were computers and monitors around the room, providing the modern essentials of communication and connectivity to stay abreast of global activity. There were no papers or pens on the table. No notetaking was allowed. Everything had to be memorized. Above the table hung a large, ornate chandelier. On the walls hung additional sconces to provide light, but still the room felt bleak. The flooring was very basic due to the remote nature of the location. It was made of brick in most places, with large stones in other areas. A huge antique rug measuring at least twenty feet by thirty feet lay under the table, handwoven from wool and depicting scenes of craftsmen creating various works of art.

In addition, no personal technology was allowed on the trip. All cell phones, laptops, and smartwatches had to be left behind. This was strictly enforced and key to remaining anonymous. The participants had also used fake documents to travel. All these details and procedures were established years ago and were very successful in keeping the organization under the radar and untraceable. In fact, just to get into this inner chamber, each member had to go through a comprehensive automated fingerprint and eye scan to have the thick metal door slide open.

No names were used in the meeting. Each person was addressed by their home country. The Spaniard opened the meeting. "I'm glad you're all here. Thank you for making the trip. It's time for an update on our latest mission. Our initial test was successful, and we've now begun the operational phase. It's going live as we speak."

BREAKING NEWS

Spine Chilling–Autonomous Electric Vehicle Car Crashes
Continue to Increase Nationwide

By Lilli M. Sullivan
November 3, 2024

A significant increase in incidents involving autonomous electric vehicles is being witnessed on city roads across the nation. These accidents not only endanger the lives of the occupants of the car but also of other citizens. In the last month alone, multiple accidents have been reported.

San Francisco, CA–*An autonomous electric vehicle came to a quick stop at a green light, causing multiple fender benders on busy Van Ness Avenue. The cause of the malfunction is still unknown, according to company sources.*

Austin, TX–*Multiple injuries when a car slammed into a self-driving vehicle that randomly stopped mid-turn. Apparently, the software believed that another car was in its path.*

Redwood City, CA–*Autonomous EV ignores right turn signal command, shuts down and activates hazard lights, backing up traffic for blocks.*

Portland, OR–*Traffic jammed for hours when multiple car crashes occurred after a self-driving electric vehicle changed lanes on a busy street, slamming into another car and pushing that car into a different lane, creating a chain reaction.*

Evanston, IL–*Mass chaos on Dempster Street and Chicago Avenue when an autonomous electric vehicle failed to navigate around a construction merge sign and side-swiped a parked construction vehicle blocking traffic all afternoon.*

SEVEN

THE IMPORTANCE OF DATA

San Francisco, California

"Good morning," said Booker Stevens, Supervisory Special Agent, Joint Terrorism Task Force (JTTF) for the FBI's San Francisco Field Office, as he addressed his regular Monday morning staff meeting. Most of his team were present in the room while those working remotely were on Zoom.

"We will come back to the topic of ongoing surveillance at the Mexico and Canada borders, but I want to focus today's discussion on a new potential alert that has come to our attention. As you know, our analyst team is constantly monitoring news reports looking for covert terrorist actions that could lead to widespread public fear and panic. One such alert recently popped up as *moderate,* and we've been asked to investigate and prepare a report in the next couple of weeks. You've probably read about the recent autonomous electric vehicle car crashes. Many of the crashes have been minor, but several have resulted in major injuries, even fatalities. The data models indicate that the rise in car crashes nationwide isn't random and goes beyond typical statistical explanations. They believe something abnormal may be occurring here. It's our job to talk with the various industry players and see if we can come up with anything that is out of place or that has occurred recently that could be causing the increase in crashes. I have organized an initial list of companies that I want you to split up and reach out to. Let's keep our eyes and ears open and see if we can uncover anything, then report back together in a few days. Thanks."

As the team of special agents gathered their equipment and streamed out of the room, Booker turned to his Senior Special Agent (SA) and commented, "Pat, let's really dive into this one. I have a strong feeling that something bigger is going on. This could be a great opportunity to make a name for us and get recognized nationally. Let's put everything behind this for the time being."

"Agreed," Pat said before walking out the door. She knew not to debate a subject when Booker got excited. He was always looking for his ticket to the next promotion.

Booker Stevens was forty-four years old and had been with the bureau since he left the military. His upbringing was dark and complex, molding him into the man he had become today. He was known for being competitive, driven, and willing to do whatever it took to get the job done. While he had done well with his career so far, he had ambitions to achieve much higher goals. Although some people viewed him as a cowboy, Booker believed that if he achieved the results, he would be recognized and promoted regardless of whether he pushed the envelope a little. He knew that the current Assistant Special Agent in Charge (ASAC) for the San Francisco Field Office was up for retirement soon, and Booker was laser-focused on being his replacement when that happened. He was thinking this project might just be the perfect opportunity to position him at the right time.

Several days had passed, and Booker once again assembled his staff for an update. "Okay, what has everyone learned? Let's go around the room and share."

One of the agents spoke up. "Not much from our team. We met with the four car companies on our list and their software teams for autonomous driving. They walked us through the changes made over the last few months to their software. They were all convinced that nothing material had changed that would cause these accidents. For some reason, however, each of the accidents had errors in the sensor readings that led to the crashes. In some cases, it was proximity sensors, and in others there were mistakes around seeing the right color at traffic lights. All areas where they have redundant systems that should have caught the issue. They are investigating the cause of the errors and will implement necessary software modifications. It was the same story at each of the car companies."

"We heard the same thing from the companies we talked with," another agent chimed in.

Frowning, Booker jumped in. "Okay, so we can rule out any one car company having bad software or a new release that is causing this. We need to step back then and look at the system-wide infrastructure. If this problem isn't occurring at the individual level, let's change tactics and look at any company's software that interfaces with all these car companies. Also, if you were a bad actor initiating a cyberattack, you'd want to impact as many cars as possible, so attacking any one car company wouldn't be efficient. You would have to compromise each car company's software which would take a long time. Any thoughts?"

Another agent on Zoom spoke up. "What about suppliers that provide parts or software? That could be a way to reach a wider audience."

"Or software companies that provide adjacent car services like Apple CarPlay, music and podcast connections, navigation software, or remote emergency and security services?" someone else said.

Booker wrote all the ideas on the whiteboard and said, "These are all plausible ideas. Let's expand the investigation and reach out to these companies. Time is critical. Send me your reports by the end of the week." Then Booker turned to Pat and said, "Let's have our analyst team identify all the types of companies that have software connected to an electric vehicle, then we can systematically rule out folks one at a time."

EIGHT

CHANGING TIDES

Santa Cruz, California

Mariana stomped up the stairs to her apartment, loaded down by her work backpack, gym duffle and a bag full of groceries she picked up after work. The physical weight of her items added to the equivalent invisible weight of work on her shoulders. While she awkwardly fumbled to unlock the front door and accidentally dropped the keys to the ground, Tess, already home, came to her rescue and opened it for her.

"Here, let me take the groceries," Tess offered as she grabbed the bag and brought it into the kitchen.

"Thanks," Mariana grumbled as she picked up her keys and trudged in behind her. She dumped her gym bag on the floor, hefted her backpack off her shoulders, and plopped onto the couch.

Tess gave her a minute to regroup and began putting the groceries away. Then it dawned on Tess that she had parked in their one and only spot that afternoon when she got back from the dentist. She usually parked on the street and would leave that spot open for Mariana because it was Mariana's apartment and she deserved to park there. Tess cringed. "OMG, I'm so sorry I parked in your spot. I was late for a Zoom call and rushed in to hop on it."

Mariana took a deep breath. It wasn't like Tess had done it to be malicious. "It's fine. Just annoying because I had to park two blocks away. Why is parking so bad right now?"

"I saw a ton of people lugging coolers and chairs down to the beach. Maybe there's some event going on?"

"Yeah, whatever–I've just had a crappy day. I'm so buried at work, our deadlines are quickly approaching, and Raj is constantly hounding me. I'm ready for Joel to get back from family leave. His timing couldn't be worse."

Tess chuckled, trying to lighten the mood. "Yeah, that baby of his should've known our work schedule and adjusted her timeline to enter this world!"

Switching gears, Mariana got up to change into shorts and a sweatshirt. "I need to relieve some of this stress. Wanna go for a walk before it's too dark out?"

"Sure," Tess replied. "Let me grab my shoes."

A few minutes later the two of them were walking down toward the lighthouse on Seabright Beach, less than a mile from their apartment. Mariana kept the pace fast and seemed lost in her own thoughts.

"Do you want to talk about it?" Tess asked Mariana.

Mariana sighed. "I'm just getting tired of the never ending to do list and how complicated this build is becoming. One minute it seems like we are on track for our release date and then we get slapped with another complication. I have so much to do. It's overwhelming."

"Can I make a suggestion?" asked Tess, not knowing how Mariana would respond to her advice.

"Sure," Mariana grumbled.

"You need to delegate more. I know Raj put you temporarily in charge while Joel's out, but you can't do it all yourself. Take some of the items off your list and ask the team for help."

"I just want it done right and show Raj that I can handle the responsibility. I want to prove that I'm ready for a promotion."

"Yes, but part of being a leader is believing in your team, letting go, and divvying up the work," replied Tess.

Mariana didn't reply, but she made a mental note to consider delegating more after this assignment. She didn't want anything to go wrong with the upcoming release.

The two of them turned left on the street that brought them down a hill to the dirt path leading to the lighthouse. They both pulled their hoodies over their heads because the air was chilly and the misty clouds were rolling in quickly.

Mariana changed the subject. "How's work going

for you?"

"It's going fine, but..." Tess hesitated, not wanting to discuss her feelings about CellSpot. Then she looked up and saw the shift in weather and the rising water. Waves crashed forcefully onto the rock jetty, spraying salt water onto their path. "Let's turn around and head home."

A few minutes later, Tess summoned the courage to share her feelings with Mariana. "Work is okay, but I need to be honest with you. I'm going to start looking for another job," Tess blurted out, then quickly continued before Mariana could respond. "I totally appreciate you helping me get this job. The pay is amazing, and I enjoy working with you. I'm just really struggling with the industry. I want to target an environmental firm. I want to work for a company that aligns with my principles."

Tess watched anxiously as Mariana opened her mouth as if to say something, then closed it again. Mariana's brow furrowed and her lips pursed. Not able to take the silence anymore, Tess added, "I'm really torn because we have a great team and I'm learning so much. For some reason I thought it would be easier emotionally for me. I'd convinced myself that we'd be working to prevent more accidents like Addie's, but our focus isn't on the safety of autonomous vehicles at all."

Mariana remained quiet as they continued their walk back to the apartment.

"Please don't be upset with me," Tess pleaded. "You know how passionate I am about environmental awareness."

"I'm not mad," Mariana responded. "I know you took

this job because it was an easy solution at the time and you needed the income. I'm just feeling overwhelmed because we have this big release coming up and we can't afford to lose you right now. CellSpot has too much riding on this upcoming release. Could you wait until after?"

"Yeah, I suppose so. Thanks for understanding," said Tess. "I'm sorry to dump this on you. It's just been eating away at me, and I felt like you should know."

Having gotten over the initial shock, Mariana said, "I appreciate you telling me. Of course I understand. Our friendship will always be more important than any stupid job or company. I'd like to find a way to make it worthwhile for you to stay, but regardless, I just need some time to backfill your role."

Tess exhaled and breathed a sigh of relief, but it didn't make the pit in her stomach go away. She still felt a sense of guilt.

NINE

CONNECTIONS

San Francisco, California

The following Monday, Booker sat in his office, reading through the latest situation reports from each of his teams. He slammed shut his laptop. It was clear they weren't making any progress on the autonomous electric vehicle crashes. His boss had pinged him twice already for updates, and he had nothing noteworthy to provide. Booker tried to put himself in the shoes of a terrorist organization and work backward on how they would have achieved these attacks. He was trying to look at it through a different lens to have a more creative perspective. But after no breakthrough, he left his office in frustration and went to the kitchenette for a cup of coffee.

When he returned, there was a light blue sticky note attached to his desk. It simply read: *Found a connection. Let's talk.* Booker's curious expression morphed into a wide smile, and he called Pat into his office. Pat had become a key player on Booker's team. Booker took her under his wing years ago, at the beginning of her career with the FBI. She joined the Bureau directly after graduating summa cum laude in mathematics at the University of Wisconsin. Booker and Pat met when she was assigned to his team as a Special Agent. It was a complex case with a large crew of agents. Being new to the team, Pat didn't feel comfortable speaking up, so she got into the habit of writing her thoughts down. She would drop a note on Booker's desk periodically, always on a light blue sticky note. Her problem-solving skills and ability to think outside the box impressed Booker. One of her notes eventually led them to breaking the case. Pat connected dots and saw a pattern that no one else could see. After they closed the case, Booker promoted her to Senior Special Agent, and they've been working together ever since.

Pat materialized at his office door. "I see you got my note. The analysts have completed their research on all the types of companies that have software that connects in some way to electric vehicles. Do you want to see it now?"

Gesturing with his hands, Booker motioned for Pat to join him at the small conference table in his office. He took a sip of his coffee and pushed aside the mound of paperwork piling up on the table while Pat pulled up the files on her laptop, then the two of them started poring through the report.

Booker looked up and said, "Here's one that I don't remember us talking about...electric vehicle charging stations. I didn't realize they had a software connection with the car. I figured they just pumped in electricity to charge the battery."

Pat looked up at Booker, smirked, and nodded, already well ahead of him. She handed him another report that she had printed earlier. "I asked the team to pull together a more detailed analysis on this category. Looks like there are several companies in this space, but the major player in the United States is a company called CellSpot."

Booker interjected, "Interesting. They would be a great entry point for a cyberattack. There's been a lot of press about this company and its stock has been on fire. I just read an article about their founder...let me pull it up." After locating the article on his phone Booker added, "Looks like they are based in Mountain View. Let's drive down. Will you reach out to them and let them know we're coming? Let's also set up time with the other companies in this space."

"I'm on it," said Pat as she collected her paperwork.

Later that day, they both sat in CellSpot's conference room.

"Impressive," Pat whispered to Booker as she looked

around the room. "They must have spent a pretty penny decorating this space!" The modern conference room was encased in glass walls and elevated a foot higher than the rest of the offices on the floor, giving it the illusion of importance. There were monitors on all four sides of the conference room with soundbars under each of them for enhanced audio. When Raj entered the room and flipped a switch, Booker and Pat noticed that the glass walls turned opaque.

"Hello, my name is Raj Anand and welcome to CellSpot. I'm the CEO. I understand you're with the FBI. How can I possibly help you?" said Raj with his infectious smile and confident tone.

"Booker Stevens," Booker announced, shaking Raj's hand firmly. "I'm the Supervisory Special Agent in charge of the counterterrorism squad in the Bay Area, and this is my senior agent, Pat Larson. We appreciate you making time for us at such short notice. We're investigating the recent increase in autonomous electric vehicle crashes. Specifically, we're trying to identify if anything more than normal software issues is occurring and if there is any nefarious activity going on. We've expanded our investigation to include companies that build software that connects to these electric cars, and we know CellSpot has the leading footprint of electric car charging stations."

Raj smiled at this comment. "Of course, we will certainly assist in any way we can," he said. "I've seen the reports but never imagined it was intentional. Who do you think would be behind this?"

"Well, we don't have any proof yet, and we don't have any suspects, however, my team is always concerned about foreign powers trying to attack America's infrastructure, energy sector, and transportation. When we look at potential threats, we analyze three areas." Booker gestured with his hands, counting visually as he said, "One–specificity. Does the threat include details of who is involved, specific targets, or where or how it may occur? Two–credibility. This includes the sources and context of the reports. And three–viability. Do we think the threat can be carried out and is technically feasible? In this case, we're only beginning our investigation, but we do believe creating a panic around autonomous electric vehicles could impact various industries and overlap into other national security areas as well. As self-guided computers and AI become more widespread, we're concerned about enemies of the United States figuring out how to implement cyberattacks that could impact the economy and disrupt the country's stability."

Raj nodded. "Well, I can assure you that our company is not involved, but we'll help anyway we can. Would you like to talk with our software development team to better understand how the charging software works as well as how we handle security?"

"That would be great," said Booker.

Raj looked up and saw Mariana walking by the conference room. "Actually, here's our lead programmer, Mariana Morales. She's one of our rock stars. I'll grab her and she can walk you through the software." Raj jumped up and left the conference room.

Because the opaque walls allowed you to see out yet not in, Booker and Pat observed Raj talking to Mariana. Mariana's eyes grew large and her smile dropped. She tried stepping away, but Raj gestured to the door, and she reluctantly walked toward the conference room.

As Mariana stepped into the room, she said hesitantly, "Hi, I'm Mariana, the lead software programmer. Raj mentioned you wanted to ask me some questions?"

Booker and Pat stood up and handed Mariana their business cards. "Yes. Hello, Mariana. My name is Booker and this is Pat. We're from the FBI, investigating the various autonomous electric vehicle crashes that have been occurring across the country."

Mariana's brows furrowed as she looked back and forth between them. "Okay...but what does that have to do with me?"

"We're trying to educate ourselves on how various software systems connect to these cars and how someone might enable a cyberattack. We'd like to better understand how CellSpot works. Could you walk us through how the software operates and how it integrates with the cars?"

"Sure," Mariana responded with a little more confidence. "Let me use this whiteboard." Mariana started drawing a picture. "It's quite simple. Here's one of our charging stations and here's a car that needs to recharge. At a high level, there are four steps that occur during charging. Step one is user authentication. The station needs to know who is charging and how they will pay if there is a payment charge. This is typically done via an app or Bluetooth since no credit card is involved. Step two is a digital handshake. A bidirectional data connection is established between the car and the charging station. This is done over what is called Power Line Communication. It's a fancy way of utilizing the same wires for electricity and data. There is a receiver in both the car and the charging station that knows how to read each other's signals and data. An example of this is the battery level. The charger needs to know when to stop charging the car's battery, so it doesn't overheat or use too much energy. Step three is the electricity moving from the charging station to the car to fill up the battery. That's kind of obvious. Step four is terminating the connections when the battery is fully recharged and letting the car know it can drive away from the station. Does that make sense?"

Booker and Pat exchanged glances. Then Booker responded, "I think so. Thanks for the overview. I didn't realize when I connected the power cable to the car that I'm also making a data connection. That sounds like an area where someone could receive personal information or send malicious software into the car. Am I wrong?"

Mariana thought about it for a moment then replied, "Well the data transmitted back and forth is only supposed to travel between the EV Supply Equipment at the charging station and the Electric Vehicle Central Control Unit in the car. I don't see how data could move beyond this point into other software systems in the car, but I guess it's theoretically possible. We use industry standard protocols that have security built in.

These protocols are extensively used in other industrial environments."

Right then, Mariana's phone vibrated. She read the message and looked up. "I'm sorry, but I have an important meeting to attend. Are there any more questions you have?"

Booker thought for a second and then spoke up, "No, I think that's enough for now. We really appreciate you taking the time to walk us through how things work. We'll meet with a few other people, and if we have more questions for you, we'll reach out."

Throughout the day Booker and Pat met with a handful of more employees of CellSpot. The meetings were informative, but nothing really stood out to either of them. As they were heading back to the airport, Booker looked over at Pat and asked, "Well, what do you think? Any smoking guns?"

"No. I feel much more educated though. Everyone was forthcoming and relatively at ease with us."

"Yeah, I agree. I'm concerned about the data connection between cars and the charging stations though. That feels like a vulnerability an enemy would focus on. But they'd probably need an inside person to help them load the malicious software. Let's do a background check on all the people we met today and see if anything pops."

"Solid plan," Pat said and immediately started typing into her phone.

TEN

SELF-REFLECTION

Mountain View, California

The next morning, Mariana and Tess followed their typical routine and went to the gym before work. After the FBI visit yesterday, the simple act of working out and sneaking looks at Shep was a welcome relief to Mariana. But when they got to the office, Raj's assistant told Mariana he wanted to see her immediately. With a deep breath she headed up the elevator to the executive floor. When she arrived, they sat down at his conference table. Raj started in, "Thanks again for meeting with the FBI yesterday. That was quite a surprise visit. What did you think?"

"Yeah, that was crazy," Mariana responded. "I've been reading about the autonomous vehicle crashes, but just assumed companies were still working out the kinks. It's an extremely complex software challenge with so many independent variables. Trying to anticipate all the different scenarios that can happen is overwhelming."

Raj smiled, sat forward in his chair, and in a raised voice said, "It is complex, but I believe with new AI methods and group learning capabilities, the industry is on the cusp of making it a broad-scale reality. This in turn will be a huge boost for our company."

"Yes, but it could also backfire if people don't feel it's safe. It's scary to think that someone or some country may be hacking into these systems and making the situation worse than it normally would be. If these crashes continue, regulators and the public will protest and slow down commercial adoption. A lot of companies are counting on autonomous vehicles for their growth projections. I can see how that would be a real terrorist threat."

Raj sat back and lowered his voice. "I agree. And not just other companies would be impacted by a slowdown. We'd be hit hard as well. Many of our potential new customers are planning rollouts of self-driving fleets. I really hope this isn't a terrorist attack. CellSpot can't afford that."

Raj shook his head and thought for a second. "Mariana, would you please look at everyone's code to ensure that CellSpot is not involved? This would be a disaster for our public relations. If you do find anything, bring it to me immediately so we can determine how best to handle it. I know I can count on you."

"Of course. I'll get on it right away and keep you updated on what I find–which is hopefully nothing."

"Just keep this confidential. We can't have our customers privy to what's going on." Then Raj added for emphasis so Mariana understood the potential implications, "If this does turn out to be a cyberattack infiltrated through our company, our investors will pull out and our stock will plummet."

"I'm sure that's not the case," Mariana reassured Raj then switched the conversation to a positive note. "Are we still on track for the big press event around Project Hover? This new release is going to be quite a game changer in the industry."

Raj's eyes lit up and a smile spread across his face in excitement, "I know! It's crazy we've been secretly working on this for over two years now. Yes, we're still on target, and I can't wait to make a huge splash with the prototype. This capability should put us in a whole new league as a company."

Not wanting to wear out her welcome, Mariana stood up to leave Raj's office, but on her way out she remembered to mention the importance of incentivizing Tess to stay at CellSpot. "One more thing Raj, we can't afford to lose any of our developers right now. Our timeline for this next release is really tight, and everyone is burning the candle at both ends."

"So, what's your point?" Raj inquired, looking up from his phone.

Mariana cleared her throat, nervous about how he would react given his current mood. "Well, Tess mentioned she's looking at positions with an environmental engineering firm. I really don't want to lose her right now."

Raj's face became pinched and he stared at Mariana with stern eyes. Then he simply nodded, looked away, and said, "Noted."

Mariana went back to her cubicle and started combing through the latest software release line by line. For the next several hours, she pored through all the production logs reviewing any error messages, exceptions, and performance issues that might indicate malicious software was causing issues. She then tried various static code analyses to determine any security vulnerabilities or inconsistencies. By the end of the day Mariana still hadn't found anything alarming.

The next morning Mariana cleared her calendar so she could continue to review the software and look for abnormalities. A few hours into the day, she was still at a loss. She exited out of the company codebase and decided to work on other things for a while. Switching over to her personal email, Mariana started to respond to friends and family and deleted unnecessary emails. As she was doing this, she went into the file manager to locate certain files she needed to attach to some of the emails. Several of them were missing.

Gone.

Her stomach tightened. She knew she hadn't deleted

them. Digging into her system settings, she couldn't find any record of the files being sent to trash. Her heart started racing and her pulse spiked. *Was it possible a virus had slipped onto her laptop? Worse, what if it had infected the company build when she submitted her last update? A worm could replicate itself silently, hiding its tracks as it spread. Some strains could even corrupt files to make tracing them nearly impossible.*

Mariana broke out in a cold sweat. *If that happened, then maybe it could have hit the official CellSpot software. And if the malicious code had spread through devices connected to the charging stations, it could find its way into a car's onboard systems, and from there, into the navigation systems and sensors.* Mariana's head spun with questions.

Could that be how accidents were happening–through a worm unleashed? Unknowingly, sure, but still...

She put her head in her hands and tried to envision every possibility. *Oh my God, what if I'm the cause of this cyberattack?* Her pulse quickened and a surge of alarming energy raced through her body. Sensing that she was beginning to hyperventilate, Mariana took big, deep breaths to calm herself.

Once she got her body somewhat regulated, she started rationalizing the very low probability of being the one that infected CellSpot software. There was no way it had been her. She was always extra careful. She decided to take a break and went for coffee. By the time she got back to her cubicle Mariana had convinced herself that she was overthinking all this. She tried to focus on regular work and chose to sit in on some of the scheduled meetings for planning the next software release, even though she was an optional attendee. Distracting herself from the theoretical virus helped, and she ended the day feeling a little better. Still, she was quiet most of the drive home with Tess, lost in thought over the situation.

When they got to their apartment, Mariana went straight to her room and pulled out her laptop to continue researching how her computer could have been compromised. This time, she reviewed more of the software commits from various programmers. There was one from her that seemed suspicious. It appeared to be from her account, but from a location she couldn't remember working at. The IP address wasn't from her home or from any known office VPN. It looked like a harmless utility file for telemetry to collect metrics, but she couldn't recall writing it. Once again, panic set in, and she became more anxious about the situation. *How could my username and password have been compromised? This doesn't make any sense. Raj will never trust me again!*

An hour later she was wearing down the carpet pacing back and forth in her room, wracking her brain trying to figure out what to do, when she heard Tess call out to let her know that dinner was ready. Mariana emerged from her room and sat down at the dining table. Silence filled the kitchen as Mariana began to eat the chicken piccata, with a faraway look in her eyes. Tess remained quiet as well, allowing Mariana to brood over whatever was bothering her.

After several minutes, Mariana finally spoke in a monotone voice. "This is good, Tess. Thank you."

"No problem. You seemed distracted when we got home, so I decided to make dinner tonight. Is everything okay?"

"I just have a lot on my mind," Mariana replied, picking up her plate to rinse it off and do the rest of the dishes.

"Don't worry about the dishes. I can clean up tonight."

"Thanks," Mariana mumbled as she walked back into her bedroom and closed the door.

Mariana stayed in her room the rest of the night. Tess chose to cuddle on the couch with Drake in her lap and watch the season finale of *The Bachelor* on TV. When the show came to a dramatic end, with the bachelor proposing to the woman that the audience was not expecting to receive the rose, Tess sat Drake on the floor and stood up to get ready for bed. She noticed the light under the crack of Mariana's bedroom door, so she decided to bite the bullet and check in on her.

Tess knocked on the door. "Are you sure you're okay Mariana? Do you want to talk about it?"

Mariana opened the door. Her hair was a mess from repeatedly running her hands through it; she looked pale, and her left eye twitched. "I'm just really stressed. There's something going on with this latest software release. I don't really want to talk about it right now; I feel a migraine coming on, and I just want to go to bed. I think I'm gonna work from home tomorrow."

"Oh, okay," Tess replied with concern in her voice. "Is there anything I can do to help?"

"No, it'll be fine," Mariana responded and closed the door.

Tess stared at the painted wood for a long moment before giving up and walking to her room. The quiet space of the apartment felt awkward and wrong. *Mariana usually tells me everything*, she thought, pulling on a t-shirt and pajama shorts. *I wonder what's going on.* She proceeded to get ready for bed, then picked up her phone to text Keith.

Tess: Hi. How was your day?

Keith: Not bad. Really busy at work but got a lot accomplished. How about you?

Tess climbed into bed, propped the pillows behind her and tucked the covers around her. She then continued to text Keith.

Tess: Fine, but kind of a strange day. Something's going on with Mariana. She's not talking about it, which is unlike her. She said it has something to do with our latest software release

Her phone displayed a fleeting "..." for several minutes, signaling Keith's difficulty in responding. Eventually his text came through.

Keith: I'm sure it's fine. Let me know if you find out more. I gotta go. Big meeting tomorrow morning and I'm exhausted. Good night

Disappointed that the conversation ended so quickly, Tess turned off her lamp and rolled over on her pillow. *What's going on? Why's everyone shutting me out tonight?*

ELEVEN

CONNECTING THE DOTS

San Francisco, California

Back in the office at Booker's staff meeting, Pat provided an update on the background checks. "Most of the people we checked had no yellow flags. But surprisingly, the one person highlighted was the woman we first met. Do you remember Mariana Morales?"

Booker said, "Of course I do, but she seemed very helpful. What did you see in her background check?"

"Well, there are a few concerning things. She has received several anonymous incoming wire transfers over the last few weeks. Each one was under the radar at around $10,000 but together it was quite a sum of money for her job level and current salary. The incoming wire came from overseas, and we can't identify the specific account or who sent it. Another thing, on her phone records, she's been receiving calls originating from Russia over the past few weeks. The calls were very short, but that doesn't mean information or directions couldn't have passed between them. The last thing we noticed, and this is only relevant due to the international wires and phone calls, but Mariana spent time in Europe studying abroad and interning through a UCLA program during college. We looked at her travel records, and she did travel to Russia more than once during that time. If the Russians are involved in messing with the autonomous electric vehicles, then potentially Mariana could be a sleeper agent for them."

"Hmmm, that's not what I expected based on our conversation with her," replied Booker. "Perhaps she's a good chameleon? Let's look deeper into her past. Give her a call to get her perspective and see how she reacts. Set up surveillance. And I'll call Raj again to get more insight into her performance and mental state."

Once Pat had left, Booker placed a call to Raj.

Raj picked up immediately. "Hello Booker. I'm surprised to hear from you so soon. What can I help you with?"

"Well, I want to follow-up with you on one of your employees."

"Sure, which one?" Raj quickly asked.

"I'd like to know more about Mariana Morales, your

lead programmer. To be clear, she is not a suspect, only a person of interest at this point. We want to know a bit more about her demeanor and how her mental state has been in the recent past. Any comments on that?"

Raj laughed. "Mariana? You must be mistaken. She's a great asset to this company. I can't imagine doing this project without her."

"Okay, that's good to hear. Perhaps it's nothing, but please inform me if you hear or see anything of concern. It may not be related to her work performance. Also, are you able to have someone confidentially review the code she submitted for the last release? We just want to take all precautions."

Raj considered the request. "Yes, of course. I'll be on the lookout for anything strange. I can have my head of security review the software and look for any anomalies. I'll let you know if we find anything."

When they hung up, Raj immediately contacted his head of IT and asked him to investigate the matter.

"Let's keep this under the radar," Raj said. "Call me when you have an update."

A while later the two of them met up. The head of IT had gone through Mariana's code and found nothing strange. Feeling much better again, Raj figured he would reach out to Booker in the coming days. For now, he wanted to focus on the next software release and the big press event that was being planned.

Mariana was sitting at home when she got a call from Pat. The FBI agent said she just had a few follow-up questions. At first, Pat started by asking about the software again, but then she switched to personal questions about Mariana.

"Great, thanks for that information. On another level, we have been doing background checks on all the people across several companies that have access to software systems. This includes yourself. There are a few questions I have regarding your background...if you don't mind?" asked Pat, then quickly added, "Purely routine. We just want to make sure we're checking all the details."

Mariana sat up straighter. A surge of adrenaline shot through her. "Of course. I have nothing to hide. What are your questions?"

Pat continued, "One of the areas we check with everyone is phone records. We noticed in your phone records that recently you received several calls originating from Russia. Can you tell me about these calls?"

After a moment of silence, Mariana spoke up and said, "I don't know what calls you are referring to, but I have been receiving several calls from international numbers. I assumed it was related to work, but when I answered, the line was quiet. I tried saying hello numerous times, but no one responded. Eventually, I just hung up and assumed they had the wrong number, or it was some type of sales call. I didn't realize the calls were from Russia."

"Okay, so you never actually spoke with anyone on

those calls?"

"Yes, that's correct," responded Mariana.

"Interesting. So, another area we routinely check is bank account activity. We noticed you have received several international wire transfers into your account over the past few weeks. Each one is around $10,000. Can you explain these transactions?"

Mariana was stunned. "What are you talking about? I'm not aware of any wire transfers and clearly, not those amounts!"

"So, you didn't even notice that your bank balance was increasing?" Pat inquired with doubt in her voice.

"No," said Mariana a bit defensively. "I haven't had any reason to go to the bank recently or to check my balance. I set it up so I only get text notifications from my bank for withdrawals over $500."

Pat was quiet for a moment and then continued, "Okay, thank you for your time. If I were you, I would contact your bank and find out more about the wire transfers. Something is going on. I'm sure you can understand from our perspective this is considered a yellow flag and something we will need to investigate."

Pat disconnected the call. Mariana sat there staring at her phone, paralyzed. She couldn't move, yet her mind raced with thoughts. *What the hell? Why is this happening? What should I do?*

TWELVE

IT'S ALL POINTING AT ME

Santa Cruz, California

Mariana decided to take a drive and clear her mind. As she went to unlock her car and open the door, she noticed a piece of paper attached to the windshield under the wiper blade. She grabbed the paper thinking it was just another marketing brochure but saw that her name was spelled out in bold ink on the front. Hesitating, she carefully opened the note and read it:

We are watching you. Do not tell anyone at CellSpot or at the FBI about your concerns with the latest software release. If you share any information about this note we will be forced to act against your parents,

Jose and Ana Morales. If you do nothing, no one will get hurt and this issue will go away.

Mariana re-read the note at least five times. Astounded, she stood there frozen in time, contemplating the implications of the note. She didn't know what to do. *Should I call Booker? No, the risk is way too high. But what on earth is happening? First the FBI called about the background check, and now this mysterious threatening note...* Mariana's blood pressure started to spike. Her sweatshirt constricted at her neck, making her swallow, so she maniacally pulled it off. She was accustomed to being in control of most situations and this was new territory for her. She brainstormed all the potential scenarios and how they might play out. None of them were good. She reflected on her conversation with the FBI. Clearly, they decided she was a suspect, given the background checks and suspicious bank and phone activities that she couldn't explain. Her head started spinning, and flashbacks of her old boyfriend Oleg came to mind. *Could his Russian background make them suspicious of me? If they've been digging into my past, they clearly discovered that we dated when I was living in Prague.*

All these things did make her look guilty. How could she defend herself? Who would believe her? She kept going through all the activities that occurred over the past few days trying to make sense of it all. She couldn't think of a single explanation.

Finally, she gave up trying to decipher the logic, and instead, called her parents to check on them. They were fine, and she didn't want to scare them, so she didn't say anything about the note. She told them she would call them again soon and made a mental note to herself to keep checking on them. Looking down at the keys in her hand, she realized a drive was not what she needed right now. She had to get to the bottom of this. She ran back up to her apartment and hopped on her laptop to begin researching, yet again.

THIRTEEN

WAYFINDER

Santa Cruz, California

When Tess got home from work, she found Mariana still closed off in her room. Once again, Tess knocked on her door to check on her. Mariana opened the door dressed in her running clothes.

"I'm going for a run," Mariana said. "But my AirPods aren't charged. Can I borrow yours?"

"No problem. They're in my running waist belt. It's on the kitchen counter. Just take the whole thing."

"Thanks," Mariana responded. "I appreciate it." She walked into the kitchen, attached the belt around her waist, and bolted out the door.

Tess watched her take off at a clipped pace through

the living room window. "Why is Mariana acting so strange?" She said out loud to Drake who was brushing up against her leg trying to get her attention. "I wonder what's going on with her." Shrugging, she walked into the kitchen to feed the cat.

Mariana didn't really think about where she was going, she just knew she needed to de-stress and think through how she was going to handle her predicament. Everything pointed the finger in her direction, and it didn't make any sense at all. *Who was doing this? Why her? How could she prove her innocence? Was she going to be thrown in jail? Why was all this happening? And why were her parents being threatened?* The same questions kept flooding her brain repeatedly, and her head spun faster than her legs could manage. As if on autopilot, she ran straight to the one place that made her feel at peace: Shep's Gym. She slowed down to a walk and raised her arms over her head to open her airway and regulate her breathing. Just then, Shep walked out of the gym and handed her a bottle of water. Pulling the AirPods out of her ears, Mariana opened the running belt and placed them in the case so she wouldn't lose them.

"I saw you out my office window. That was quite the pace. Were you running off steam or running for your life?" Shep joked.

"Actually both," Mariana replied between breaths. "Thanks for the water."

"What do you mean? Are you okay?" Shep asked.

Mariana gave him a look of pure anguish, and an uncontrollable tear spilled down her face. "I...I don't know what to do," she stuttered. "I feel so out of control."

Shep grabbed her arm and guided her away from the gym. "Let's go for a walk and you can tell me what's going on."

The two of them walked slowly down the dirt path that led to the outside CrossFit training grounds, and Mariana revealed the massive mess she was in.

After listening to her story Shep jumped in. "If you didn't do anything wrong, why can't you just tell the FBI and help them figure out what's happening?"

"Well, there's more to it...I actually think I'm being set up." Mariana continued to explain the extent of the situation, including the threat to her parents.

"Can't you go to the FBI in confidence? Won't they protect you and make sure nothing happens to your parents?"

"I feel like they won't believe me. It's like they just assume I'm involved. I spent the last couple days reviewing all my code in production to see what could be amiss. I can't find anything obvious, but there are some anomalies that appear to have erased themselves after executing and some code has been checked in from my account from remote locations. I can't get to the source of what's happening, but some malicious software could be transferring itself from the charging node in the car to the car diagnostics and sensors themselves. If this is happening, then there's a chance bad data is being sent to the real-time navigation system, and this is causing the accidents with the self-driving software." Mariana paused and took a deep breath. "I'm getting concerned that the FBI thinks I downloaded the cyberattack, and I'm afraid our CEO will be more than willing to make me the scapegoat for all of this to take the spotlight away from the company. He's a brilliant leader but obsessed with making this company even more successful. He won't let this disrupt our progress. If it ends up that the attack was somehow initiated through my code that I sent to production, I could go to jail for a very long time. And if I say anything to the FBI, I'm worried someone will harm my parents."

"This is absolutely crazy!" Shep responded. "Okay, I'll be straight with you. You need to find a way to clear your name–and do it quickly!"

Then Shep added, "I haven't told you about my family, but believe me when I tell you that I have the means to buy you some time until you figure out what's going on. I can help you if you want, but you need to trust me and keep everything I tell you about my family confidential. There's a valid reason why I keep my past private."

Mariana shook her head side to side. "I'm sure I can find a way to handle this myself. I'm sorry I dumped all this on you. I just needed to get it off my chest."

"Mariana, you don't have to deal with this by yourself. This is a big deal, and you need help. I can at least help you prove your innocence."

Mariana thought about what Tess had said earlier about delegating and letting others help her. She felt so isolated and alone. She finally looked up at Shep and said meekly, "Honestly, Shep, I'm so overwhelmed. I would really appreciate your help. I just don't see how

I'm going to clear my name! I've been set up, and I don't know what I did to deserve this."

Shep's mind started racing, thinking through the logistics. "Alright, we need to move fast. We don't have time to waste. Give me a sec to tell Amy to close the gym tonight and grab my car keys. My black truck is parked on the side of the gym by my back-office door. I'll meet you there."

A few minutes later Shep was driving them to Mariana's apartment while he explained the plan. "Pack a bag with enough clothes for a few days and all your essentials, then we'll swing by my place so I can do the same. I think it's best if you get out of town until you figure out who's after you. We can drive to Las Vegas. My family has a lot of connections and can help us out. I'll explain on the drive down."

"What do I tell Tess? My family? What about my cat?" Mariana implored.

"Keep it vague. Just say you are heading out of town for a few days, then disconnect your phone. No one can know where we're going, who we're seeing, or what we're doing. I don't even want them to know that you are with me. It's critical that we keep our whereabouts confidential. Once we know what you're dealing with and have a plan of action, we can determine when to let people know."

"Why are you doing this, Shep? Why are you helping me out when you could get dragged into this mess and get in trouble as well?" Mariana asked.

"Because I know this would be hard for anyone to

handle alone. I have connections and a lot of people who owe me favors. I believe you're innocent, and I want to help you clear your name."

As they pulled up to her apartment complex, Mariana took her keys out of Tess's running belt and promised Shep she would be quick. While Shep stayed in the car, Mariana bolted up the stairs and into her home, nervous about telling Tess a lie regarding where she was going. Fortunately, there was a note on the kitchen counter.

6PM–Ran to the grocery store to get some food for dinner. Text me if you want anything. Be back in an hour

I already fed Drake

I have a bottle of Kim Crawford chilling in the fridge. I think we need a glass or two tonight! :(

With a huge sigh of relief, Mariana looked at the clock. Tess had only been gone for twenty minutes, but regardless, Mariana had to hurry. She ran into her room, grabbed her suitcase and started yanking clothes out of her drawers and off the hangers, then she added her laptop and shoes. Per Shep's instructions, she powered off her phone and placed it in a drawer. When she entered the bathroom to grab her toiletries, she took one glance in the mirror and realized what an awful state she was in. After her fast-paced run, she was still a little sweaty, and her flushed face didn't mask the scared, manic look in her eyes. She quickly removed her damp clothes, took a fast rinse in the shower, then pulled on jeans and her favorite, well-worn UCLA sweatshirt for good luck. As she was about to exit the apartment, she remembered to email work to say she needed a few days off and then scribbled a note to Tess.

Had to head out of town for a few days. Long story. Will explain later. Please take care of Drake for me. I'll be in touch asap!

As if he knew that she was writing about him, Drake jumped up on the table, meowing for attention. She picked him up, gave him a big hug, and whispered, "I'm going to miss you buddy, but I'll be back soon!" Then she set him on the floor, picked up her suitcase, and ran out the door to Shep's truck.

It only took about five minutes to get to Shep's house. While he lived close to Mariana and Tess, his waterfront condo on West Cliff Drive had a completely different look and feel. Santa Cruz was a typical beach town made up of streets filled with run-down beach shacks intermixed with decent apartment buildings and pristine waterfront homes. Mariana's place fell somewhere in the middle of the spectrum, while Shep's was clearly on the higher end. When they stepped into his condominium, Mariana's jaw dropped. The massive window in the main room boasted an expansive ocean view. Immediately drawn, Mariana walked over to the window and looked down on the beach while Shep went to pack a suitcase. Waves crashed on the shore below. Surfers swam hard to catch the last few sets before sundown. Couples walked along the water's edge holding hands. Children ran away from the surf as it swallowed their sandcastles. Dogs chased each other in the sand, ignoring their owners calling out to them. It was a spectacular evening, and the setting sun highlighted an array of color–a dramatic union of blue, purple, red, orange, and yellow.

"This view is incredible, Shep. I can't believe you live here–it's amazing," Mariana said, then turned around to register the room she was standing in. The family room was decorated in a deep grey and white palette with pops of color in various shades of blue to complement the ocean panorama. The plush couch made Mariana wish she had the luxury to crawl in it and read a book or watch a movie on the massive television screen hanging on the opposite wall. The room opened to a chef's dream kitchen, complete with high-end appliances, granite countertops, and a kitchen nook with glass walls overlooking the ocean.

"Change of plans," Shep said as he emerged from his bedroom. "I need to go back to the gym to take care of a few things because we might be gone for a few days. I'm also exhausted and don't think driving all night is a smart thing to do. Let's spend the night here and leave early tomorrow morning."

"Are you sure about this?" Mariana asked, feeling a bit awkward about the idea of sleeping at his home.

"Absolutely. No one knows that you're here. Just stay inside, eat some dinner, and watch TV," Shep replied, pointing to the remote control on the coffee table. "I have a ton of pre-cooked dinners in the refrigerator."

Mariana looked at him quizzically.

"I use a meal delivery service," Shep explained. "I'm so busy at the gym I never have time to cook. Eating healthy is important to me, and I don't like going out all the time."

Mariana nodded, "Okay. Thank you." *He really was Mr. Perfect.*

"I may be gone for a few hours. Just make yourself at home, and call me if you need anything," Shep replied while heading out the door and locking it behind him.

Hungry from her run and the nervous energy burning inside of her, Mariana turned on the news station, then entered the kitchen in search of dinner. When she opened the massive Sub-Zero refrigerator, she found various labeled boxes lining the shelves, ranging from fully prepped entrees to healthy snacks, including organic fruit and vegetables.

What on earth? Mariana voiced aloud to herself. *He has enough meals here to feed an army!* Then thinking of how big he was and how hard he worked out all the time, she figured he probably consumed all these meals himself. Mariana grabbed a chicken curry salad and fruit smoothie, then flipped through the channels looking for a lighthearted movie to watch. She needed something more uplifting than the news to escape into.

By the time Shep got back to the condo, Mariana was deep asleep on the couch. Not wanting to disturb her, he added another blanket over her and quietly entered his room to finish packing and get ready for bed.

FOURTEEN

ON THE ROAD

Santa Cruz, California

The next morning, they got a later start than expected because there was a bad accident on the CA-1 South and the freeway was shut down temporarily to clear the road. When they were finally able to leave, Shep plugged in his Las Vegas home address to see what route would be fastest, then switched to Spotify and handed Mariana his phone.

"Pick whatever you want to listen to, we've got a long drive ahead of us. It will take about eight hours to get there."

Mariana scrolled through his playlists and selected *Imagine Dragons–Top Hits*.

"One of my favorite bands," she smiled, tapping her

fingers to the beat of their hit song, *Whatever It Takes.*

"Me too," Shep replied. "I just went to their concert at Shoreline."

Mariana turned towards Shep with wide eyes. "Tess and I were there! We were crammed up on the lawn with general admission because we bought last-minute tickets, but it was still a great show."

Mariana sat back in the seat, closed her eyes, and listened to the music, allowing herself to temporarily escape the situation she was in. It didn't last long. Her mind started racing again, questioning why all of this was happening to her. Sensing her distress, Shep tried to distract her by asking her about her childhood.

"Where did you grow up? Have you always lived in California?"

"Yes. My parents moved to California after they married. I was born and raised in Chula Vista, just south of San Diego. My mom and dad opened a restaurant when I was little and worked around the clock to make ends meet. They still do, work around the clock I mean. Their restaurant is successful now, but they devote all their time to running it. I wish they'd take a break and travel more. My aunts and uncles, and now many of my cousins, help run the restaurant and are more than capable of taking over."

"Sounds like quite the family affair. Did you work at the restaurant?"

Mariana laughed. "Since I was old enough to wash dishes, crush garlic, and dice tomatoes! My mom is an amazing cook. She taught me a lot, but while I may have developed a passion for cooking, I have no interest in the restaurant business." Mariana shrugged, then added, "Mom and Dad respect that. They were thrilled to discover I was not only a good athlete but also a straight A student. Neither of them had the luxury of going to college, and all their money was tied up in their restaurant, so they couldn't afford to pay for my education. By the time I was a sophomore in high school, Mom and Dad refused to let me work in the restaurant outside of Saturdays. They wanted me to focus on excelling at school and winning my track races. They believed in me, and I appreciated that, so I poured all my energy into studying and running. It paid off. When I was offered a full scholarship at UCLA, they shut down the restaurant for the night and had the biggest party. I think they invited the entire neighborhood and all their regulars to celebrate with us. It was a night I will never forget. When I was racing in my track meets at UCLA, I would picture everyone at that party cheering me on at the finish line. It was great motivation to always perform my best."

"That's pretty inspirational," Shep said. "Now I see where you get your competitive spirit. What races did you run?"

"I ran the 100 and 400-meter hurdles."

"Why did you pick those events?"

"I liked the fact that I was in control. I either performed at my best or I didn't, but I wasn't depending on other people as well."

"Did you run all four years?"

"Yeah, it was intense, but I tried my best to have a

full college experience. I was even able to participate in UCLA's Global Internship Program for engineering students in Prague between track seasons."

"That's so cool. I wish I did a semester abroad in college. Were you able to visit a lot of other countries while you were there?"

"A few," she responded, then quickly redirected the conversation. "What about you? Clearly you were an athlete. What's your story?"

"Well, I was a football player in high school. I was good, but two concussions prevented me from playing in college. My second one was the worst. I recovered fine and could've made it back on the field, but my parents were adamant that I quit. It really scared my mom to see me stuck in bed for weeks. I had to keep my room dark because the light really gave me headaches, and I ended up missing a lot of school. In the end, I promised to stop playing."

After a short pause, Mariana asked, "So, when did you start getting involved in CrossFit?"

"Well, my high school football buddies and I started it during the off-season to keep in shape. When I was getting ready to graduate, I saw that the University of Reno had a CrossFit Club Team. I met with the coach, and he was fired up to have me join. I figured it was the perfect solution–keep my parents happy because I was staying close to home while continuing to be involved in a sport I enjoyed."

"And then you opened your gym?"

"No. Initially I did what my dad expected me to do,

and I went to work for him. He and my uncle run the family business my grandfather built a long time ago. I lasted several years but eventually found a way to escape."

Mariana absorbed the heavy comment, then asked, "Why did you feel the need to escape?"

"Now that's a long story...let me just say that a part of our family business borders the line on ethics. I learned my uncle became involved with several somewhat questionable business partners that I am not allowed to talk about. This is why I have connections and can protect you while we figure out what the heck is going on at CellSpot."

"So...what's your family business?" Mariana asked.

Shep cleared his throat. "Well, we own a resort hotel and casino."

"Seriously? What's the name?"

"The Argyll."

Mariana gasped and leaned forward, looking over at Shep. "Your family owns The Argyll? Isn't that one of the most exclusive casino hotels in Vegas?"

"Yeah...," Shep sheepishly replied.

Mariana sat back in her seat, staring straight ahead, absorbing what he had just said. "I don't even know what to say. That's crazy."

"I know, and please keep this confidential. In addition to the fact that I don't really like everyone knowing my background, there's a valid reason why I walked away from the business."

"Absolutely. Mums the word," Mariana responded,

then let out a long, slow breath as she turned her gaze to the window. The scenery was nothing special, just a long, monotonous stretch of dry dirt and pale, dusty brush. She found the colorless landscape calming. The sheer absence of life allowed her mind to go still. Shep sensed that she needed a break from the conversation, so he turned up the music. Eventually, Mariana spoke up again.

"This is all so overwhelming–I cannot thank you enough. As soon as we figure out my next steps, I promise I'll do this on my own, and you can get back to the gym." Then she added, "Do you mind me asking how you were able to walk away from the family business?"

"Like I said, it's a long story, but here's the short version. Basically, I was injured badly trying to protect my brother, Joe. One of our business partners became shady. He took advantage of a situation, and when Joe confronted him about it, the guy pulled out a knife. I stepped in to protect Joe and ended up getting stabbed in the stomach and almost lost my life. When I was finally released from the hospital, my father and brother promised that if I really wanted to step away from the business, they'd support me. They helped me create a new identity and fresh start. So, I changed my name, moved to Santa Cruz, opened the gym, and the rest is history."

Mariana shook her head and tried to make sense of the thoughts swarming around. "Well, I'm glad you survived! So, what's your real name, and how did you choose Santa Cruz?"

"Trent McCallister," Shep replied, holding out his hand to shake hers as if meeting her for the first time.

Mariana's fingers tingled when her hand joined his, radiating throughout her body. When she looked up at Shep, she could tell that he was feeling the same intense connection.

Shep cleared his throat and continued, "Choosing Santa Cruz was super easy. I love the ocean, and the weather is significantly better than Las Vegas. My parents used to take us to Los Angeles when I was little to escape the heat and enjoy time on the beach. I liked it a lot, but when I first came to Santa Cruz in college, I loved the relaxed, laid-back environment–I found it much more down to earth than LA and Vegas.

Mariana and Shep continued to talk about their upbringing, families, friends, and interests. Conversation came effortlessly between the two of them, and the hours quickly passed. When they pulled into a gas station to fuel up, Mariana raced into the restroom and then bought a couple more bottles of water and snacks for the road.

Shep eyed the pile in her arms as she walked back to the truck. "So...you have a sweet tooth?"

Mariana laughed. "I just need some good anxiety relief and road trip fuel. You can't go on an eight-hour drive, under the most stress of your life, without having some Hershey Kisses and Hot Tamales."

Shep laughed as they both climbed back into the truck to hit the road. Mariana's sugar high didn't last long. Soon the gravity of the situation and the vibration of the car lulled her to sleep.

Shep, on the other hand, was wide awake. He was thinking about the upcoming reunion with his family. He had left in a hurry after the injury healed, and hadn't really kept in touch with anyone, especially his brother. He held his older brother in high regard, so it deeply troubled him to think his brother was still permitting illegal actions within the family business. His brother tried to contact him many times over the recent past, but Shep dismissed him. Part of Shep was excited to see his brother again, while the other part still felt extremely betrayed and angry. He wasn't sure how this reunion would play out, and he didn't trust his own emotions.

As he contemplated what lay ahead, Shep realized he was humming along to the lyrics of one of his favorite Imagine Dragons songs, *It's Time*.

It dawned on him that these lyrics reflected his own life. Emotionally, he knew he was at a low point with his family. Deep down, he wanted to rebuild it, but he wasn't sure if he could. He was stubborn and principled, and he wasn't willing to change his beliefs to be close again with his family. He wondered how the passage of time would impact his relationship with his brother.

FIFTEEN

TRACKING MARIANA

San Francisco, California

Booker walked into his office early in the morning and saw one of Pat's infamous light blue sticky notes, with a cryptic message stating, *On the run?* Booker immediately called out for Pat to come join him when he saw her walking back from the coffee station.

"Good morning," Pat greeted him. "As you requested, I put a surveillance team on Mariana to keep track of her. They arrived at her place last night and didn't see her enter or leave the apartment building. This morning, they saw her roommate leave for work by herself. Since then, Mariana hasn't left the apartment. Her car is still in the parking lot. What would you like them to do?"

Booker considered this news for a second and then

responded, "Have them keep tabs for a bit longer. If nothing changes, let's contact Raj at CellSpot and see if he knows where she is."

Later that day, Pat caught up with Booker again to give him the update. "Looks like she took off. I talked with Raj at CellSpot, and he said she had called HR to let them know she needed to take a few personal days. He checked with her roommate, Tess, who also works at CellSpot. I guess Tess got a note from Mariana last night saying she had to leave town for a while and would explain later."

Booker looked up, rolled his eyes, and scoffed. "Okay, let's officially make her a suspect. Check the airports and other transportation locations to see if she has bought a ticket. Also, send out a bulletin to local police forces in surrounding cities where she might have gone. Let's include her hometown, San Diego, as well as Los Angeles, Las Vegas, and Portland to start with. That should cover most of the areas she could easily get to driving."

SIXTEEN

THE KNOTS

Continuation of Secret Meeting–Undisclosed Location

The Spaniard opened the meeting. "I'm glad you're all here. Thank you for making the trip. It's time for an update on our latest mission. Our initial test was successful, and we've now begun the operational phase. It's going live as we speak."

Everyone shifted in their seats. This mission was the most brazen to date. While critical in their eyes, they also knew the risks. The Spaniard was adamant that they were on the right path, and excited to share the progress.

"AI is the biggest threat our organization has faced. Without knowing it, humans are in essence demoting themselves from the top of the food chain. Other technological advancements in the past have been tools to amplify what we can achieve as humans. AI is different. It mimics what human intelligence can accomplish, and potentially does it better. Where does that leave us? We know we can't stop it forever, but we can try to slow it down and prevent mass chaos in society. If we don't, we'll see a massive shift of wealth creation for the very few at the expense of tremendous unemployment for the rest of the population."

There was silence in the room as none of the others wanted to interrupt the Spaniard's flow and risk his wrath.

The Spaniard continued, "Autonomous vehicles are the perfect AI application to attack. The pace of innovation is accelerating at an alarming rate, the media loves talking about it, and it has high visibility with consumers. Most importantly, it will drive large numbers of unemployment in the near term."

The American jumped in and said, "Commercial drivers in the U.S. make up approximately 3% of total employment–that's over five million people. And most of these folks come from lower-income demographics. Eliminating these positions will contribute even more to the wealth divide between technology conglomerates and the working class."

The Spaniard looked across the room to gauge everyone's reaction and then took over again. "These stats are similar in other countries as well. This is unacceptable. We need to stop the greed and power play of these tech titans! These advancements come at the expense of the broader population, and we can't allow it."

The Brazilian woman spoke up, "That's easy to say, but what can we do to stop it?"

The Spaniard lowered his voice to add drama to the next part. "We've been looking for ways to exploit this market. We found it. Insert bad data into the AI models. We can't impact the AI engines–they're robust. But just like any machine, garbage in, garbage out. We figured out how to gain access to the software systems in these vehicles and create erroneous sensor data that will lead to crashes. This will become a wake-up call for the government to enact harder legislation and slow everything down. Our plans are in action as we speak, and results are already paying off."

"How are you controlling the car crashes? Are innocent people getting hurt?" the Italian asked from across the table.

Everyone looked at the Spaniard as he stood up and began pacing. He then stopped, leaned over to grip the edge of the table forcefully and said with a confident tone, "We aren't trying to control them. And yes, people will get hurt as an unfortunate side effect. It's unavoidable but necessary to create urgency. Let's not forget who we are: The KNOTs. The ends justify the means."

The room was silent for a moment as the members reflected on their mantra. The woman from Brazil hesitantly asked another question, "How have you gained access to the vehicle software systems?"

"Good question," answered the Spaniard, regaining his calm, scholarly demeanor. "We're using the specialist again and taking advantage of his resources. His team has shown great creativity in discovering exploitable vulnerabilities. We've been testing various approaches in other industries first to prove out the capability. Those tests were successful, and we've now started to roll out the approach through electric charging stations. We found a vulnerability with the data connection while cars are charging, and this allows us to insert algorithms to drive incorrect sensor readings to confuse the cars at random times."

"Tell them how we got access to the software," exclaimed the Russian, glancing at everyone around the table with an animated expression.

The Spaniard looked across the room with a smirk. "Young love. In America, we have had agents recruiting software developers from charging station companies through web forums and dating apps. One of our agents was successful in gaining the trust of a developer. He sent her a photo with an embedded malicious payload which silently executed a worm and installed a keylogger. The keylogger provided us with usernames and passwords to access the company's software. The specialist purchased what's called a zero-day exploit for image-processing software from the Dark Web with crypto to keep the transaction anonymous."

The Dutchman jumped in. "But how many of the reported crashes are from us?"

The Spaniard nodded. "Just enough to make the headlines. Exactly as we have predicted, car companies are pushing too fast to commercialize self-driving cars, and they're experiencing their own number of crashes due to the immature software. This only supports our case, and we're just making sure enough crashes occur to draw the public's attention."

The woman from Brazil chimed in, "Why are we only targeting autonomous vehicles? I'm concerned we need to target more industries where AI is being deployed."

The Spaniard commented, "Yes, yes. You're correct. We're extremely concerned about AI in general and what it will do for structural unemployment. All in due time. Let me remind you of what our predecessor, John Maynard Keynes, said about this topic. He coined the phrase, *technological unemployment*, where technology leads to significant unemployment in the short term and that certain groups will suffer during the transition. In the long run, advances in technology will lead to new job creation, and overall, society will be better off. He evolved our thinking not to try to stop the change, but to manage its velocity. This is now our purpose, as we don't believe companies will do it themselves and governments will react too slowly. Labor unions have tried to play this role in the past, but they don't have enough leverage. That is where we come in. We create the forcing functions that can't be easily swept under the rug. We stay anonymous and behind the scenes, but our fingerprints touch everything."

All the members pounded the table with their fists to display agreement and unity. The meeting ended, and the individuals each headed out separately according to the protocol.

SEVENTEEN

AGAINST THE CLOCK

San Francisco, CA

Pat burst into Booker's office. Booker was just getting off the phone, sitting at his desk. He looked up at Pat.

Pat said, "We got a sighting of Mariana! She was at a gas station buying food, heading east out of California near Bakersfield."

Booker clapped his hands. "Way to go. Did you find out what car she's driving?"

"Unfortunately, no," said Pat. "The cameras by the pumps are non-operable, so the only camera shot we have is when she went inside the station to buy food. She used cash to pay."

Booker frowned in disappointment.

Pat continued, "Well, we know she isn't driving her car since it's still back at her apartment. Regardless, based on her direction, I'm betting she's headed towards Las Vegas. I'm going to put the authorities in Vegas on high alert. If she switches back and goes south again, we'll probably pick her up in LA or San Diego on some camera surveillance. There are so many down there."

Booker contemplated the news. "Okay, great job. Keep me posted. There's no way she's sophisticated enough to evade us for long. I predict we'll catch her before tomorrow is over."

EIGHTEEN

SIN CITY

Las Vegas, Nevada

Shep gently nudged Mariana, who had been deep asleep for the last couple of hours during their drive to Las Vegas. The stress of the past forty-eight hours had taken its toll, and her body finally shut down. Mariana looked at her watch and couldn't believe it was 7:30PM.

"Yikes, Shep. I'm sorry I slept for so long! Are you doing okay? Do you need me to drive for a while?" Mariana asked, rubbing her eyes to wake up. When she opened them again and focused on where they were, she quickly realized why Shep had started laughing. Bright lights, flashing billboards, massive buildings, and the chaos of people on the streets overwhelmed her instantly as they traveled down Las Vegas Boulevard. Having never been to Vegas, she was quickly intoxicated by the overstimulating environment.

Shep witnessed her eyes grow large as she took in the surroundings. "Welcome to Sin City, the entertainment capital of the world. I wish I could show you around more, but to be safe, we need to head straight to my family's hotel. They know we're coming."

He steered the truck into a garage on the backside of a very tall, sprawling building and drove up to a side door. A large man in a black suit with an earpiece walked out and opened the car door for Mariana.

"Good evening, Miss," he greeted Mariana, then looked over and addressed Shep. "Mr. McCallister, we're all excited to see you again. It has been too long." The man paused for effect, letting the words hang in the air. "I'm going to take you straight up to the office. As you know, your parents are in The Caymans, but your uncle is here to see you and go over the logistics."

"Where's Joe?" Shep asked, while he took the suitcases out of the car.

"Your brother already left for the evening, but we've arranged for you to meet up with him. Your uncle will explain everything."

Mariana quickly gathered their items from the front seat. "Oh no," she grumbled. "I forgot to put Tess's running belt and AirPods back in the apartment." With a deep sigh she shoved the items in the outside pocket of her suitcase, hoping she would be home soon to return them to Tess. After handing the car keys to the guard, they were ushered into the elevator and taken up to the offices on the sixty-seventh floor. The doors opened to an expansive reception area beautifully decorated in rich masculine colors with elaborate furniture and modern art decorating the walls with pops of bright color. Because it was evening, the rooms were dark and quiet, but Shep's Uncle Bob walked out of his office, arms open to greet them. He gave Shep a huge bear hug, pulled away, and looked intently into Shep's eyes with a compassionate smile. "It's been a long time, Trent. We're glad you're back."

Shep stiffened, but regained his composure and said, "Thanks, Uncle Bob. We'll only be here for a short visit though."

Bob smiled and shrugged. "Well then, we'll make the most of the time we have to catch up with you," he said, turning toward Mariana. "And who is this lovely lady?" he asked, grabbing her hand to place a kiss.

"Uncle Bob, please meet Mariana Morales. We appreciate you staying late to meet us tonight. Where's Joe? I thought he was going to be here."

"Joe is at the Jason Aldean concert at the Sphere," Bob explained. "We have some clients from Texas he's entertaining, and it wasn't easy for him to cancel on them last minute. No worries though, I have tickets for you. They're in our suite at the Sphere so you'll have a private area to talk with Joe. The concert starts soon so our driver will take you over there now."

Shep and Mariana made their way back to the parking garage and hopped in the back of the blacked-out

Escalade to head to the concert. Mariana sat quietly looking out the window. She wasn't used to being ushered around, and the whole experience unnerved her even more. She couldn't believe how luminous Vegas was at night. As they approached the Sphere, Shep watched her eyes grow even larger. The ominous globe was a hypnotic sight, all lit up with revolving pictures changing scenes every few seconds. It reminded Mariana of the atlas globe that sat on her history teacher's desk in fifth grade, but this one was a thousand times larger and done up Vegas-style–flashy and bright.

They were driven to the exclusive West VIP Entrance and ushered out quickly because the concert was about to start. The driver had informed them to go straight to Suite 19 and ignore their ticketed seat numbers. After Shep scanned their tickets at the check-in, they rushed up the escalator to the third-floor suites.

Once they entered the private room, they found the view was surreal. It was as if they had stepped back outside, into a whole new world. The stage was set for the band to play at the base of the enormous dome theater. Displayed all around them was an eerily realistic cinematic experience, transporting them to a horse ranch in the sprawling backcountry of Georgia. Looking left and right as far as they could, as well as up and down, their reality had changed to an immersive outdoor landscape.

With a nod to his guests, Joe, an almost identical version of his brother, quickly approached Shep with open arms and a huge grin, but then hesitated. Aware of the awkwardness, Shep extended his hand, leading to a clumsy handshake between them. Joe put his other hand on Shep's back, embracing him with a soft pat. He looked intently into Shep's eyes, trying to register his feelings. Then, Joe shifted his gaze to Mariana, formed a big smile on his face, and gently squeezed Mariana's hand. "It's nice to meet you, Mariana. I'm Joe, Trent's brother."

Shep interjected, "Joe, you can call me Shep now. That's the name I go by."

Joe nodded in tacit acknowledgement. He then looked over at the other guests across the room and stated, "No need for introductions, I told my guests you were arriving to deal with some quick family business. Mariana, I wish we were meeting on better terms, but hopefully we'll have time for that later. Let's move over to the corner where it's a little quieter and you can fill me in. Mariana, enjoy the show. It's about to start."

Mariana started to insist that she join their discussion when Shep whispered in her ear, "Please. Just give me a minute. I haven't seen my brother in a long time."

Mariana looked up and saw the pleading in Shep's eyes, so she walked over and sat down in the chair Joe had pointed at. The guests were all at the private bar getting more drinks before the concert started. Mariana was shocked at how realistic the virtual scene was in front of her. She felt like her chair was sitting in the middle of the open field as she watched the leaves on the trees blow in the wind and the horses meander completely at ease, eating the grass and warming themselves in the sun. The sky was a vibrant blue and the puffy white clouds floated across the screen. Mariana wanted to reach down and touch the blades of grass that somehow seemed as if they were tickling her ankles. Suddenly the sky darkened as the sun fell behind a set of dark clouds. Thunder boomed and Mariana's seat felt like it was vibrating from the raucous, dramatic weather change. The horses in the field were spooked and started charging away, kicking up dust, hooves pounding on the ground. The rhythmic beat of drums, synchronized with their hooves, grew louder. Then, a spotlight hit the stage, revealing the band as they launched into their opening song for the crowd. They chose to play *Dirt Road Anthem,* and as the music began, the dome screen changed once again to a pickup truck driving down a winding country road. Mariana felt like she was a passenger in the truck. Before she knew it, she was singing along to the lyrics while she felt herself bouncing and swerving along the dirt road.

A genuine feeling of nausea washed over her as she watched the truck accelerate over the undulating landscape, its path winding along the curving road. The burger that she ate for lunch stirred in her stomach, and she knew she needed to get up and step out into the hall for a change of environment.

Outside the suite, in the hallway, Mariana steadied herself on the railing. She looked down through the vast open atrium three levels below to the main lobby just as police officers were charging into the reception area at the main entrance. They began corralling the Sphere security team, showing them a picture on their phone.

The hair on Mariana's arms stood on end as a pricking sensation ran across her skin. She had an eerie feeling they were looking for her. Mariana ran back into the suite, interrupting Shep and Joe from their discussion.

"We gotta go...like NOW!" Mariana blurted. "The police are here, and I have a strange feeling they're looking for me. Maybe I'm overreacting, but I'm scared."

Joe and Shep had clearly been in the middle of an intense discussion, and it took them a moment to focus on Mariana's words. Joe finally said, "There are lots of cameras when you check into the Sphere with your tickets. I wonder if one of them captured you and triggered something on the FBI watch list through facial recognition. Just in case, let's get both of you out of here right away." Registering the need to act, Joe quickly pulled two wide-brimmed cowboy hats off his guests' heads. "Sorry guys, I need to borrow these," he told them, then plopped the hats on Shep and Mariana's heads. "Keep your face hidden and avoid any security cameras," Joe directed them. "Don't use the escalator. There's a stairwell across the hall that will take you down to the nearest exit. The Venetian Hotel is walking distance and will be crowded this time of night so it should be easy to lose any tail. Go through the hotel casino and follow the signs to the valet drop-off. I'll tell our driver to meet you there and take you back to our hotel. I'll meet you at the office."

Shep and Mariana descended the stairs quickly. With each flight they raced down, it felt like another one magically appeared. Mariana looked down at the center opening of the stairwell and felt a wave of nausea all over again. A long, steep maze of stairs loomed below. There wasn't anyone on the stairwell though, so they were able to run down as quickly as they could manage without tripping. Thankfully, the police took the escalators as Joe had predicted. When Shep and Mariana finally made it to the bottom, they burst out the exit door and sprinted toward the Venetian.

NINETEEN

TESS

San Francisco, California

After Booker learned that Mariana had a roommate who also worked at CellSpot, he decided to connect with the roommate. That evening after work, Booker stopped by Mariana's apartment and rang the doorbell. A woman who looked to be the same age as Mariana cracked open the door, keeping the chain attached. She wore yoga pants with a sports bra and had a towel around her shoulders.

"Can I help you?"

"Yes," Booker responded, trying to keep eye contact with the woman and not look down at her revealing outfit. "My name is Booker Stevens, and I'm with the FBI. I spoke with Mariana a few days ago and was hoping to follow up with her on some additional questions. Here's my badge." Booker flashed his badge for Tess to read.

"Oh, yeah, Mariana told me about you," Tess stated. "Mariana isn't here right now. I'm her roommate, Tess. Can I pass along a message when she returns?"

"Do you happen to know where she is? I was hoping to speak with her tonight."

Tess leaned against the side of the door. "Actually, she left me a note saying she had to leave for a couple of days, and I'm not sure where she went. I tried to call her, but it went to voicemail. It's strange that she left in such a hurry. I hope she's okay."

Booker took the opportunity to engage with Tess. "Would it be alright if I asked you some questions since you also work at CellSpot and work with Mariana?"

Tess was stunned for a moment, but she managed to compose herself quickly. "Sure, what do you want to know?" She stood firm, not intending to invite him in.

Booker cleared his throat. While it was awkward to converse through the crack in the door, it was nighttime and he wanted to respect Tess's privacy.

"I'm sorry I'm calling on you so late, but it's urgent we clear a few things up. So how long have you been living with Mariana?" Booker asked.

"Umm, it's been a little over a year. I'm kind of crashing on her office futon to save money," Tess responded as she glanced over her shoulder at the room behind her. "Mariana's been so nice to help me out."

Booker bit down on his lower lip and tilted his head. "I'm confused. I would imagine a software programmer would make enough money to pay rent, no?"

"It does, but I'm saving as much money as I can to help pay for my sister's ongoing medical bills."

Booker's expression became sympathetic. "Do you mind me asking what happened to your sister?"

"A while back she was hit by a self-driving car while she was riding her bicycle. She's now in a wheelchair and trying to do a lot of physical therapy to gain enough strength to walk again."

"I'm really sorry to hear that," Booker replied, then added, "I'm surprised you'd work at CellSpot after that."

Tess was unfazed by his comment. "Yeah, a lot of people ask me that. To tell you the truth, I wasn't sure I should. But I decided I could be a force of good, helping the industry to make sure this doesn't happen again."

"That's very commendable of you," Booker said. He shifted his stance, put his hands in his pockets, and leaned against the outdoor pillar. "If your sister got hurt by the self-driving car, why is she responsible for her ongoing medical bills?"

With a deep breath, Tess responded, "The company should be, and my parents did sue them, but they had a ton of expensive lawyers. They were able to reduce the settlement by arguing it should be 'no fault' considering it was a four-way intersection, and my sister also didn't stop before entering the intersection, even though she was only riding a bike."

"Sounds like a really tough situation." There was an awkward silence between them, and then Booker changed the subject. "Speaking of CellSpot, do you like the company?"

"Sure," Tess replied, not wanting to share her growing frustration with the situation. Then, sensing that he expected her to expand on her comment she added, "Even though the hours can get long and grueling, I really like the team of people I work with."

"That's great to hear," Booker replied. "I'm sorry to have bugged you this evening. Can I leave you my card, and if you happen to connect with Mariana, will you please let me know? We really need to speak with her." He slipped his card through the crack in the door.

Tess grabbed the card and looked down at it with a furrowed brow. "Is everything okay with Mariana? What's going on at CellSpot?"

"Oh, we're just trying to investigate some things across the industry, and she's been a great source of information for us. That's all."

"Of course," Tess responded, but looked unconvinced.

Booker thanked her for her time, then turned to walk back to his car.

"Nice to meet you," she called out as Booker descended the stairs.

He turned and gave her a passing wave. "Nice to meet you as well, Tess."

Booker sat in his car, thinking about their conversation. He pulled out his phone and sent a text to Pat before driving home.

Booker: Met with Mariana's roommate, Tess. Did you know her sister was hit by a self-driving car? It seems strange that she chose to work at CellSpot and that she's living with Mariana given her salary level as a software programmer. It doesn't add up to me. Let's do a thorough background check on Tess and look for any red flags.

Within seconds, Booker received a text back from Pat. He immediately regretted sending her a text so late, but he was also relieved that she was online.

Pat: Sure thing. I'll start the process in the morning. I wonder if they're working together on this, or if Tess is setting up Mariana. Could be an interesting twist.

TWENTY

NARROW ESCAPE

Las Vegas, Nevada

"Ha! It's a good thing you were a track runner. I bet you never thought you'd be running away from the police," Shep said, panting between breaths.

Fortunately, they didn't have to run for long because the Venetian was only half a mile away. But the streets were crowded, so they had to weave in between the people meandering on the sidewalk. When they reached their destination, they bolted up the escalator and into the massive building only to find themselves in what appeared to be a shopping mall rather than a hotel. Mariana searched in all directions, confused as to what building they entered.

Shep guided her toward the directory on the wall. He located which direction they needed to go and led Mariana quickly down the corridor. By the time they made it to the valet garage, the black Escalade was waiting for them, so they hopped in and the driver sped away.

"Thank goodness you made it out of there in time," Joe exclaimed when Shep and Mariana walked into the office back at the Argyll. "Security really fanned out searching everywhere. I'm just glad I gave you random seat tickets located on the other side of the Sphere. They had no idea where to find you. My Texas clients were angry that I snatched one of their favorite possessions but promised to keep quiet if I gave them back."

Mariana handed over the two hats. "Thank you for helping us. That was a close call."

Mariana and Shep collapsed onto the leather couch in Joe's office. Joe tossed them bottles of water, then poured them all whiskey on the rocks. Overwhelmed with the emotions flooding through her, Mariana took a sip of the very strong, but smooth liquor. She was a self-confident woman, used to fighting her own battles, but the events that had taken place over the past several days finally reduced her to silence. She was afraid to depend on Shep and his family for support, but she didn't know what else to do. She had to find a way to prove her innocence, even if it meant fleeing from authorities until she had more information to clear her name as their key suspect.

A moment later, a man entered the room with a camera and a box full of supplies.

"Hey, Trent," the man said while setting his equipment down. "Long time no see…didn't think we'd be having to do this all over again."

Shep got up to shake his hand. "Hi, Robbie, this is my friend, Mariana. We really appreciate your help. We don't know our next destination yet, but we need to be fully prepared and ready to go anywhere."

"No problem. What do you need? I'm assuming new identification cards, passports, and credit cards."

"Yes, but make that two for each of us, just in case we need to switch gears and ditch one along the way."

"Alrighty. Let me just get some pictures of you two and I'll start the paperwork. It's going to take me some time because it's already so late tonight."

"That's fine," Joe said. "You two need to figure out a plan and where you're headed. Let me know and then we can make travel arrangements for you. If you need to fly out anywhere, it's best if you take the company jet tomorrow night. It will be a lot easier for us to get you out of here unnoticed in the evening."

"But what if we are seen here?" asked Mariana.

"No chance of that," Joe replied. "We self-monitor all our security cameras here on property. If you do not step out of this building, we can keep you safe. I will have a few bodyguards tracking you as well."

Joe handed each of them burner phones and a hotel key card, then added, "I've arranged to have an unregistered room set up for you so no one can track you to this hotel. Your bags were already put in the room so you should be set for tonight. I also took the liberty of ordering some room service. You both look like you need to eat and get a good night's sleep."

Mariana glanced at the key cards and noticed they were for the same room. When she looked up with surprised, inquiring eyes, Joe said, "Yes, I have you staying in the same room. It will be a lot safer this way. Sorry, we didn't have any open suites available–it's a busy weekend here–but you have a nice room set up on the 59th floor."

Then Joe reached into the box Robbie brought in and handed Shep two laptops. "I'm assuming you will need to do a little research. These computers are VPN-secured, and you can keep them for your travels. The password to get into both is Peekaboo!2010."

Shep smiled. "Man, I miss that goofy mutt!"

"Your dog's name was Peekaboo?" questioned Mariana.

"Yeah, he used to love hiding around corners and jumping out at us when we were kids. He would start barking and running in circles when he scared us. His original name was Bear, but we kept calling him Peekaboo because of his crazy antics, and it just stuck."

After Robbie finished taking the photos of Shep and Mariana for their new identities and left the room, Joe turned to Mariana. "Why don't you go get settled in the room? I'd like to talk with Trent, I mean Shep, for a moment if you don't mind."

Mariana looked back and forth between Shep

and Joe. She realized she wasn't wanted for whatever they were going to discuss, and she nervously smiled, thanked Joe again, and walked out.

Joe started in as soon as the door closed behind Mariana. "Shep, we didn't get to finish the conversation at the Sphere. I've been trying to talk with you for a long time about what happened, but you keep shutting me out. Will you just sit down and listen to me for a moment, and then you can decide to ignore me again if you want?"

Shep studied Joe for a few seconds and then begrudgingly sat back down on the couch. "Okay, but I don't see the point. We both know what happened that night and that you were following in the footsteps of our family."

Joe sat down as well and slowly composed himself before he spoke. "That's not true. You've always been so stubborn, and I admire that about you, but it can also make you blind. You only saw what you wanted to see that night. Truth is, I'd been working hard to remove us from all the illegal activities we were involved in. It's complicated though, and I needed to do that deal to get leverage on another person. I know it was distasteful, but I was playing the long game. I wish you had let me explain before you left."

Shep stared at Joe with a look of disbelief. "Why would you keep me in the dark if this was true? We always confided in each other. There were no signals for me to think anything but that you were keeping the business going in the usual manner."

Joe took a deep breath. "I'm sorry. You deserved

better. I wasn't confident I could pull it off, and I didn't want to get you in trouble as well if things went South. Clearly, they did, and you got injured regardless, which was completely my fault. I will keep apologizing, but at some point, you need to believe me, given our history together."

Shep's hands and arms were shaking. He had so many emotions that he was grappling with. Finally, he looked up at Joe, and the words came out fast. "I was so angry with you. I thought you'd betrayed me. I'm sorry I didn't give you a chance to explain."

Joe leaned forward and looked intently into Shep's eyes. "That was the past–let's just move on. I'm excited to tell you that we've stopped investing in those old activities. We have no more ties to those partners anymore."

Shep's features softened. "That's great to hear, Joe. I miss you, Brother. I'd like to try to make this right again."

The two men stood up and hugged each other for several moments, taking in the strong bond between them that was still there and not wanting to let it go again. Eventually, Joe stepped back. "Why don't you go help Mariana get situated in the hotel room. We can talk more tomorrow. I know everything won't change with one conversation, but I feel like this is a good start. I miss you, and I want you back in my life."

Shep nodded approvingly to Joe, taking in everything he had said, but not responding. He turned around and headed out the door to find Mariana.

TWENTY-ONE

ONE COZY BED

Las Vegas, Nevada

While room 5911 was not one of the hotel's grand suites, Joe was correct when he said it was still luxurious. When Mariana entered the room, the curtains automatically opened revealing sweeping panoramic views of the city. The colorful city lights illuminated the sky making the dimly lit room dance with vibrant colors. A table was placed in front of the window with a full spread of food, and a plush library chair with an ottoman was tucked in the corner. The space was decorated in thick cornflower blue carpet and curtains, striped wallpaper in various shades of white, and one massive king-sized bed topped with a fluffy white comforter, lavish pillows, and a throw blanket so soft Mariana couldn't resist running her hand across it. Mariana made herself comfortable while she waited for Shep. She didn't have to wait long.

Shep opened the door, looked around, and coughed. "Ummm...looks like they didn't have a room with separate beds. I can sleep in the chair tonight."

"Don't be silly! You're way too big for that chair to be comfortable all night. I'm so exhausted I will barely move from my side of the bed. We can just share," said Mariana. "I'm going to wash my hands then let's eat–I'm starving."

When Mariana stepped into the expansive bathroom she was dumbfounded. "Check out this bathtub," she yelled out, pointing to the deep claw-footed tub adorned with spa soap and bath salts. "I know what I'm doing after dinner. I haven't taken a bath in years. My apartment only has a shower."

They sat down to feast on the various pastas and salads Joe ordered for them. Mariana had to scoot her chair away from the window as she was still feeling a bit of vertigo from the concert. She found being on the 59th floor just as stomach dropping. Ironically, they were high above the Sphere now, looking down on it. Their hotel window had the perfect view...for someone whose stomach could handle it. Focusing only on the food in front of her, Mariana piled her plate high, and the two of them began to eat as they discussed their next plan.

Shep started, "So how are you thinking you want to clear your name with the FBI? Do you have any idea who did this to you?"

Mariana's face tightened, and she slowly closed and opened her eyes. "Not really. The shock is wearing off, so at least I can focus better now. I've been thinking about the various clues. Someone has been sending me international wire transfers and calling my phone from Russia. Also, somehow someone got access to my laptop and inserted a computer virus that transferred to CellSpot and then to the navigation system of a car during charging. I'm thinking I should use these clues to search on the internet for similar cyberattacks in other countries."

Shep nodded. "That sounds like a good place to start. I can help. Do you want to start now?"

"No," replied Mariana. "It's late and I'm too tired. I want to take a bath and pretend that none of this is happening."

"Okay, I need to respond to a few emails and find someone to cover my upcoming CrossFit classes."

"I'm so sorry to inconvenience you, Shep. I feel awful I pulled you into my mess."

"Please stop. I'm more concerned about you and the threat to your parents. Go take your bath and try to relax. I'm sure we'll get to the bottom of this tomorrow."

Mariana started to walk towards the bathroom but then turned around and looked at Shep with concern on her face. "Shep, what were you discussing with your brother? Anything to do with me and bringing all this mess to your family?"

Shep shook his head and looked at the ground. "No Mariana, it has nothing to do with you and your *mess.*

I haven't spoken to Joe since I left, and we needed to clear some things up. I felt betrayed by him. We were just talking about that and clearing the air. If it wasn't for you, I may have waited a lot longer before I came back."

Mariana took a deep breath and exhaled. "Phew. I thought it was because of me." She walked over to Shep and placed a comforting hand on his shoulder. "I'm sorry you've been estranged from your family. Family is extremely important to me, and I can't imagine not being close to them. If you need to go back tonight and keep talking, it's okay."

Shep reached up and squeezed Mariana's hand. "No, it's fine. We had a good talk, and we agreed to discuss it more tomorrow. I think it's better to have several short discussions anyway. I need to process this information and understand his side of the story. Go take your bath. I'll be fine."

After a long hot soak in the most sumptuous bath Mariana had ever had, she put on the hotel robe and almost melted in its soft inner lining. She stepped into the main room with wet hair, rosy cheeks and a subtle smile on her face.

"I'm sleeping in this robe tonight. It's so incredibly soft I can't take it off. And..." Mariana continued, "I kind of forgot my pajamas when I was rushing to get ready."

Shep laughed, "No problem. We can get you some tomorrow at the boutique."

"I don't think I could afford *anything* that this hotel would have in their shop. Plus, you told me not to use my credit card so it can't be traced."

"Oh, don't worry about that. I'll just put it on my family account. And please don't stress about money. My grandfather left me more than I will ever use in this lifetime."

Mariana pushed the bedside button to close the curtains. One closed the sheers and one the thick blue curtains. "I can't believe all the buildings are still lit up and so many people are still out on the streets. It's 1:45AM for goodness' sake!"

"That's why they call Vegas *the city that never sleeps.*"

"Well, I'm going to sleep. I can't keep my eyes open any longer," Mariana replied, crawling between the crisp white sheets. And before Shep could even shut down his laptop she had already fallen asleep. Shep gazed at her and breathed in the fresh scent of lemon verbena bath soap. She looked so beautiful and peaceful–he knew it would take every bit of willpower tonight to stick to his side of the bed. He took a deep yoga breath to calm his nerves then hopped in the shower to wash away the stress of the day and relieve himself from the pent-up energy he'd been suppressing since the moment she hopped in his truck for this wild adventure.

TWENTY-TWO

CHARTING A COURSE

Las Vegas, Nevada

When Mariana woke up the next morning she was mortified for several reasons. First, the bedside clock read 10:15AM–an hour she hadn't slept to since high school. Second, her pillow was *not* made of feathers, but a very large manly chest decorated with a small tattoo of an angel with ornate, widespread wings. Third, her long leg was wrapped around Shep's waistline. But worst of all, Mariana realized that in her sleep she must have overheated and shed her cozy robe because the only thing she had on was her underwear. In a panic she slowly peeled herself off Shep's body and rolled to the other side, careful not to wake him up. She then eased her way back into her robe and faced the opposite direction.

She hadn't really escaped the situation though. Shep woke up when Mariana first stirred, but he pretended to be asleep to spare her the embarrassment. He was a little embarrassed as well. Clearly his body was not listening to his mind when he promised to control himself. With a sigh of frustration, he quickly rolled off the bed and went into the bathroom, hoping she didn't notice the bulge in his pants. He changed into sweatpants and then came out to make them some coffee. Mariana was waiting and quickly bolted into the bathroom after him.

"I can't believe we slept in so late," he yelled to Mariana. "I think the past 48 hours finally took its toll on us. I'm making some coffee."

A few minutes later Mariana emerged from the bathroom, looking down to avoid Shep's eyes and hide her beet red face. The smell of the freshly brewed coffee perked her up though, and she rushed to grab the cup he held out for her, pretending like nothing happened.

With only his sweats on, she couldn't help but notice his broad, bare chest sculpted to perfection. Then she saw the massive scar running down his stomach and instantly registered that it was from the fight he told her about in the car ride. She reached out and gently traced a finger from his scar up to his inked chest.

"Is that why you have a tattoo of an angel?" she asked.

Shep glanced down with a look of deep sorrow. "That was the worst night of my life, and honestly the best. I almost bled out, but an angel saved me."

Impulsively she placed a quick kiss on the tattoo as if

thanking that angel for saving his life. Embarrassed by her gesture she quickly changed the subject and asked, "So, what's the agenda for today? I know I need to figure out the next steps and where to go, but are we stuck in this room all day?"

"Not at all," Shep replied, glad to change the conversation. "As long as we stay on hotel property, we are safe. Trust me, my family has more security than the President. I suggest we both spend the rest of this morning researching what the heck is going on at CellSpot and meet with Joe to finalize logistics. Then, if we have time, we can take advantage of some of the amenities here. I told Joe to secure one of the private poolside cabanas for us. We save a few for special guests who are trying to avoid the public. No one can see us there–it's separated from the main pool with private access."

"Wow, do you get a lot of celebrities here?" Mariana inquired.

"Oh, all the time. The hotel prides itself on being very discreet and the guests know that they'll receive impeccable service. When VIP guests stay on the property they are given royal treatment."

Mariana shook her head in disbelief. "I can't believe this world you grew up in. It seems like the opposite of life in Santa Cruz. I feel a little out of my league."

"Yeah, it's another reason why I walked away from it," Shep responded then grabbed his bag of clothes and excused himself to shower and get ready for the day.

An hour later they were so focused on researching and looking for similar cyberattacks that they barely heard the door chime announcing the room service they ordered. A bowl of fresh berries artfully displayed on top of homemade granola and yogurt was placed in front of Mariana, while Shep's plate consisted of the largest omelet Mariana had ever seen.

"Chef's special, Mr. McCallister," said the waiter with a smile, then he placed a basket of warm homemade croissants and muffins on the table. "Can I get you two anything else?"

"All set. Thanks," replied Shep. The waiter nodded politely then left them to eat their scrumptious breakfast in peace.

As they got back into the rhythm of researching, Shep could tell that Mariana was getting frustrated. They had been looking for similar attacks for hours and nothing seemed promising. Eventually Shep spoke up, "Maybe we need to think differently? Is there anything about the CellSpot infrastructure that we could search for, even if it's not in the car industry?"

Mariana was quiet for a moment and considered the question. "That's not a bad idea."

Shep continued, "Explain to me how the car charging system works. Maybe we can identify a similar situation in another industry?"

"Well, when a car plugs into an electric charger, there's a data communication handshake that occurs. There are no wires, so the connection happens over the existing electrical current. This technology is called Powerline Communications, or more commonly known as PLC. It's been around for decades and has very established industry standards. Once the handshake is completed, then data is passed back and forth using Modbus Communications. Modbus is a simplistic and reliable communications protocol for sending and receiving data. It's been used extensively in the industrial automation industry, especially with sensor data. In our car chargers, it's important that we know exactly what the charge level is and the temperature, so it doesn't overcharge or overheat. We also need to pass back and forth information on the user, their payment method, and other car information. When the charge is complete, the data communications connection is terminated and that's really it." Mariana looked over at Shep wondering if he understood her explanation and if he had any new insights.

"Okay, got it," said Shep. "You said Modbus is used in industrial automation environments, so maybe we search for cyberattacks where Modbus and PLC were compromised?"

Mariana thought for a second, "That's a great idea. Let's focus on international situations first."

Both were silent as they continued to refine their searches on the internet and read postings about various cyberattacks. About thirty minutes later, Mariana blurted out, "Hey, I may have found something. There were a couple attacks that originated from the same cybercriminal. One in Kiev, Ukraine and one in Prague, Czech Republic. They both compromised PLC and Modbus. It looks like there were centralized control buildings in both locations that served hundreds of apartment complexes for heating and cooling."

"That sounds promising," Shep said. "Tell me more."

"Well, I guess the individual or company that did this got remote access to the central control unit. They were then able to send incorrect temperature sensor information to the heating units. This meant the heaters didn't turn on during the middle of winter. I guess it took several days for authorities to figure it out and fix it. I can't find any reference to it happening again anywhere else."

"Isn't that really similar to what may be going on with autonomous vehicles where the sensor data is inaccurate and causes random crashes?"

"Yes, exactly. It's just the opposite approach of causing the navigation to do something it shouldn't have done rather than ignoring it. This is interesting. Let's keep looking for other industrial cyberattacks and then we can come back to this one."

They kept searching for other instances but after another thirty minutes, they both gave up after coming up empty. Mariana decided to do more research on the previous cyberattack.

"Shep, I found a cybersecurity consulting firm that did a detailed analysis on these attacks. They claim it was the Russians, but they couldn't continue the investigation as the Russian authorities weren't responsive. The consulting firm is in Prague," said Mariana excitedly. "Why don't I call them and try to find out more details and why the investigation stopped?"

"I like it, but I'm not sure how well a phone call will work. We can't stay in Vegas much longer. Like Joe said, the police may have already found you through video surveillance when we went to the Sphere. I'm sure they're continuing to search the rest of the city. How about we get out of here, fly to Prague, and talk to the company in person? They'd probably share more information that way."

Mariana gave him a skeptical glance, forgetting the conversation the night before with Joe and Robbie. "How would we get to Prague? I don't even have my passport."

Shep said, "It should be okay. Our company jet is well equipped for international flights. Robbie said our new passports will be done by the end of today. I'll call Joe and have him get all the necessary arrangements in order."

Mariana didn't look convinced with eyebrows pinched and a frown pulling at her lips. "I'm shocked it's that easy to create fake documents."

Shep scoffed. "Trust me, Robbie knows what he's doing. He's done it many times before."

Mariana considered the plan and then said, "If we can get there safely, it buys us time, and I do think we're really onto something with the cyberattack. I feel bad though. I told you I would do this on my own as soon as we developed a plan. Asking you to come to Prague feels like too much of an ask."

"I already told you. I want to help you. I can handle the logistics of being away from work for a while, and no offense, but it really does seem like you could use the support."

It was clear to Mariana that Shep was correct. She

convinced herself this would be the last time she would ask Shep for help and reluctantly agreed.

After they finalized their plans and Shep informed Joe's team of their travel needs, they decided to take a break and de-stress by enjoying the beautiful, sunny day. En route to the private pool cabana, Shep steered Mariana into the boutique to pick out a bathing suit and cover-up. Mariana, appalled at the high prices, quickly grabbed the least expensive two-piece in her size with a matching sarong. She pulled the tags off and handed them to Shep then went into the dressing room to change while Shep picked out a suit for himself and put the items on his account. When she looked at herself in the dressing room mirror Mariana winced at the skimpy bathing suit, then with a sigh, resigned herself to wearing it.

Not only did the pool cabana have a private entrance, but Mariana was also shocked to see that it had a private plunge pool as well. They were completely isolated from the other hotel guests. The area included four lounge chairs in the sun with umbrellas, a covered patio with a sitting area and firepit table, a fully stocked bar, and a television. She grabbed a magazine off the table and headed over to one of the plush blue and white striped chaise lounges.

When she untied her sarong, it dropped to the floor, revealing a soft pink bikini that did not leave much to the imagination. Shep's jaw dropped, and he quickly sat down and looked the other way before his body, once again, did not listen to his brain telling it to calm down.

When she started slathering sunscreen on her amazingly long, toned legs, Shep couldn't take it anymore and jumped into the pool to cool off.

Mariana smiled to herself. She knew he was looking at her, and she relished the fact that he clearly liked what he saw. He wasn't so bad to stare at either when he emerged from the pool with water trailing down his tan torso. He shook his wavy brown hair highlighted from the sun and grabbed a towel to wipe down his stunning, muscular body. Mariana was glad to have a brief distraction from her situation, so she sat back in her lounge chair and tried to relax.

"You obviously enjoy working out, but what drove you to open your own gym?" she asked.

"Honestly, CrossFit kind of changed the course of my life. I had so much fun competing in college and I learned so much about the impact of fitness on our health and wellbeing, I wanted to share that with others. Plus, I figured why not create a job out of one of my passions."

"What are your other passions?"

"Oh, you know, women, sex, rock & roll," Shep said with a laugh.

"I'm being serious! What are your hobbies, your passions...your favorite things in life?"

"Let's see, surfing, jogging on the beach, carne asada burritos, suspense thrillers, dark chocolate, the color pink...," he said, eyeing her bathing suit with a sexy smile.

Mariana blushed and squirmed in her lounge chair

uncomfortably. "Have you ever been in a long-term relationship?"

"Not really. I've dated a lot over the years; I just never had the time to get too involved with anyone. Or maybe I just haven't found the right person to put in the effort. How about you?"

"I thought I was in love once–dated a guy for quite some time in college. It was during my internship abroad."

"Was he a student in your program?"

"No, he was a little bit older. He worked for the company I was interning at."

"Oh, so he's European?"

Mariana cleared her throat then responded, "He's from Russia. He was on assignment for the company and based in Prague that summer. A nice guy, and we had an intense relationship, but it was too complicated."

"Was it a mutual breakup?"

"Kind of...eventually. He proposed to me. At first, he wanted me to move back to Russia with him at the end of my program. I told him that it was important for me to finish college, and I wasn't ready to end my track career. He said he understood and was willing to wait. We continued to stay together for a while, but the long-distance relationship was hard to manage with the time zone differences and being so far apart. After a couple months the reality of it all really started setting in. While I was in love with him, the idea of marrying him and moving to Russia scared me. I couldn't see myself moving so far away from my family and friends permanently."

"Do you still talk to him?" Shep asked.

"No. When I officially called it quits; he didn't want to communicate with me anymore. He said he found it easier to move on if we didn't talk. I agreed."

Tired of talking about herself, Mariana stood up and announced that she was ready to get out of the sun and was going to go back to the hotel room.

"That's fine," Shep said. "I need to go find Joe and finish our discussion. I'll come back to the room in a bit."

By the time Mariana got back to the hotel room, she convinced herself that she should call the FBI agent, Booker Stevens, to make a plea for her innocence. She was grappling with the idea all day and figured he wouldn't believe her, but she felt like she should try anyway. She walked into the room and sat at the table to write down some notes on what she wanted to say, then searched in her backpack for the business card that Booker had given her. Before she could change her mind, she quickly dialed his direct number using the burner phone. Booker picked up right away.

"Hi Booker. This is Mariana Morales from CellSpot. I wanted to call you and let you know why I left the area and didn't tell you."

Booker patiently said, "I'm glad you called. You do know that you're a prime suspect now?"

Mariana continued, "I figured as much. Whether you believe me or not, I want you to know that I'm innocent.

I had *nothing* to do with any software virus, and I have no idea who has been depositing money in my bank account. I realize it looks bad though. Everyone seems to think I'm the one who did this. I decided the only way to prove my innocence is to figure out who's framing me. As I get closer to the answer, I promise to let you know, but I'm not coming back until then."

Booker's voice grew stern. "Mariana, this is the wrong way to go about this. It only makes you look more guilty and hurts your case. Just let me know where you are and we can sit down and discuss. I want to get to the truth behind this case as well, and I'll keep an open mind about your involvement."

Mariana said, "No. I need to do this my way. I need to go now, but I'll try to stay in touch as I learn more." Without waiting for a reply, Mariana hung up the phone and threw it on the bed. She was shaking but felt like she had done the right thing, even though it probably didn't help.

Booker put his phone down and contemplated the conversation. *Why would Mariana risk reaching out to me just to convey her innocence? There are too many clues pointing to her involvement. She probably just wants to make me think twice and slow down progress. That won't happen.* He proceeded to call Pat to ask her if there were any more sightings of Mariana in Vegas or leads to follow. Still nothing new. It was like she disappeared into thin air right after the escape from the Sphere. It didn't make sense. Booker concluded that she must be getting help to stay hidden so well.

An hour later Shep knocked on the door to room 5911 and announced himself to let Mariana know he was coming in. When he entered the room, he saw her sitting in the chair by the window with a distant look in her eyes.

"Is everything okay?" he asked.

"I called the FBI agent," she announced in a matter-of-fact tone, knowing Shep would be mad.

Shep closed his eyes, took a deep breath and silently prayed she didn't compromise their location.

Before he could speak, Mariana jumped in, "I wanted him to understand I'm innocent and just trying to find clues as to what is really going on."

"How long were you on the phone?" Shep asked.

"Very briefly–I knew I shouldn't stay on long and potentially reveal our location."

Shep nodded, still frustrated she placed the call without mentioning it to him first. Finally, he said, "I'll have my family get you a new burner phone before we leave." Then he went into the bathroom to get changed.

TWENTY-THREE

I'LL GO WITH BLACK

Las Vegas, Nevada

Around 5:00PM, Joe called to let Shep and Mariana know that Robbie had just dropped off their new passports and information. When the two of them walked into his office, Joe was packaging up the items along with credit and debit cards to an account in their new fictitious names, a wad of cash, a new burner phone, hotel reservations, and a list of overseas contacts in case they ran into trouble.

"Here's everything you should need," Joe said, handing the manila envelope to Shep. "Your new names are Nick and Samantha Jones, and yes, you two are married so you need to act like you are a couple in love." Then he placed rings on each of their fingers.

Joe turned to Mariana and pointed to the corner of the room. "There are several bags of new clothes for you both...including some pajamas," Joe said with a wink, referencing that he was aware she'd forgotten them. Mariana blushed as Joe continued speaking. "You'll find in there an outfit for this evening and a few items to help you disguise yourselves just in case we have any undercover agents walking through the casino tonight. My wife, Nicole, took the liberty to select some items for you Mariana. You two are about the same size so it was easy for her."

Shep laughed, much more at ease around Joe than he had been the day before. "Nicole could've selected items from her own massive closet. I've never seen anyone have so many shoes and outfits!" Then he proceeded to inform Mariana that fashion was a passion of Nicole's, and she was the buyer for the family's hotel boutiques.

"Be ready for dinner at six," Joe informed them. "I have the private dining room at the steakhouse booked for the four of us–Nicole is excited to see you Shep and meet you, Mariana."

"The boys aren't joining us?" asked Shep. "I miss those two little rascals!"

"No," Joe replied. "I think it's best to keep your presence here quiet. Who knows who they'd tell. They can't contain themselves when you're around."

Joe hesitated and looked at Shep. Both men gave an imperceptible nod to each other making it evident that things were better between them and it was time to move on. The discussion they had earlier that day cleared up a lot of their tension. They still had some repairing to do, but Shep realized that the assumptions he made came at a big cost. He lost years of time with his brother and family because he chose to walk away and shut them out versus listening and giving his brother the opportunity to explain his actions.

An hour later Mariana completed the final touches to her make-up and secured the platinum blond wig Nicole bought her. Looking in the mirror, she took a big deep breath to calm her nerves. Nothing about this felt normal, and now she didn't even look normal. *Whatever,* she thought. *Just stay calm and go with the flow.* Then she added some large silver hoop earrings and walked out of the bathroom to show Shep her transformation.

"Wow!" Shep exclaimed as his eyes traveled from her three-inch knee-high black boots to her very short black halter dress topped with a silver beaded band around her neck. The dress hugged her curves just enough to reveal her sexy body while leaving some to the imagination. Embarrassed, she quickly spun around displaying the low cut back of her dress which made it apparent that she was not wearing a bra.

Her blunt-cut bob wig swung as she turned. "Maybe I should become a blonde permanently."

Shep grunted and grabbed the faux fur coat to put it on her. "You definitely look like you belong in Vegas now. Let's get going or we're going to be late," he said gruffly.

Mariana noticed how handsome he looked in his dark grey suit, tailored to perfection. While she was getting ready, Shep went to the hotel salon and had them cut his wavy brown hair to an inch thick but kept the recently growing scruff on his face to switch up his own appearance. The Justin Timberlake style looked good on him. Instead of masking his chiseled jawline it accentuated it even more.

The private dining room in the hotel's Michelin Star steakhouse was located on the third floor of the resort. The restaurant was dark and romantically decorated like a 1920's Speakeasy. Located on the side by the hostess stand, a door camouflaged like a bookcase opened to a private dining room complete with a fireplace, ornately carved mahogany dining table, and walls lined with bookshelves and candles. Mariana felt like she stepped into an intimate version of Hogwarts library in Harry Potter.

"Oh, you look lovely," squealed Nicole in delight while approaching Mariana with open arms. "Joe showed me your picture, and I just knew this dress would be stunning on you!" Then she turned to Shep and kissed him on the cheek.

Nicole was exactly how Shep described her–tall and lanky with long, wavy red hair, porcelain skin, and an air of elegance about her. Her statuesque figure looked graceful in her cream silk dress, softening her features.

"Please come sit." Nicole motioned to the table. "Tell me how the gym is doing, Shep. Did you add those hot yoga-strong classes I told you about? Such an amazing workout! It's like a sauna and body toning class all in one. In fact..." Nicole babbled on, and the evening was full of much-needed light conversation and laughter.

When they finished dinner, the four of them meandered to the casino. Walking away from the little oasis of the private dining room brought a twinge of fear to Mariana. She scanned the crowd, wondering if the police were looking for her.

"Relax," Shep whispered in her ear. "You don't want to draw attention by looking scared and anxious. Just try to act normally and blend in with the crowd. We have an hour before our flight; let's try to have a bit of fun before we take off and feel like fugitives."

"We *will* be fugitives," Mariana hissed back under her breath while walking forward, pretending to not have a care in the world.

Joe turned to Shep and said, "Since you've been gone, you'd be amazed at how technology has changed the casino business, both with customers and in back-office operations. AI has opened so many dimensions of data analysis that we never had access to in the past. Just like how your Netflix service learns about what you like to watch and personalizes your user guide and recommendations over time, casinos now do the same thing. We track all the history and behaviors of customers, and we can provide unique experiences at the individual level driving more enjoyment and, of course, more betting."

"How has AI helped back-office operations?" Shep asked.

"We can do so much more with less people to reduce our costs. But we're starting to run into issues with the unions as employees are concerned about job displacement. I think it's a foregone conclusion that we'll be significantly reducing our workforce soon. I don't like it, but I don't know how to avoid the situation as we need to stay competitive with other casinos."

Shep shook his head and said, "It's a shame. Technology as a tool to help humans do a better job is a great model. It sure seems like AI is different and has the potential to take jobs away from humans. I see the same trend happening in gyms with back-office jobs being replaced with AI."

As they walked into the main casino, Shep gently grabbed Mariana's arm and pointed to a sea of gaming stations. Mariana was surprised by the infinite rows of slot machines and gaming tables. She had never gambled before, so she wanted to take a baby step and try out a slot machine. She figured it would be easy to use. She walked up to one called *Magic Treasures*, a bright blue machine with flashing lights and a picture of a tiger wrapped around piles of gold coins. She put the gaming card Shep handed her into the slot and quickly discovered it was anything but easy. The instructions were vague, she had no idea what button to push, and she instantly felt overwhelmed, so she pulled the card out. Laughing, she turned to Shep and said, "How about that gaming table over there?" pointing to a Blackjack table on the other side. "Perhaps the nice gentleman behind the counter will explain what I'm supposed to do."

After several more unsuccessful attempts at gambling, Mariana moved away from the table in frustration. "I don't understand, what's the point of just throwing your money away?" she complained to Shep. "Who has this kind of frivolous money anyway?"

Shep smirked, "Oh you'd be surprised at how much money casinos take in daily. The profit can vary from $500,000 to a few million dollars. It's amazing how much money people will throw down trying to make it big." Then he guided Mariana over to the Roulette Wheel and handed her the last stack of chips. "This is an easy game to play. The simplest thing you can do is choose black or red. Then you have almost a 50-50 chance of winning."

"Why do you say *almost*?" Mariana asked.

"Because there are two slots of green that make the odds less than 50 percent and make the odds more in favor of the house."

"Interesting, okay...I'll choose black," Mariana pronounced, placing the stack down on the table. The casino dealer waited for everyone to place their chips then spun the wheel. The metal ball went around and around the circle. Mariana felt like it took forever to slow down, then eventually it moved at a snail's pace rolling and bouncing from one colored number to the next.

"Red five, black twenty-four, red sixteen...and the winner is...Black 33," the dealer called out to the participants around the table.

"I won!" Mariana yelped in excitement.

Laughing, Shep pulled her away from the table with her winnings. "We better get going before you get the gambling bug...and we have a plane to catch." Mariana tucked one of the casino chips into her pocket, praying luck would be on her side moving forward.

TWENTY-FOUR

UP, UP AND AWAY

Las Vegas, Nevada

Once again, Shep and Mariana were back in the blacked-out Escalade, but this time they were headed to the private jet terminal at the McCarran International Airport. They drove straight to the tarmac to board the plane. Petrified they were going to be caught leaving, Mariana raced up the stairs and stepped inside. Mariana was dumbfounded by the luxuriant interior of the plane. Even though it was just the two of them traveling, the jet was large enough to make the transatlantic flight. It had a seating area for several passengers made up of enormous cream leather chairs that also turned into beds, a dining section, a bar, an enclosed kitchen area, and a full-sized master bedroom.

Mariana had never been exposed to such luxury before, and she was shocked that this was considered normal for Shep. Shep knew she was overwhelmed by the plane. He brushed the opulence of their travels aside and focused on getting them out of there as soon as possible. They quickly sat down and buckled up. Then Mariana tried some of the buttons on the chair and realized she could swivel the chair almost 360 degrees. Another button allowed the chair to slide back and forth several feet. When she was done trying the buttons, she looked up at Shep and sheepishly smiled. Shep rolled his eyes and went back to looking at his phone. He secretly smiled, happy to see Mariana in a playful mood, if only for a brief moment in time. Soon they were off. It was an exhilarating takeoff with a steep, aggressive climb—very different from commercial airline takeoffs. Mariana couldn't believe they were on the way to their next destination: Prague.

Once the plane levelled out, Shep broke the silence by reminding Mariana that they had a lot of work to do. He grabbed two water bottles and placed them on the table in front of them, then pulled out his laptop to research. "Okay," said Shep, "remind me again about the potential cyberattack in Prague."

They proceeded to discuss the details of the cyberattack and the information they found online.

"Maybe the Russians were practicing this cyberattack prior to bringing it to the United States and applying it to electric vehicles to cause widespread panic?" Mariana suggested. "I'm hoping to find some information that ties these two events together. Then I could get the FBI to focus on the Russians and not me."

After more research and debate, Mariana grew tired. It had been an intense, long day, and the weight of the situation made her exhausted. She looked over at Shep who was squinting with tired eyes at his laptop. He too had an overwhelming day, and Mariana was riddled with guilt for dragging him into her problems.

"I can't thank you enough, but there's no need for you to stay with me once we land, Shep. You've done so much for me already."

Shep sighed, exhausted from the day and tired of having the same circular debate with Mariana. "What are you talking about? Of course, I'm not going to drop you off in Prague and leave you alone to deal with this."

"I can handle it. I know my way around Prague–I used to live there. It was wrong of me to pull you into this. I can figure it out on my own."

"Why can't you just accept help? You aren't Wonder Woman," Shep countered in frustration, then he decided to shut the conversation down before he said something he would regret. Mariana was fiercely independent and not used to relying on others, but she was in a big bind and trying to solve this alone would be impossible for anyone. "Please take a break and try to get some sleep," he said. "You can take the bedroom. We can discuss this when we land, but you need to rest up so you have energy for tomorrow."

"Yeah, I'm a mess," Mariana admitted as she got up and retreated to the bedroom. She understood Shep needed to rest also. The polite thing to do would be to invite him to sleep on the bed beside her, but she just wanted to be alone to stew over her feelings.

After another twenty minutes, Shep realized how tired he was, so he powered down his laptop. While he was putting it back in his backpack, he overheard Mariana crying in the bedroom. It was a punch in the gut–Shep didn't know if she was crying because of what he said or if she was just upset about her situation. He slowly opened the door to peek in on her. She was lying on the bed with her back to him. Shep crawled on the bed and hugged her from behind attempting to comfort her.

"I can't tell you everything is going to be okay, but I will do my best to protect you and help you figure out what the hell is going on," Shep told her and squeezed her tightly.

She turned in his arms to face him. She wiped her tears dry and stared into his eyes. No words could describe how grateful she felt for his presence. She lifted her head and placed a gentle kiss on his lips to thank him and apologize for pushing him away earlier. Seconds later that gentle kiss became manic and then quickly so passionate Shep had to pull away.

"I don't want to take advantage of this situation," he said to her. "While every fiber in my body wants to continue kissing you, I think it would be best if we hold off. We're both emotional now, and I want us to be together...for the right reasons." Then with all the muster he could manage, Shep left the room to make up a bed in the main area.

TWENTY-FIVE

FALSE ALARM

Mountain View, California

Tess was at the office working on the next software release when Raj stopped by unannounced.

"Good morning, Tess," Raj said. "How are you?"

Tess looked up at him from her desk with big eyes and a nervous smile. "Ummm, Great. Just working on the next software release. Excited to get this one in production. How are you?"

"I'm doing well. I agree with you, I'm excited to get our next release out to the world. I can't wait to talk about these revolutionary innovations publicly." Raj paused for a minute and then went on, "I understand you're roommates with Mariana." Tess nodded, so Raj continued. "I heard from HR that she is on leave for a few days. Did she tell you why?"

Tess sat still, hesitant to answer. She wondered if she should share how stressed Mariana seemed to be lately but decided not to. Instead, Tess said, "She left a few days ago. She told me she had to take care of something and would be out of town for a while. I haven't heard from her since."

Raj said, "That's strange. I guess that's why we haven't been able to reach her. When you hear from her, please let her know I'd like to talk with her. We have a huge press event associated with this next release and we're all depending on her."

"Do you plan to push out the release date?" Tess asked.

"Absolutely not," Raj said with a defiant tone. "We've made commitments and everything is riding on this release." With that, Raj didn't wait for a reply. He turned and walked away, waving and smiling to a few other employees along the way.

As Raj walked down the hall, he made a mental note to call Booker. Raj figured the background check had turned out to be nothing serious for Mariana, and he really did want her to oversee the next software release. Approaching his CFO's office, he forgot all about Mariana and the FBI, and instead became laser-focused on discussing the latest negotiations with the new clients on finalizing the nationwide contract. They were so close to completing the deals which would give CellSpot a huge boost with investors. His issues with the capitalization of the company would be easy to solve then.

TWENTY-SIX

JET LAG

Prague, Czech Republic

It was late in the day when they landed in Prague. Remembering to use their new names, Nick and Samantha Jones, they went through passport control. Shep and Mariana both breathed a sigh of relief when the customs agent didn't question their identities. As they walked out of the terminal, they searched for a ride. There was a line of black cars that said Uber Airport on them. A man in an Uber shirt came up and explained that the Uber app was still required to secure one. Not wanting to use his real information, Shep quickly grabbed his new phone to create a second Uber app using his fake ID and credit card. He then requested an Uber, and a pin number popped up on the screen. The Uber driver of the first car in line got out of his vehicle and walked over to Shep to compare the pin number now displayed on both of their phones, then gestured for Shep and Mariana to get in the car.

"I wonder why other airports don't use this process with Uber," Shep commented. "It's quick, and you don't have to wait around looking for the right Uber driver to pull up."

"It's fast but still seems inefficient. Soon this'll be automated by AI," said Mariana. "There'll be a line of self-driving Ubers and all you need to do is place your phone against the door and the trip will be initiated. No app or human involvement needed."

Shep's brother had made a reservation for the two of them at the Four Seasons Hotel Prague since it was close to the cyber security software company they planned to visit. The hotel overlooked the Vltava River with views facing both west and south, highlighting the Charles Bridge and the Prague Castle. Their room, which faced the front entrance of the hotel, was decorated in a neo-classical design with muted shades of beige and gold. Jet lag made Mariana want to crawl into the king-sized bed, but she knew that she needed to press on through the evening to get her body regulated to the time zone.

"It's almost sunset," Mariana observed as she looked out the window. "How about we go for a walk along the river before dinner? It's gorgeous out, and even though

I wish it were for other reasons, it's so nice to be back in Prague."

"That sounds like a great idea," Shep replied while yawning. "The fresh air might wake us up. Let me call down and make a dinner reservation."

Leafing through the hotel information booklet Shep said, "I'll get us a table at the CottoCrudo. Their menu has a variety of options."

After they unpacked, the two of them decided to walk over the Charles Bridge to Malá Strana, one of Prague's most historic neighborhoods. Malá Strana, known as the "Lesser Town," was a picturesque neighborhood made up of cobbled side streets filled with boutique shops, Czech pubs and quaint cafes.

"These shops used to be where the wealthy merchants lived," said Mariana. "One of the classes I took when I was here in college was an art and architecture course. We learned all about the different architectural styles over the centuries."

"So what style were these houses?" Shep asked.

Mariana laughed. "I don't remember. That was so long ago." Then she quickly looked it up on her new phone.

"It says they are called ancient burgher houses, and their style depends on what year they were built or rebuilt. The current homes existing today are a combination of Renaissance, Baroque, and Gothic styles. That's what makes the city so historically rich and architecturally diverse." Then she put her phone back in her pocket.

"I thought you were a computer science major."

"It was an elective course. They offered it to international students because it was a way to learn about and experience the city. We mostly walked the streets, looked at the different architectural styles and sketched the buildings. It was a lot of fun."

Mariana grabbed Shep's hand and guided him down one of the side streets. "Let me show you the Lennon Wall. It's such a cool site to see."

As they walked toward the secluded square where the famous graffiti wall stood, Mariana explained its significance and how it evolved.

"It's unbelievable how many times this wall has been repainted. It's layered with so much history. I heard they opened a museum called the Lennon Wall Story that features photos of the various artworks.

Shep and Mariana stood in front of the colorful monument.

"Wow," Shep stated, taking it all in. "It's like a constantly changing canvas mirroring what's going on in society currently." He pointed to a painting on the wall protesting the rising power of tech. It was an image of robots and computers barred by a diagonal line.

"Yeah, it's a wall of free expression related to human dignity. What's ironic though is John Lennon had never been to Prague. It was just named after him."

During dinner both Shep and Mariana battled waves of fatigue. Their goal was to stay awake for a couple more hours in hope of sleeping through the night. Initially they tried to keep the conversation light, discussing Mariana's time in Prague during college and her relationship with her boyfriend, Oleg, at the time.

"What was your favorite thing about living here?" Shep asked.

"Honestly, I loved everything about it. I was sad to leave. It's such a vibrant atmosphere and so different from California. Oleg and I loved walking around and soaking in the historic buildings and charming cobblestone streets. It's so different from Los Angeles."

"Do you miss him?" Shep asked.

"Yeah, he's a great guy, but it would never have worked out. At the time our cultural differences were attractive, but I think in the end it would have put a strain on our relationship. Plus, his family didn't really accept me."

"So, you met them in person?"

"Several times. His parents visited Prague one weekend and took us out to dinner. I was so nervous to meet them because Oleg made a big fuss about what I should wear and how I should act. It was pretty evident that he was nervous to introduce me to them. His mom was extremely protective and her idea of the perfect woman for Oleg was not an American."

"Definitely his loss," Shep said.

"His family wasn't very welcoming when I visited them in Russia. They were old-fashioned and very reserved. It made me uncomfortable. It didn't help that several family members were government officials and didn't like that I was an American."

"Maybe it's best how this all played out. It seems like it would have been extremely challenging to keep that relationship going. Okay, not to jump to conclusions, but do you think the Russians *could* be behind the cyberattack? Do you think Oleg or someone related to him could be involved?" Shep asked.

Mariana responded with a deep sigh. "I don't know, but someone put money in my bank account, placed international phone calls, and hacked my computer."

"I still can't figure out how your computer was compromised. But let's discuss next steps and create a plan. You said the company we need to contact is Cyber something...?'

"Yes, Cyber Membranes. They wrote the analysis on the attack on HVAC units in Kiev and Prague."

"We need a credible reason to get them to share their findings. How do you think we should connect with them?"

Mariana pondered his question for a moment then said, "How about we pretend we're journalists seeking more information on their analysis and how it might potentially relate to recent activity in the U.S.? Maybe we can get more details from them that aren't in the report. We need to find concrete facts that tie the Russians to this attack and to the one with CellSpot. That's what we'll need to convince the FBI that I'm innocent."

By the time dessert was ordered, jet lag was hitting them, and they couldn't wait to escape to their room and crawl in bed. When they got back to their suite, Mariana announced, "Why don't you shower and get ready for bed first. I want to look up the phone number for Cyber Membranes so I can call them in the morning."

Shep grabbed his toiletries and closed the door to the bathroom. Fifteen minutes later he emerged, looking like a sleep deprived zombie, then pulled back the feather duvet and climbed into bed. By the time Mariana closed her laptop to head into the shower, Shep was sound asleep. The toll of the last couple of days plus the jet lag finally caught up with him. Mariana was not far behind him. After she rinsed off the stress of the day, she pulled out the new pajamas Nicole bought her and had to laugh. Technically it was *not* pajamas; it was the sexiest, softest lingerie Mariana had ever put on. Made of fine cream silk, the tiny lace trimmed shorts and camisole left nothing to the imagination. Exhausted, Mariana decided not to fight it and climbed into the bed, already warmed by Shep's body.

At 2:15AM Mariana woke up, sensing movement on the other side of the bed, and rolled over placing the pillow over her head. Feeling bad that he disturbed her sleep, Shep carefully got up to use the restroom then tried to sneak back between the covers. It didn't matter. Mariana was wide awake now. While the clock read the middle of the night, it was only early evening in California. Mariana lay there, unable to fall asleep, wondering what to do. She knew she needed to sleep longer to regulate her body's clock, but that seemed impossible. It didn't help that anxiety kicked in as her mind started racing with the reality of why they were in Prague and the predicament she was in. She decided to get up for a glass of water and aspirin to help her relax.

Before climbing back into bed, she took a few minutes to stretch out her muscles. Sitting on the airplane for hours and the lack of exercise the past few days made her feel tight all over. The full moon and city lights peeped through the crack in the thick curtains casting a faint light. Not realizing her silhouette was on display for Shep, she continued to stretch and flow through her yoga poses. Shep secretly watched her as she reached her arms to the ceiling, bending backward in *Sky Reaching Pose*. Her short camisole rose up through her stretch exposing the base of her breasts. The smooth material highlighted her soft curves and hard nipples. Then she slowly bent at the waist, reaching down to her toes and completed her *Vinyasa*, ending in *Downward-Facing Dog*. Shep's eyes trailed up her long legs and settled on her firm ass. Aroused and embarrassed that he was watching her, he flipped over and tried to fall back to sleep. Mariana completed her yoga routine and slipped between the sheets.

"Are you awake?" she whispered.

"Yes," he responded gruffly. "Damn jet lag."

"Should we just get up now?" she asked.

"No, that won't help. We'll end up being a complete mess by midday. I think it's best if we find a way to relax and fall back asleep."

"How do we do that?"

Shep chuckled with a sly smile, "I can think of a few ways."

Mariana grabbed her pillow and whacked him. "I'm being serious. I'm wide awake and ready to go."

"Well, I'm ready to go any time you are," Shep continued the teasing banter.

Mariana turned toward him and softly said, "I really am trying to keep my distance from you, but I do have to admit that it's getting harder the more time we spend together. Especially when you're sleeping in your boxers, bare chested right next to me."

"Well maybe we should quit fighting it," Shep replied, inching closer.

"Hmmm...maybe," Mariana responded, looking Shep deeply in the eyes, signaling her approval.

Within seconds Shep brushed his lips softly against hers. Mariana reciprocated a little more firmly, holding their lips in place as if she didn't want the spell to end. What started out tentative between them soon became decisive, and the kiss morphed into a passionate expression of desire. Mariana couldn't remember the last time she had been kissed so deeply. Wanting to savor every minute, she slightly pulled back. Sensing her desire to slow down the momentum, Shep guided her to flip over to face the other direction.

"Let me give you a massage. I know your back is tight from the long plane ride."

Shep began kneading her shoulders then worked his way up her neck to the base of her skull.

Mariana moaned, "Oh my God that feels so good!"

Feeling encouraged to continue, Shep's fingers gently rubbed down her spine, finding all her knots across her back and massaging them out. An inch at a time he worked his way down to her lower back and over her buttocks. The penetrating massage lightened to soft caresses as Shep's desire grew. Mariana felt the shift and began to flip over.

"That was amazing. Now let me do you," she exclaimed while nudging him onto his stomach. She proceeded to climb over him, straddling her legs across his back and began returning the favor by massaging his broad shoulders. Feeling his warm soft skin beneath her fingers turned her on, making her lightheaded while desire radiated deep within her.

Sensing her increasing pleasure Shep flipped her onto her back in one swift move. Towering over her now, he leaned down and kissed her so passionately she could barely breathe. When he started to back away, she grabbed the sides of his head and pulled him back down, wrapping her legs around his waist securing him tightly to her. She was not about to let him go now–they clearly already had crossed the line.

TWENTY- SEVEN

FIND MY DEVICE

Santa Cruz, California

It had now been several days since Tess had heard from Mariana. Tess was continuing to go to work, feed Drake and keep the apartment clean.

"Something doesn't seem right," Tess blurted out loud to herself as she sat on the couch with Drake on her lap.

Drake purred and nudged her as if he agreed. Tess scratched him under his chin and behind his ears, his favorite spots, and continued sharing her thoughts with the cat. "Mariana should've been back by now or at least called to let me know where she was."

As she was stewing about what to do, Tess remembered that Mariana had borrowed her running bag with her AirPods inside the night she left. Then a thought occurred to her. Tess quickly unlocked her iPhone and searched for the *Find My* app. She first searched for Mariana in the *People* section on the bottom navigation bar, but the last known location was the apartment several days ago.

That's strange. Tess thought. *Mariana always has her phone on and with her.*

Now she was getting even more nervous and worried. She switched the navigation menu to *Devices* and scrolled down to find her AirPods Pro. Tess saw that it said *Las Vegas, NV–36 hours ago*, and there was a small icon of a battery showing that the AirPods Pro battery was extremely low. Shocked, Tess couldn't think of any reason why Mariana would have gone to Vegas, especially without her phone. She got up and Drake jumped to the ground, hurrying off to the other room. Tess started pacing back and forth trying to determine what to do. Remembering the card the FBI agent gave her, she searched for it in the kitchen drawer. *Maybe Booker will know where Mariana is, or at least I could give this information to him, and he could find her faster than anyone else.*

Booker answered on the third ring, "Hello, this is Booker Stevens."

"Hi Booker. This is Tess Givens. I'm Mariana Morales' roommate. You stopped by a few days ago and told me to contact you if I heard anything."

"Yes, hi, Tess," said Booker. "What can I do for you?"

"Well, I still haven't heard from Mariana, and I'm getting worried. I can't figure out where she'd go. And more concerning, I realized she must've left her phone here at home. At least, that's the last place I can track it. She would never go anywhere without it, and she always keeps it charged, so something isn't right. Anyway, I remembered that she borrowed my AirPods to go for a run the evening she left. I went on my phone just now to see if maybe she'd taken the AirPods with her, and I could locate her. It doesn't show anything recently, but it indicates the last known location was Las Vegas around thirty-six hours ago. Maybe someone else has my AirPods now, and it's not Mariana, but I thought I should call you and let you know." Tess paused to take a deep breath from her monologue and let Booker soak in all the information.

Booker considered his response as he already knew that Mariana had been in Vegas. "Thank you for calling and letting me know. This is very helpful. We're still looking for Mariana ourselves and we'll make sure we check Las Vegas."

He hesitated then asked, "Quick question...If Mariana doesn't have her phone, how can you still track your AirPods through the app?"

Tess thought for a second and replied, "Actually I'm not sure how the *Find My* app works, but somehow my AirPods must've connected to the internet and logged that she was in Vegas."

Booker responded, "Okay, I'll check it out. Thanks again for the information. Can you please keep checking the location of the AirPods and call me immediately if you receive an update?"

"Will do," Tess proclaimed.

"I'm sure Mariana is okay. If we locate her, I'll call you and let you know."

"Thanks," said Tess as she hung up.

Booker was in his office with Pat who had been watching him intently while he was on the phone. He turned to her and said, "Do you know how the Apple iPhone *Find My* app works? How do devices check in with their location?"

Pat thought for a second then said, "I'm not sure. Hold on." She quickly researched it on her phone.

A couple minutes later Pat announced, "Okay, I got it. It says devices will periodically connect to a linked iPhone via Bluetooth and send their location. I guess if you are not close to the device with your phone, then the device is able to connect to any other close iPhone using Bluetooth through a proprietary Apple network. Interesting—I didn't realize Apple did that. Does that answer your question?"

"Yes, that's perfect," replied Booker. "I was just talking to Mariana's roommate, Tess. I guess Mariana borrowed Tess's AirPods before she took off. The AirPods must've connected to another iPhone in Vegas and logged that information on the *Find My* app on Tess's phone. We already know Mariana was in Vegas, so it doesn't help us now, but Tess is going to call back immediately if the AirPods register themselves again in a new location. This could be the perfect way to catch Mariana without her realizing we're even close."

Pat asked, "Do you think we can trust Tess? What if

this is a way for them to misdirect us and point us in the wrong direction?"

Booker slowly nodded. "Good point. It does seem a little odd that she took her roommate's Air Pods. Let's keep that in mind if Tess calls back with more information."

Tess hung up the phone with Booker. The call hadn't made her feel any better. She decided to text Keith and try to have a conversation with him. That might make her feel better. Tess logged in to the app and texted him.

> **Tess**: How are you? I'm good. Been here all alone though. Mariana left town for some reason. I'm worried as I haven't heard from her

She stared at her phone hoping for an immediate response but after a minute or two she gave up and focused on making dinner. Halfway through the preparation, she heard a ping from her phone. She stopped what she was doing and walked over to check it out.

> **Keith**: Great to hear from you! All's well here. Busy as usual. Sorry to hear you're alone. Wish I could visit. Why do you think Mariana left?

Tess: I wish you'd visit too! That's the weird thing. Mariana didn't tell me where she was going. I figured out she was in Vegas of all places because she borrowed my AirPods before she left and I was able to track them. Just hope she's okay

TWENTY-EIGHT

LOOKING FOR CLUES

Prague, Czech Republic

Early in the morning, Mariana and Shep finally fell into a deep sleep. When the alarm went off at 9AM Mariana bolted upright, disoriented and shocked to find herself alone in bed. She slapped off the alarm, and the sound of running water filled the room. Just the thought of Shep naked in the shower made her smile, bringing back a surge of memories from last night. Then she remembered why they were in this hotel room and anxiety washed over her, turning her smile into a frown.

She climbed out of bed, grabbed her cozy hotel robe, and crossed the room to the coffee station to make a pot of coffee. Realizing it was just an espresso machine she rolled her eyes. *Well, nothing like a quick jolt,* she mumbled to herself. *I'd kill for a latte right now.* She drank her shot then collected her tablet with the Cyber Membranes contact information, hoping to set up an appointment as soon as possible.

She dialed the number and waited for someone to answer. After several rings, someone finally picked up.

"Dobrý den," greeted a woman's voice.

Mariana said, "Hello, my name is Samantha Jones. Do you speak English?"

"Yes, of course," the woman responded in almost perfect English.

Mariana continued, "Great. I'm an American reporter working on a story that relates to the cyberattack your company documented last year in Kiev and Prague. I'm only here for one day but would really appreciate it if I could interview someone at your company for the story. I will make sure to add the name of the company and give you credit in the final version."

The woman on the other end paused for a moment and then said, "Hold on. Let me go talk with our managing partner who just got into the office."

A few moments went by, and then a man's voice came on the line. "Hello, Ms. Jones. This is Tomás. I'm in charge here at Cyber Membranes. How can I be of assistance?"

"Hi, Tomás. Please call me Sam. I am working on a story for a TV news network in the U.S. As part of the story, we would like to highlight the cyberattack that occurred here last winter in Kiev and Prague. I saw that your company did a comprehensive analysis of the attack and thought it would be great to interview you and add you in the story. Of course, we will give you and your company credit when it's released. The challenge is that I'm only here today."

Tomás took a moment to process her request. "Of course," he said in a raised voice. "We can accommodate you. Can you come to our office around noon?"

"That would be fantastic," she replied.

"Will you have cameras to set up for this interview?" Tomás asked.

Thinking quickly, Mariana replied in a reassuring tone, "No, I'm just doing some initial background research on this trip. The camera crew will come later and take videos depending on how the story develops."

"Yes, yes that sounds great," answered Tomás. "Just ask for me when you get to the lobby and I'll meet you."

Mariana thanked him and hung up the phone, then turned to Shep who had come out of the bathroom.

"All set–I have a meeting with Cyber Membranes at noon. Fingers crossed that I can uncover something helpful. I looked up their address and it's about a fifteen-minute walk."

Shep hesitated, realizing Mariana was pushing him away once again, and she intended to go to the meeting by herself. "Sounds great," Shep said. "How about room service first? I'm starving and want a bite to eat before working out." Then he bent over and placed a gentle kiss on her lips, letting her know that last night was not a one-off.

After returning the kiss, Mariana smiled. "Will you

order a pot of coffee please? This espresso shot isn't going to do it for me this morning," she asked, holding her tiny cup up for emphasis.

As she turned her back to enter the bathroom Shep announced, "By the way, I plan to join you for this meeting. We already discussed working on this together."

Mariana chose to ignore his statement and proceeded to head in for a shower.

After breakfast Shep went to the gym for a quick workout. Mariana stayed back, claiming she wanted to do some more research. Before he returned to their room, she grabbed her notepad and purse, then proceeded to leave the hotel. Mariana knew Shep would be upset with her, but she was adamant that she should handle this meeting on her own. This was her mess to resolve, not Shep's, and while she appreciated his offer to help, she found it was best to seek the answers on her own and keep him out of it.

Mariana found walking to Cyber Membranes quite pleasant. Not only was there a spring in her step due to their late-night activities, but the sun was also out, and trees were beginning to bloom marking the beginning of the season. It was a short walk through the Old Town of Prague. Tourists were everywhere and she passed several Easter markets set up in the main square. As she followed the directions on Google Maps, Mariana suddenly realized that Cyber Membranes was in the heart of the

Old Town, right next to the famous Tyn Church. *I can't believe this security company is located here,* she thought to herself as she looked all around in search of where to go.

Shep quietly came up from behind her then startled her when he announced, "I think we go through this narrow walkway into the courtyard right in front of the church."

Mariana whipped around in frustration. "Shep, I told you I could handle this meeting on my own."

"That's great, but *I* told *you* that I was coming. You don't know what kind of situation you're walking into, Mariana. Quit pushing me away!"

"Fine," Mariana relented, recognizing she had no choice. They both looked around the area and noticed an unmarked black door leading into a building next to the church.

Just then the door opened and a short man with dark wavy hair and spectacles asked, "Are you Sam?"

Mariana quickly responded, "Yes, and this is my husband and partner Nick."

"Pleasure to meet you both. I am Tomás. Welcome to Cyber Membranes." Then he guided them to the staircase. "Let's head up to my office on the 3rd floor."

Once in his office, Mariana and Shep sat on the two chairs facing his desk.

Mariana started in, "As I mentioned on the phone, we're doing some preliminary research for a story on cyberattacks perpetrated by the Russians. We read your analysis of the attacks on centralized HVAC control units for apartment complexes last winter. We think this is very similar to what we believe is being initiated by the Russians in other locations. We were hoping to get more information and details from you so we can add it to our story."

Tomás responded, "We can help, and I agree, this clearly has Russian fingerprints all over it. Since you've read the report already, I'll jump into some of the interesting findings. There have been numerous industrial control system malware attacks over the past, but this was the first one we are aware of that targeted vulnerabilities with Modbus communications. As best we can tell, the Russians got access to an externally facing router that wasn't properly protected from the internet. Once they got into the router, they were then able to access various network servers and the heating system controllers. The attack caused inaccurate temperature measurements which resulted in several hundred apartment buildings not receiving heat for many days during sub-zero outdoor temperatures."

"Why do you think it was the Russians?" Shep asked.

Tomás continued, "When the attackers infiltrated the router, they still had to send commands from an external destination. We uncovered Moscow-based IP addresses."

"What did you do with that information?" Mariana asked. "Did you determine who in Russia started this attack?"

Tomás responded, "Unfortunately no. We tried to partner with the Russian Embassy here in Prague to work on this together. I know they started their own investigation, but shortly after, they came back to us and said they found nothing and couldn't determine who or what was behind the IP addresses in Moscow. Clearly, they were withholding the information. We don't have great relationships with the Russians these days, so we weren't surprised. That led us to a dead-end though."

Mariana and Shep looked at each other for a moment, then Mariana said, "Tomás, who did you work with at the Russian Embassy? Do you think if we approached him, he might give us some information?"

Tomás gave them a skeptical glance. "I highly doubt it, but I believe they know more than they're telling us. My contact was named Alexei Sokolov." Tomás jotted down his name and contact information and handed it to Shep. "I hope this has been helpful for your story?"

"Yes, you've been extremely helpful, Tomás," Mariana said. "We'll follow-up with you regarding background details and potential videos and audio recordings that they would like to make for the story."

Tomás nodded, then asked, "Oh, I meant to ask, what is the name of the news service you are associated with?"

Mariana quickly stood up, reached her hand out to thank him for the meeting and replied, "We're independent journalists working on this story for one of the big networks. As we get closer, we can provide more information."

"Thank you so much for your time," Shep added. "We can see ourselves out." Then the two of them made their way down the stairs swiftly. When they got outside,

Mariana leaned into Shep and said quietly, "Well that was close, but we got some good information and a new lead. Let's go find a cafe and talk about how to follow-up with the Russian Embassy and this Alexei person."

Shep and Mariana walked down the street looking for a good quiet place to get something to eat and discuss next steps. They saw a cafe and found an open table in the corner to sit down.

Pulling out her notes, Mariana said, "I obviously don't have enough information to give to the FBI yet to clear my name. Should I try to talk with his contact, Alexei, at the Russian Embassy and see if he will divulge anything?"

Shep shook his head and carefully switched the discussion from *I* to *we*, to remind Mariana that they were in this together. "I think that's a dead end as Tomás stated. There's no reason why Alexei would share their investigation with us. However, I do think there's a strong chance they have the information we need. It's probably in some file within the Russian Embassy. The question is, how do *we* get it? If we ask them for it, and they say no, then we'll be on their radar."

Mariana leaned over and put her head in her hands. "I have no idea. I can't believe we came all this way and have nothing to show for it. What's worse is I'm definitely a suspect so if I stop now, I'll be put in prison and blamed for everything! I have to dig up some credible information that shows I was set up. There must be another way."

Mariana became somber and bit her nails thinking

about how best to proceed. Reflecting on her true feelings she looked up at Shep and said, "I need to tell you something else. I don't trust the FBI. When my family came here from Mexico, my parents worked hard to make a living yet always were afraid of the authorities. They wanted a better life for me but were paranoid we may be sent back to Mexico where we had nothing. I spent years listening to my parents whispering about their concerns to each other and trying not to show that I was afraid. I even saw several relatives sent back. I guess I developed an irrational fear of the authorities, and when the FBI started asking me questions and becoming suspicious, all those feelings came flooding back."

Shep listened intently, processing what she said. "I can only imagine how you and your family felt. I do think you need to keep an open mind though. We may need the FBI by the time we figure this all out and they may be our best chance of identifying who's behind all of this."

There was some awkward silence. Shep began typing on his phone then said, "I have an idea." He leaned forward. "I just looked up reasons why an American would need to go to the Russian Embassy. It says we need a Visa if we're planning a trip to Russia and we must go to the Embassy to get it. Here's my idea...How about we make an appointment for a Visa, then when we get into the Embassy, we try to figure out where Alexei's office is? After the appointment, we find a place to hide within the Embassy until the night when no one's there. Then we can search his office and find the investigation file on the malware attack. That might be enough evidence to share with the FBI and show them that you're innocent and only trying to track down who framed you. What do you think?"

Mariana was silent for a moment, thinking through what Shep proposed. Then she said, "It's extremely dangerous. What if we get caught? And even if we don't, what are the odds we find the right information? I don't know...It sounds like a big risk."

"I agree it's risky, but I also think we have a good shot. Why would the Russians expect anyone to hide in the Embassy after hours? If they have a security guard on site, he'd be manning the front entrance, not the back offices. If we notice that they have monitoring cameras throughout the building, we can adjust. Also, if Alexei works there and he was responsible for the investigation, it seems highly likely all the files will be there." Then he added with determination, "I don't see another way."

Mariana squeezed Shep's hand on the table and said, "I guess you're right. We've come this far; we might as well go all the way and figure this out."

Shep smirked as Mariana looked down at her phone to find the website for the Russian Embassy in Prague. She finally acknowledged that they were in this together.

"Looks like we need to make an appointment online before we can enter. Hold on a sec." She kept typing for a while and then looked up at Shep, "I can't believe it, but they have an opening tomorrow afternoon at 4:30PM.

There must've been a cancellation. This is perfect. I'm filling in the online form now. Looks like we have a day to figure out our plan."

The next day, Shep and Mariana went shopping. They bought clothes to make them look more like students and purchased backpacks to complete the look. The backpacks would be perfect to carry any documents out of the Embassy assuming they found the right files. They also bought flashlights and some small tools in case they needed to break into the file cabinets or open doors. Finally, they grabbed two cans of mace in the event they ended up running into someone and needed to escape.

At 4:00PM, they were ready. They walked over to the Russian Embassy and rang the bell at the entrance. They told the security guard their fake names and informed him that they had an appointment at 4:30PM. As they went through security clearance, they looked at each other with concern that their equipment would create an alarm, but somehow it didn't. With a subtle sigh of relief, they got in line to check in with the front desk clerk. Shep scanned the room and spotted a directory on the wall that listed the various offices in the building. One of the lines listed *Alexei Sokolov, Foreign Relations Minister...401*. Shep made a mental note of the office number and elbowed Mariana, so she saw it as well. They smiled at each other and continued to wait in line.

When they finally got to the counter ten minutes

later, Mariana repeated their appointment details. Fortunately, the woman spoke English and told them to go
down the hall and enter office 202 where someone would
process their Visa application. As they walked down the
hallway, Shep asked someone where the bathroom was.
Continuing past them clearly in a rush, the person motioned that it was at the end of the hall and to the right.
Shep and Mariana decided it would be a good excuse to
each go to the bathroom to check out the rest of the floor
and look for a good hiding spot. Eventually, they found
a door that opened to a storage closet. They looked at
each other and nodded in agreement that this was the
place to hide until closing time. They backtracked to
office 202 and went in to fill out the paperwork for the
Visa. At this point, it was 5:15PM. As they left the office,
they turned right instead of left towards the bathrooms.
When they passed the bathrooms, the hallway was still
empty. They didn't see any surveillance cameras, so they
believed they made it to the storage closet undetected.
Shep looked both ways, quickly opened the door and
guided Mariana in, then followed behind her while closing the door quietly.

It was dark inside the closet, so they fished around
for their flashlights and turned them on. Surprised at
how large and deep the storage closet was, they started
looking for a good place to hide for a few hours. They
found the perfect spot at the end of the closet, which
was lined with large, floor-to-ceiling cabinets. Moving a
few of the items from one cabinet to the next, Shep created space just large enough to fit them both. They were

wedged tightly up against each other, but the intimacy of the confined space was not a problem. They were in this together–in every way. They turned off their flashlights and waited.

Shep managed to make a seat atop a stack of boxes with Mariana on his lap. In any other situation he would have enjoyed their position but tonight was not the time to do anything other than pray that they make it through this unharmed. They sat in silence, too afraid to speak–the only sound, the relentless pounding of their hearts. Shep's mind was racing. *What have I done? Why the hell did I push to do this? Who knows what the Russians will do if they catch us?* When the adrenaline finally faded, they drifted into sleep, lost in thoughts of survival. It was hours later when Mariana felt Shep stir.

"I haven't heard anyone for a while," Shep whispered while opening the cabinet to step out. "I think we should be okay. Man, my back is tight from sitting in the same position for so long. How are you feeling?"

Mariana tried to smile and made her way out of the cabinet as well. "I'm fine. Just sore all over."

Shep smiled and gave her a comforting hug, "Let's hope this works. Grab your backpack and let's go find Alexei's office."

They slowly opened the door and looked in both directions for any movement. They proceeded to head down the hall. As they got to the corner, Shep spied a camera angling down one of the halls. He grabbed Mariana's hand and turned away from the camera, down a different hallway. Halfway down, they found a door leading to a stairwell.

"Let's take the stairs to the fourth floor," Shep said. "I think we should avoid the elevators in case there's someone still in the building."

When they got to office 401, they found the door locked. Shep opened his backpack and pulled out the tools he bought at the hardware store. He started fidgeting with the lock, and after a minute, he heard it pop, allowing him to turn the knob and open the door.

Mariana gasped. "How'd you know how to do that?"

Shep replied with a smile, "One of my family's security guards showed me a while back. I guess you never know when some skills will prove useful."

They entered the room and looked around. Mariana said, "I don't see any security cameras here, do you?"

Shep shook his head, "I think we're okay now."

Mariana took in the surroundings. There was a desk in the middle of the room with a big window behind it. Two chairs were on the other side of the desk. Stacks of papers lined the edge of the desk beside a computer display monitor and lamp. A coffee mug that stated in English, *IF YOU DON'T HAVE ANYTHING NICE TO SAY, SAY IT IN RUSSIAN,* sat atop another stack of papers in the opposite desk corner. On one side of the room, there was a table with a few glasses and several bottles of liquor which looked like different types of Russian vodka. On the other side of the room were several file cabinets. Shep was already leaning over one of them with his toolkit, trying to open it. Mariana decided to rifle through the stacks of paper on the desk to look for words that related to the cyberattack. After several minutes of not finding anything interesting on the desk, Mariana heard a crack.

She looked over at Shep and said, "Be careful–that was pretty loud."

"I know. I'm trying," said Shep. "I had to snap the lock. But I got the drawers open. Why don't you start looking through these files and I'll try to open the other cabinet. Hopefully, that one's easier."

Mariana started leafing through the files. Most of them were labeled in Russian so she skipped those. As she was sorting through the second drawer, she noticed one of the files was labeled *Cyber Membranes*.

"Shep," she blurted out in excitement.

Shep turned from working on the other cabinet and put his finger to his mouth and motioned *Shhh*.

Mariana continued more quietly, "I found something."

She took the file out and walked over to the desk. They both sat in the chairs and started looking at the various documents.

"This is great," said Mariana. "There are a ton of documents here. I'm sure some of this will be helpful. We can get the documents translated and then reach out to the FBI based on what we find."

Just then, the door slammed open and three men burst into the room. The first two held guns pointing at Shep and Mariana while the third man was following behind. Shep stood up and started to reach in his back pocket for the mace he brought when one of the men pistol-whipped him on the side of his head. Shep went down immediately. Mariana could tell he had passed out and there was a trickle of blood coming from the impact on the side of his head. Mariana quickly raised her hands and exclaimed, "Okay, okay. We're unarmed!"

TWENTY-NINE

CAUGHT

Prague, Czech Republic

Mariana woke up and heard the shallow breathing coming from Shep a few feet away. She had no idea how long they had been held captive. She was stiff from sleeping upright in a chair. She also couldn't tell how hurt Shep was because the lights were off. She recalled how the men forcefully dragged them away from the office. She knew they were taken downstairs, and the cold, damp air around her gave her the impression they were underground. Their arms and legs were tied to chairs. Mariana tried to wake up Shep by calling his name, but eventually she gave up and just let him sleep. She also tried multiple times to break free from the bindings, but they were tied way too tight.

Time dragged by while Mariana waited for Shep to wake up. Alone in the dark, her mind started racing.

Why did I allow Shep to help me? Now he's really hurt, in a foreign country, and being held by the Russians. This is all my fault. Then she cried out loud in frustration, "Ugh!"

Shep grunted, beginning to come to, and clearly in pain.

Mariana whispered, "Shep, are you awake? Can you hear me?"

After a few seconds, Shep stirred and said gruffly, "Yeah, what the hell happened? Where are we? I can't move and I have a horrible headache!"

"They found us in Alexei's office. They knocked you out and took us down here hours ago. We're tied up. I think we're in the basement of the Embassy, but I can't really tell because it's so dark."

Shep moaned in response.

"Shep, I'm so sorry. This is all my fault. I never should have allowed you to help me and take all this risk."

"It's not your fault," Shep groaned. "I volunteered to help you. Did they say anything to you before they left?"

"No, nothing, but they took our backpacks."

Shep started to reply, "Okay, let's make sure we..." but he couldn't finish the sentence because just then the door opened and the lights switched on.

The three men entered the room. The man without the gun spoke calmly as he looked at Shep. "What is your name?"

"Nick," Shep said.

One of the other men leaned over and punched Shep

forcefully in the gut. Shep cried out and doubled over in pain.

"Wrong answer," barked the man in charge. "Let's start over. My name is Alexei Sokolov. It was my office you were snooping around in. We found your passports, but clearly, they are fake, so we know that isn't your real name. You are most likely American spies, and we don't take to American spies very kindly. We can't confirm your identification in any of our databases so do me a favor and be honest with us before we must use more forceful means of extracting the information."

Mariana didn't want them to hit Shep again, so she blurted out, "My name is Mariana Morales. This is my friend Ben Shepman. We are *not* spies. We're just trying to find some information. Please don't hurt him again!"

Alexei looked over at Mariana with menacing eyes. "We will check those names with your faces. If you are telling more lies, you will both pay." And with that, all three men exited the room, turned off the lights, and locked the door.

As they sat there contemplating their situation, Shep finally broke the silence with a joke. "I sure could use another one of those amazing massages from you right about now."

Mariana couldn't help but smile. "Yeah, me too. Feels like a very long time ago now. I promise I'll make it up to you *if* we get out of here."

Close to a half-hour later, the bright lights came on again, making both squint as the three men entered the room. This time, the two armed men stood behind Mariana and Shep with their guns pointing, intensifying the tension in the room. Shep and Mariana both stiffened while they stared up at Alexei who stood in front of them stoically.

Alexei tossed a folder onto the table next to them with a loud slam. The noise echoed in the eerily quiet, concrete-lined room making Mariana jump in her seat. He proceeded to look from one of them to the other, his stare unwavering. Then finally he spoke in a gruff tone. "We found both of your records and looked at your backgrounds. You *must* be working undercover. Your actions are too suspicious. Why did you break into the Embassy and my office in particular?"

Mariana glanced over at Shep and sucked in a deep breath, hesitating to answer.

"There's no point in lying to me!" Alexei barked.

In a shaky voice she said, "It's kind of a long story..."

Alexei just stared back at her with cold eyes. Shep remained silent. His head pounded from the blow and the punch to the gut just accentuated it. Mariana realized she had no choice but to explain their actions.

She filled them in as much as she could, starting with her being a computer programmer and ending with her being framed for a cyberattack. Mariana had been talking very fast without any pauses. She stopped to catch her breath and looked into Alexei's eyes to judge his reaction.

Alexei showed no response but began pacing the room. Finally, he said, "This is ridiculous. What is the connection between the cyberattack here in Prague with an electric car charging station company in California? Why did you remove the file on Cyber Membranes? Did you plant something in my office? Your story makes no sense." Alexei then nodded to the man behind Shep, and the man stepped forward aggressively, pressing the gun against Shep's head.

Recognizing the escalating threat, Mariana yelled out, "No. Stop! It does make sense. Let me explain. The cyberattack in the U.S. has the same characteristics as the attack here in Prague. I think the one here was a test prior to the U.S. attack." Mariana was getting even more emotional and continued in a manic voice, "Are you the person behind all of this? Why are you doing this to me? Why is Russia making me look like a suspect? I didn't do anything to you! I don't understand!"

Alexei considered her comments. He motioned for the man behind Shep to step back. Then he said, "Well I know something that you don't. And I had no reason to share it with the authorities. Our relationship with the Czech Republic is very tense these days, and we would prefer to hold information and make their life harder. Let them think it's us. That only helps us build more fear and uncertainty."

Mariana and Shep glanced at each other in confusion. Alexei kept talking, "Yes, we did our own investigation. The IP addresses that initiated the attack in Prague did come from Moscow. That is true. However, what we didn't share is that the IP addresses didn't originate in Moscow. They were redirected through Moscow, but they trace back to Amsterdam. It wasn't Russia that caused these attacks. We had nothing to do with it and turning off the heat to various apartment buildings doesn't really get us anything. Since my investigation determined Russia was not involved, we found it unnecessary to support the ongoing Prague investigation, and we dropped it. The Czechs mistook our actions as admission that we were responsible. In truth, we didn't investigate who might be involved in Amsterdam as it isn't our jurisdiction. Let the world think it is the Russians. We don't care. That is fine by us."

"Well, if it wasn't Russia, then who is behind this and why are they setting me up?" Mariana asked.

Alexei shrugged. "I don't know, but I can assure you that my country is not behind it." At that moment, the door opened, and another man popped his head in.

"Alexei, can I speak with you for a few minutes? It's urgent."

Alexei and the two other men exited the room, leaving Mariana and Shep once again alone, but this time the lights stayed on. Mariana glanced at Shep and gasped. The gash on the side of his head was significant. Dried blood marked a trail down his cheek. A large bump had formed where the pistol had hit him. "Are you sure you're okay, Shep?" Shep looked over and tried to focus, "I'll survive. I just have a raging headache."

Just then, Alexei came back into the room by himself and dumped their backpacks on the floor. Instead of going to his normal spot, he walked behind Mariana and Shep and untied them. He then grabbed his chair and sat in front of them.

"Do you know the history of this building?" Alexei asked.

Shep and Mariana stole glances at each other and then looked back at Alexei in bewilderment. Alexei continued, "It's fascinating. A long time ago, this building was owned by Jiri Popper, a prominent Czech banker. However, in 1939, a day after the Germans occupied Czechoslovakia, the building was confiscated by the Germans and used as the Prague headquarters for the Gestapo during the War. Over this time, the Nazis built a series of tunnels and secret passageways under the building. Then, in 1945, after the liberation of Czechoslovakia, the building was given as a gift to the Soviet Union for their role in freeing the country. The Soviets continued the work of the tunnels, and it's reported that the KGB used them extensively for espionage and counterintelligence over the years."

Alexei rolled his eyes, then continued, "I have no comment on those rumors. Recently, the relationship between the Czech Republic and Russia has deteriorated significantly with lots of tit for tat back and forth. In 2020, the Czechs changed the name of our street address to the name of a Russian opposition leader that was killed in 2015. We accordingly changed the address of the Embassy to an adjacent street, but then the Czechs turned around in 2022 after Russia attacked Ukraine and renamed that street to what is known in English as

Ukrainian Heroes."

Alexei stopped his historical discourse and looked at his watch. He then continued, "You may wonder why I'm telling you this story. Well, I think it's relevant. Your FBI caught our search for you and notified INTERPOL that they believe you're being held here. INTERPOL is on their way to pick you up and take you back to the U.S. Embassy. Given the camera surveillance around these streets, we had to acknowledge that we caught the two of you breaking into our Embassy and we said we'd hold you until they arrive. They should be here in about ten minutes."

Alexei noted the worried expressions on both Shep and Mariana's faces. He smiled. "As I have made clear, we're not interested in supporting the internal affairs of the Czech Republic or the United States. I'm not at liberty to actively help you, but I will give you some information that may prove useful."

Alexei pulled out a pen and paper. "I'm writing down the address in Amsterdam where we discovered the IP addresses were rerouted. You may want to look there for your next set of clues as to who is behind this."

Mariana reached over and grabbed the paper. "Thank you so much Alexei. This is extremely helpful, but I'm not sure we'll have the opportunity to pursue this once INTERPOL picks us up."

Alexei sighed. "I'm sorry to hear that. Maybe you will find a way to continue your investigation. I must go take care of other business now. The authorities will arrive shortly to take you into U.S. custody. However, in the meantime, I would like you to know that the third door down the hallway to the right opens to a secret passage, part of the underground tunnels. You might be inclined to take that path and see where it leads. I wish you well. Goodbye for now." With that, Alexei stood up and left the room, leaving the door propped open.

Shep and Mariana looked at each other questioningly. After hesitating for a moment and registering what just happened, they jumped up, collected their belongings, and left the room. They found the third door down the hallway, entered it, and started down the long, dimly lit passageway for what seemed like several hundred yards. When they got to the end, they decided to go left because the hall to the right led to a barricaded door. The narrow hallway turned in multiple directions, back and forth as if they were traveling through a maze. After a few more minutes of fast walking, they found a staircase that led to a door. The door was locked from their side, so they unlocked it and cracked it open quietly to see what was on the other side. Cold air rushed in. They stepped into a courtyard leading to another building—much smaller, with narrow windows. Shep and Mariana could see people inside walking back and forth and a group of people in a reception area sitting in chairs. People looked up but thankfully no one took any interest in the two of them. Shep grabbed Mariana's hand and guided her across the courtyard to the black metal fence on the side of the building. They opened the gate and stepped through to what appeared to be the driveway to the front entrance.

"Look at that," Mariana said as she pointed to the sign she saw posted on the main door. "The tunnel we took runs from the Russian Embassy to the Russian Consulate building. I wonder where else it leads."

"Well, we don't have time to figure that out," Shep responded as he looked at their surroundings. To the right was a residential area with large luxury homes, while down the street to the left there were a variety of office buildings, apartments and restaurants. "I don't see any police. Let's head this way and try to get an Uber back to the hotel. We need to get out of Prague as fast as possible."

THIRTY

THE KNOTS

Undisclosed Location

The message was encrypted and written in code. After the Spaniard decoded the message, he sat back and contemplated what he had read. He was half alarmed and half in admiration. The message read:

```
Target       located      in     Prague,   Czech
Republic. Traveling with unknown man.
Escaped the FBI in Las Vegas. The two
subjects are currently being held in
the Russian Embassy. Russians performed
background checks on both persons. FBI
alerted during the checks. INTERPOL
intercepting targets and taking them to
```

```
U.S. Embassy. Requesting instructions.
```

The Spaniard typed back a response in code.

```
Have local agent get to location asap
and   monitor   activity.   Report   back
regularly.
```

He then put down his encrypted phone and went back to entertaining his guests at the cocktail party.

THIRTY-ONE

ON THE RUN

Prague, Czech Republic

Shep turned to Mariana in the Uber and whispered, "Let's grab our stuff at the hotel. We need our second set of passports. I'm sure the Russians have told INTERPOL the current names we're using. They can easily figure out where we're staying, so if we're going to escape, we need that second set now."

Ten minutes later, they were back in their hotel room. As they were collecting their belongings, Mariana looked out the window and saw several police cars pull up.

"Shep, we need to go now. They're here."

"All set," he said as he threw his bag over his shoulder. "We can take the back stairwell and look for an exit behind the building."

They left the room and headed to a staircase used to access the spa area and private event spaces. They went down to the first floor and ran through an empty meeting room, then saw an exit door heading outside. They opened the door slowly and realized they were behind the hotel facing the river. They tried to act like normal tourists walking along the pathway admiring the views. Shep led them to the right, and they made their way a couple blocks to a bridge with a busy street. They stood on the corner trying to hail a taxi.

Shep said, "Let's go to the train station and get on the first train headed in the direction of Amsterdam. We should also try to find hats, so we aren't so easy to spot through camera surveillance."

Mariana looked over at Shep. "Sounds good. Oh, I forget...what are our new names?"

Shep didn't remember either. He set down their bags, pulled out the passports and read them aloud, "Mike and Lisa Roberts. Not very creative, but easy to remember."

A taxi pulled over. They looked around and didn't see anyone following them, so they jumped in. Little did they know, they had already been spotted. The taxicab had been shadowing them.

"Praha Hlavni Nadrazi," said Shep in broken speech to the driver, naming the main railway station. While the driver sped off, Shep pulled out his phone and began researching cafes at the station.

"Okay, here's the plan. When the driver stops at the train station let's split up and enter through different doors to avoid anyone spotting us. Keep your head down and walk in as quickly as possible without causing attention. Let's both try to find stores where we can buy a hat. Then meet me at the bookstore called Luxor. It looks like it's in the middle of the station. Go to the second level and there should be a small cafe in the corner."

Mariana nodded, biting her lip, clearly nervous and at a loss for words.

"It'll be okay," Shep assured her, giving her hand a squeeze. "Just act natural and don't look anyone in the eyes."

The driver slyly looked in the rear-view mirror at his two passengers in the back seat. Traffic was heavy so when he had to stop at the next red light, the driver quickly shot off a text:

```
Směr Praha Hlavni Nadrazi
(Direction, main railway station)
```

The driver took the long way to the train station to buy some time. Eventually, he pulled up to the main entrance. When they exited the cab, the driver quickly sent another text, naming the cafe he heard the male passenger speak. The driver figured his contact could find the subjects there.

```
Kavárna Luxor Knihkupectvi
(Luxor Bookstore Cafe)
```

Shep and Mariana headed in opposite directions and entered the building through separate entrances. Shep found a sporting goods store called INTERSPORT and picked up a navy-blue Yankees hat.

I can't believe all they have are American baseball team hats for sale, Shep thought as he weaved through the crowded train station looking for Luxor Bookstore. Then he chuckled out loud when he realized he had just passed three different men all wearing Yankees hats while other people were sporting Brooklyn sweatshirts.

Meanwhile, Mariana walked around the train station and couldn't find any stores with hats. Finally, she walked into a women's clothing boutique, Orsay. There was one blue denim hat for sale. She paid for it, secured it low on her head, then walked around looking for Luxor bookstore. She went down the escalator and saw the bookstore directly in front of her, so she walked in, took the stairs to the second level, and looked around for the cafe. Eventually she located it behind a wall of books on display and spotted Shep sitting at a back corner table with two cups of coffee in front of him. Mariana scanned the area for anyone eyeing them suspiciously but didn't see the man standing a little distance away pretending to be looking at various books on one of the racks. As she sat down at the table, Shep was busy looking at online tickets. He found an overnight train that was leaving in twenty minutes. The whole trip would take around twelve hours. He quickly booked two tickets on the European Sleeper for a first class, double sleeper compartment.

"We're all booked. Gotta hurry," Shep said downing his coffee. Then the two of them rushed off to board the train.

When they got on the train, they found their way to compartment 61. It was tight quarters with bunk beds on one side and a pull-down chair next to a small desk on the other. Privacy curtains hung on the two windows facing the outside as well as the sliding door to the center aisle of the train. Shep and Mariana stored their luggage and prayed that the train would depart on time, with them undetected. When the whistle blew and the engines accelerated, they were finally able to relax. Shep pulled Mariana in his arms and gave her a huge hug, wincing slightly when she crushed up against his stomach, bruised from the punch he endured only hours before. Sensing his discomfort Mariana looked up at him with concern in her eyes.

"How are you feeling? Let me see your stomach," she said, gently raising his shirt. Eying a bruise forming on the right side of his gut she added, "He may have broken one of your ribs."

Shep brushed it off. "It'll be okay. I still have a bad headache from the blow to my head though. I'll take some aspirin. Let's go to the dining car and get some food." Then he tilted her head up and gave her a soft kiss. "I'm looking forward to more of that after we eat."

Mariana smiled in response with a twinkle in her eyes and led him out of the compartment.

The dining car was "reservation only" but fortunately it wasn't that crowded, so they were able to get a table. While they were eating, Shep noticed a man sitting alone a few booths away staring at them intermittently. He tried to brush him off as a businessman heading home, but Shep thought it was odd that he looked a little rough around the edges and wore a big coat throughout dinner. When he and Mariana got up to leave, Shep observed the man close out his check as well, even though he hadn't finished his meal. And when they approached the sliding door to exit to the next car, Shep saw in the reflection in the window that the man began to follow them out.

"Why don't you go back to our compartment? I think I left my credit card on the table," Shep told Mariana.

Confused because she was pretty sure he had it, Mariana shrugged and headed back to the room. She was anxious to research how they were going to get to the Amsterdam location Alexei gave them and was excited to put on some more comfortable clothes.

After she left, Shep pretended to go back to the table but continued progressing through several train cars. His goal was to guide the *stranger* away from Mariana. When he got to the fourth gangway between trains, Shep stepped aside into the shadow and waited for the man to emerge. As Shep predicted, the man came through moments later. Shep lunged at him and pinned him against the door.

"Why are you following us?" Shep blurted out.

The stranger didn't answer. Instead, he pulled a gun hiding underneath his coat and pointed it at Shep. Just then, the train lurched around a corner, forcing both men to try to regain their balance. Shep took the opportunity to swat the gun away. The two of them started to struggle. The stranger was skilled, but Shep was in amazing shape and could hold his own in combat. A punch by one was quickly reciprocated by the other. The stranger tried to land a right cross to Shep's head. Shep saw it coming and quickly stepped to the left and blocked the punch with his left arm. At the same time, Shep grabbed the stranger's right wrist with his free hand, twisted him and shoved him against the wall. As he did this, Shep registered that the stranger had a unique tattoo on his forearm: a square knot. Gaining his balance, the stranger twisted around breaking his arms free and proceeded to push a button on the wall, opening the doors to the outside. He attempted to push Shep out the door. Aware of what the stranger was hoping to accomplish, Shep feigned that he was falling but then got under the man's arm and slipped around him. He then shoved the stranger through the door and out the train. Shep, paralyzed for a moment, realized what just occurred, then looked down and saw the man's gun on the ground next to his feet. Shep kicked it out of the train, not knowing what else to do, and pushed the button to close the door. With a deep breath, he took a few minutes to gather himself.

When Shep got back to compartment 61, Mariana immediately knew something was wrong. He was pale in the face and clearly in shock.

"What is it? Are you okay?" she asked.

Shep, breathing heavy and looking ashen, sat on the bed. Mariana sat down by his side and gave him a moment to respond. Eventually his racing heart calmed down enough for him to speak.

"I didn't want to alarm you during dinner, but I saw

a man sitting by himself observing us. When we got up to leave, I noticed he did the same thing. That's why I told you to come to the room without me. I wanted to confront him."

Shep proceeded to relay what transpired, not leaving out a single detail. Voicing his actions made him woozy and the shock of it all began to settle in, causing him to involuntarily shake. He muttered, "I seriously thought I was done for."

Mariana gasped, "What! Are you hurt?" She eyed him up and down. "I don't see any blood anywhere."

Shep shook his head, "I'm fine. Just a little in shock. Oh my God, Mariana…Do you think I killed him?"

Mariana stared intently into Shep's eyes and replied, "I don't know Shep, but it's his fault, not yours. He pulled a gun on you for God's sake! You were just defending yourself."

They sat in silence for a moment and then Mariana continued, "I doubt he's with the police, or he would have told you. Who do you think he is?"

"I have no idea. Maybe he's part of whoever is trying to frame you?"

Mariana grabbed Shep's hands, "I'm so sorry, Shep. I know that you must be in shock. Whoever he is, he's a bad person. Thank you for protecting me."

She leaned over and kissed him quickly. Shep looked at Mariana, grabbed the back of her head and pulled her back in for a longer, more sensual kiss, hoping to erase what just happened from his mind. The kiss morphed from gentle sensation to passion to unspoken desperation. Their hands and arms groped around each other, frantically touching, squeezing, and grasping to show that they were present in the moment, and this was not a dream. Caresses gave way to tugs as they pulled and yanked each other's clothes off, never stopping the connection between their lips. Passion overtook the awkwardness of being confined below a bunkbed. They didn't care where they were. They just wanted each other. Clothes off, naked and exposed, Shep's heart raced, but for a much better reason this time. He pushed Mariana down and allowed his body to take over, entering her without hesitation and losing himself in the sensation of their union. It didn't take long for him to be pushed over the edge. The release of emotions was desperately needed after all that had just happened. After a few minutes of relishing in the moment and regulating his heartbeat, Shep rolled to his side and hugged Mariana tightly.

"I'm sorry. I didn't mean to rush that," Shep said. "I just needed to get lost in the moment and make the image of that man falling onto the track go away."

"Don't be sorry! Trust me, I'm just as overwhelmed with all of this."

Shep smiled and took a moment to slowly scan her naked body. He had spent so much time imagining what she looked like without her gym clothes on that he loved being able to finally take in everything. His manic gestures from moments before switched to soft fingers tracing across her breasts and down her stomach, then moving back up to her face. He leaned in and kissed each of her breasts, allowing his tongue to play with each of her erect nipples. Mariana threw back her head and smiled, enjoying the sensation. Feeling more impatient than Shep, she put her hands around his head and pulled him up to her so they could kiss again. With him lying on top of her, she ran her fingers down his back and over his butt feeling his strong muscles contract as he slowly moved back and forth. She slid her hand under him and started caressing him, stroking him slowly to see if his body was up for another round. Clearly it was because she quickly felt him grow stronger under her fingers. She guided him toward her and eased him into her. The moment he pushed inside they both cried out in delight. This time they started with a slow, sensual pace, taking their time to enjoy every sensation, until their pleasure overtook them and their rhythm continued to accelerate. Shep tried to back off and slow down the pace again to make it last even longer, but the day had been exhausting and emotional, and the passion between them now was just too much to control. Hitting the peak, they both escaped into ecstasy. As they lay there exhausted, side by side, Shep was overwhelmed with emotions. He couldn't believe their sex could get even better. He couldn't believe that he just pushed a stranger off the train. He couldn't believe he may have killed the man. He closed his eyes and hugged Mariana even tighter.

"Let's see what tomorrow brings," he thought, not realizing he said it out loud. Mariana responded by wrapping her body around him even tighter. Exhausted, they both immediately fell asleep.

THIRTY-TWO

CONVERGENCE

San Francisco, California

Booker looked over at Pat. "After the fiasco in Prague, we need to get to Europe ourselves so we can be there in person."

Pat nodded. "I agree, but how do we get approval to travel? The local CIA office has already claimed ownership of the investigation now that it has moved to Europe and involves Russia."

Booker said, "They'll just screw it up. We know the situation better than anyone else. We also won't be laser-focused on Russia. We still don't know that they're behind this. It doesn't look good that the Russians allowed her to *escape* from their embassy. However, if they were already working together, why would the Russians need to do background checks? There's something we're still missing."

Pat nodded but couldn't think of anything additive to say.

Booker kept going, "We have enough extra budget in our travel expenses for you and me to fly over there, but we don't have time for approvals. We can deal with that later. Let's go to London and then we'll be closer to the action and able to go wherever Mariana pops up. We still have an ace that no one else has–the AirPods tracker from Tess. I'm not going to let the CIA take over and get all the credit for this case. I'm the one who started it, and I want us to be the one closing it. We both deserve that."

Pat fidgeted in her seat. "Looks like we're going to do this the *Booker Way*," she said. "Making reservations now."

THIRTY-THREE

THE KNOTS

Undisclosed Location

The Spaniard received another ping on his encrypted phone. He went into his office and decoded the
message. It was from the same contact as before.

```
Agent   in   Prague   located   targets.
Followed  them  onto  a  train  headed
to  Amsterdam.  We  were  tracking  his
location on the train when it suddenly
stopped moving. Found agent by side of
tracks. Dead.
```

The Spaniard was irate as he thought about the implications. *How was the agent spotted? Also, why are they*

headed to Amsterdam?

He sent a curt reply.

```
Get a local agent in Amsterdam to meet
the train and continue surveillance.
Absolutely   no   interaction   though!
Report   back   immediately   with   any
updates.
```

He then notified the Dutchman that the targets were en route to Amsterdam.

THIRTY-FOUR

ARRIVAL

Amsterdam, Netherlands

"Aandacht alle passagiers! We zullen binnen één uur aankomen op het centraal station van Amsterdam"

"Attention all passengers! We will be arriving
at Amsterdam Central Station in one hour."

The announcement over the intercom blared into the sleeping compartment jolting Shep and Mariana awake.

"Wow–I can't believe how hard I slept," Mariana commented.

"Me too. Must've needed it. But we only have an

hour, so we better get ready," Shep responded, untangling himself from her and climbing out of the twin bed while trying to avoid hitting his head. They both had fallen asleep on the bottom bunk, intertwined and indifferent to how small the bed was.

"I forgot to tell you last night that I did some research on where to stay. We have a bit of a problem," Mariana informed Shep. "Apparently there is a big 'King's Day' Festival this weekend. When I looked online, every hotel was sold out. I don't know what we're going to do."

"Damn. Well, why don't you hop in the shower and get ready? I'll reach out to my family and see if they have a local contact who can help us find a place."

Mariana grabbed her toiletries and clothes then entered their small, but private, shower stall. By the time she emerged, Shep had a hotel room secured for the next several nights.

When they departed the train, they decided to hop in a taxi. On route Mariana read her notes to Shep regarding what she learned about the area.

Pointing to a map of the city on her phone she said, "Amsterdam has an interesting network of canals that form a semicircular ring around the city center. Narrow streets, bridges, and old houses line all the waterways. Our hotel, The Dylan, in an area called the *9 streets*, and the location Alexei gave is only a few blocks away."

"Why is it named that?" asked Shep.

"It says the area was known for its trade and where all the craftsmen lived. Now it's considered a hip location. The number 9 refers to the nine small streets that connect the city's main canals."

Mariana added, "How on earth did you get a hotel room there when every place is booked out for the festival?"

Shep responded, "Family. And what's up with this King's Day Festival?"

"It's a Dutch national holiday to celebrate King Willem-Alexander's birthday on April 27th. Amsterdam is the center of all the festivities. More than a million people arrive in the city to celebrate. There are music, dancing, open markets, and parades. Supposedly everyone wears orange to show their pride in the royal family. They call it *orange madness*. Here's a picture." Mariana handed Shep her phone showing a massive crowd. It looked like a sea of orange adorning the streets.

"That's a crazy amount of people," Shep said. "Looks like we need to buy some orange shirts for this weekend, so we blend in."

Mariana pondered Shep's comment. "Isn't it ironic that while we're going to spend the weekend stressed out looking for clues, everyone else will be relaxed and celebrating?"

When they stepped out of the taxi to enter the hotel, a car pulled over behind them and the driver snapped their picture on his phone.

THIRTY-FIVE

DE TIJDMAKER

Amsterdam, Netherlands

Shep and Mariana arrived at the hotel before check-in time, so they stored their bags with reception. They ventured over to the hotel's restaurant to get some breakfast, and the hostess seated them at a table for two by the window. Aware that others may overhear their conversation, they spoke quietly as they reflected on the events of their train ride.

"Do you think that man is okay?" Shep asked, clearly concerned that the fall off the train was fatal. He was not really expecting an answer from Mariana, Shep understood her guess was as good as his.

Mariana picked up her menu and replied, "I think it's best if we assume he survived and only look forward.

The one thing I've learned from all of this is that you need to focus on what you can control in the moment and compartmentalize the rest, otherwise it will eat you up inside."

"Agree. It's just hard not knowing," replied Shep as the waitress walked over to take their orders. Feeling overwhelmed with emotions, Shep stood up, told Mariana to place an order for him, and then excused himself to regroup.

When he returned to the table, hot coffee and eggs benedict were waiting for him. The waitress hurried over to remove the silver dome cover keeping his breakfast warm and asked if they needed anything else. Both Mariana and Shep shook their heads and began to eat.

"Shep, I'm sorry I placed you in this situation," Mariana declared. "Do you want us to go back home? I can meet with Booker, explain what we've learned, and I would leave out the part about the train incident. We can..."

Shep cut her off by gesturing with his hand and said, "Stop. I just needed to clear my head. We're going to see this through. What happened on that train validates that someone or some group is trying to stop us because we're on the right track. Whoever's behind this clearly wants us derailed, no pun intended and will do whatever it takes."

Mariana nodded. "Well then, let's try to stay one step ahead of them and figure this out. I looked up the address Alexei gave us again and it appears to be a shop in the middle of the art and antique district called 'Nieuwe

Spiegelstraat'...Wow that's a mouthful to say. The shops don't open for another hour so let's head over there after breakfast. It's only a couple blocks away."

"What do you think we'll find at this antique shop?" Shep asked.

"I have no idea. Maybe the owner or someone who works there is involved in this? Seems like a peculiar place to operate out of, but maybe it's all a front?"

"Hmmm, it could be, I guess. Well, we'll soon find out. I do think we should be extra careful from now on and watch our backs."

They finished breakfast and confirmed with the front desk that their room would be ready by 2:00PM. When they exited the hotel, they noticed that several people were already starting to sport their *orange attire* in preparation for the upcoming King's Day festivities.

The walk to the street lined with antique shops and galleries was quite quick. Numerous tourists meandered through the street, popping in and out of the various shops hoping to find something unique, rare or beautiful. Each establishment offered different collections ranging from 6,000-year-old Egyptian relics to 17th-century Dutch delftware to abstract modern art. Wanting to blend in with the crowd and not be too obvious that they were looking for a specific shop, they chose to enter a random store. It was an art gallery. Mariana and Shep took a few minutes to admire the lithographs, etchings and paintings. As they stood by the window toward the front of the gallery appreciating Picasso's work on display, Shep noticed a man standing on the sidewalk outside watching them.

"Don't look now, but there's a man outside who seems suspicious. Maybe I'm overreacting after what happened on the train, but let's leave and go to another store. I want to see if he follows us," said Shep.

They exited and walked down the street passing a couple more shops then entered one filled with antique Delft and Dutch ceramics. The walls and countertops were lined with blue and white tin-glazed earthenware. Mariana walked over to the wall of plates adjacent to the storefront window and pointed to them as if she was excited to purchase one. While they were feigning interest and Mariana babbled about the intricate design of the windmill on one of the plates, Shep slyly stared out the window to see if the man had followed them. Sure enough, Shep saw him waiting across the street.

"Okay, it's confirmed, we have a tail," Shep told Mariana. "We need to ditch him before we get to the antique shop. I saw a cafe around the corner, let's go in there and see if they have a back door exit. The guy doesn't seem to find it necessary to follow us inside so hopefully he will wait out front while we slip out the back."

Mariana grabbed his hand and they proceeded to walk out of the store. Fortunately, the cafe was crowded, and it had a back door leading to a courtyard garden. Shep and Mariana casually weaved around the people and acted like they were going to stand in line to order a drink, but then quickly bolted down the narrow hallway and exited.

"Great idea!" Mariana exclaimed as they crossed the

courtyard and entered the back door of a clothing store then out the front entrance. They both continued to scan the area to make sure they weren't spotted again.

"Yeah, we got lucky," Shep concurred as he quickly researched on his phone the directions to Nieuwe Spiegelstraat 60. "Looks like the shop we're looking for is at the end of this block and around the corner."

They walked down the busy street. As they turned the corner, they both looked to see if the man was anywhere in sight. He was not. It helped that the street they turned onto was even more crowded with tourists. Mariana and Shep located the address. It was a narrow, brick building with a shop on the ground floor displaying antique clocks in the windows. When they walked in the door, they were instantly greeted by the chime of clocks marking the top of the hour.

"Hopefully this means we're right on time," Mariana joked, trying to make light of the situation. Between their discussion at breakfast and the fact that someone was still tailing them Mariana was on edge and felt even more terrible about burdening Shep with her problems.

The shop was filled with a variety of antiques, but the primary collection on display was grandfather clocks. The room was lined with tall, ornate wooden cases, each with a unique clock face and prominent pendulum. They walked around the shop slowly absorbing their surroundings to see if anything seemed unusual. Just then the salesclerk approached them to offer assistance.

"Do you speak English?" Shep asked.

"Of course," the woman responded with a kind smile

on her face. She was maybe in her mid-fifties and had naturally blonde hair, just beginning to turn gray, pulled back into a tight bun at the back of her head. Her facial features were strong with a well-defined jaw and cheekbones that gave her face a sculpted appearance. She was dressed in a flattering, but conservative, gray tweed dress that almost matched her eyes perfectly.

"May I be of assistance?" she asked them politely.

"We're just looking for now, but thank you," Mariana chimed in.

"Please take your time and let me know if you have any questions. My name is Olivia."

Mariana and Shep continued to browse, commenting on various items and pretending to be interested in purchasing something. They headed toward the back of the shop where a long display case featured antique jewelry and watches. While Mariana was admiring the beautiful rings and necklaces, Shep noticed a door ajar behind the counter. Just then another couple walked in and asked for assistance. Olivia proceeded to help the new customers, highlighting all the features of the ornate clock the couple was interested in. Taking advantage of the fact that she was distracted, Mariana blocked Olivia's view of them while Shep maneuvered around the counter, pretending to be looking at the jewelry from a different angle, and pushed the door open further with his foot. Peeking inside he saw a very large back office lined with dozens of computer servers, and multiple desks covered with stacks of paperwork and computer screens. *That's odd*, he thought to himself. *Why would an antique shop need such a big back office filled with so much computer equipment?*

Mariana motioned to Shep informing him that Olivia and the customers were walking to the back of the shop toward them. He quickly moved back to Mariana's side, pointed to a ring, and said in a loud voice, "Yes, that's a beautiful piece, but let's continue looking. We can always come back this afternoon." Then he grabbed her hand and guided her out of the shop, thanking Olivia as they walked out the door.

"What did you see?" Mariana asked as they walked briskly down the street.

"A back office that looks like it's running more of an operation than a simple antique shop, that's for sure. I didn't see an additional security lock on that door, nor did I detect surveillance cameras in that room, but there is one at the front entrance."

"What do you think we should do?"

"Let's go to that huge park we heard about...what's it called?"

"Vondelpark?"

"Yes," Shep replied while signaling for a taxi. "I think it's best we get out of this area in case that man is still looking for us."

The taxi driver took them to the entrance near the park center. Shep and Mariana proceeded to watch their backs while they located a park bench surrounded by trees and bushes near the open-air theater. A children's dance group was performing on the stage, and there was a large crowd assembled around watching them. Feeling confident that they were alone, Shep and Mariana sat down on the bench and mulled over their options.

After brainstorming several ideas that all had major flaws, Mariana said, "What if we go back this afternoon like you mentioned out loud before we left the shop? We can pretend like I really want that ring in the display case. Clearly Olivia was the only one working in the store. I'll distract her by asking if I could look at the ring in the natural light. I can embellish the importance of seeing how it reflects in the sun. I'm sure she would want to walk out front with me for security reasons. While we're outside you can slip into the back office quickly and check it out further."

"That could work," Shep responded, "you'll just have to keep her out there long enough. Maybe ask to look at several rings so I have enough time. The door will chime, so I'll be notified when both of you come back inside."

An hour later the two of them were walking into the shop. They made their way to the display case full of antique jewelry.

"You've returned," Olivia announced with a big smile on her face.

"Yes," said Mariana. "I'm really interested in some of your rings. I just can't decide which one l like more."

Olivia took the tray that Mariana was pointing to out of the case and said, "Yes, these are lovely. All heirloom jewels. Would you like to try one on?"

"Actually, I really like these three," Mariana responded. "They're all so beautiful it's hard to choose."

Shep chimed in, "You should look at them in the

natural light. Perhaps viewing how they sparkle in the sun will help you make up your mind."

"Oh yes!" Mariana exclaimed. She looked up at Olivia with pleading eyes and asked, "Would that be okay?"

Taken aback, but wanting to make the sale, Olivia nodded. "Of course, let me accompany you." She grabbed the three rings off the tray then placed the tray with the remaining jewels back in the case and locked them up. Olivia turned to escort them outside. As they started to walk toward the front, Shep looked at his phone and announced that he had to take a call.

"You two go ahead," he said, motioning them to proceed. "I need to take this call. I'll be right out."

Shep stayed back while they exited the front of the store. As soon as the two women were deep in conversation and looking down at the rings, Shep slipped behind the counter and into the office. Once again, he was shocked by the number of computer servers lining the back wall. He quickly scanned the room looking for anything else of interest. He noticed several pads of paper with a lawyer's name and firm written across the top. He ripped off the top sheet and pocketed it. Then he saw a stack of envelopes, all addressed to the same bank in England. He quickly snapped a picture with his phone. Just then the front door chimed. Shep raced out the door to the corner of the main room and pretended to be talking on the phone.

"All right, all right. I'll get the paperwork to you as soon as possible. I want to review it one more time," Shep said into the phone, loud enough for the two women to hear him as they walked in. He pretended to hesitate for a minute then continued, "Yes, I understand it's urgent. Let me go so I can finish up here and I'll review it as soon as I get back." Hanging up and pocketing the phone he turned to Mariana and Olivia.

"My apologies, I have a pressing issue at work, and we need to get going." Then he kissed Mariana on the forehead and added, "Did you decide on one, Love?"

Mariana smiled and showed him the ring on her finger. Not even looking at the price, Shep handed Olivia his credit card under his fake name, Mike Roberts. Olivia took the card and tapped it on her portable payment terminal, confirmed approval, then handed it back to Shep.

"Would you like me to box it up?" Olivia asked.

Mariana smiled, "Oh, no thank you, I'll wear it out." Then she hugged her pretend husband in excitement over their purchase. Olivia handed her a small bag containing the receipt and an empty box for Mariana to store the ring in the future.

Shep wrapped his arm around Mariana's shoulder, and they walked out the door. The man, still staking out the general area in case they returned, saw them as they emerged from the shop. He followed Shep and Mariana as they walked back to The Dylan, but this time he was a little more careful about concealing his identity. When Shep and Mariana entered the hotel the man hung back, pulled out his phone and messaged his contact:

```
Subjects   spent   the   day   in   Nieuwe
Spiegelstraat. Entered many shops but
appeared to only place a purchase at
```

one store. An antique store called De
Tijdmaker. Will let you know if they
leave the hotel again.

225

THIRTY-SIX

CHOICES

Amsterdam, Netherlands

Back in the hotel Shep and Mariana approached the reception desk to get the keys to their room and collect their stored bags.

"Good afternoon, Mr. and Mrs. Roberts," the front desk clerk greeted them, as he recognized them from earlier that morning. "Your room is now ready. You were on the upgrade list but unfortunately, we are quite full this extended weekend because of the King's Day Festival. We have you in a lovely double room with a view over our secluded garden. I'm sure that it will meet all your needs. Our porter will show you to your room now and bring your luggage."

As they started to walk to the room, the porter

explained the history of the hotel. "The building dates to the early 1600s and was the very first theater in Amsterdam. Unfortunately, the building caught fire during a performance in 1772 and completely burned down. The main entrance gate is the only remaining original structure. You may have noticed the inscription on the gate. The English translation is *the world is a theater stage; each play their role and get their chance.*"

Mariana reflected on her own situation sarcastically. *I wonder what my role is in this absurd charade, and how this will all play out.*

The porter continued his practiced speech as they proceeded down the hallway. "The site was then used as a Catholic charity until 1998 when it was completely renovated and reopened as this boutique hotel. It's named after the Welsh poet, Dylan Thomas. You probably know his poem, 'Do not go gentle into that good night.'"

Mariana scoffed out loud but was lost in thought. *Yeah, I'm not going quiet into the night. I'm going to fight!*

When they got to their room the porter opened the door and gestured for them to enter. He followed them in with their luggage, pointing out the amenities and highlighting in detail the significance of the design style of the room.

Mariana took a deep breath to calm her frustration. She just wanted the porter to leave so she and Shep could discuss what he saw in the office at the antique shop. Not wanting to be rude, she smiled at the porter as he continued his practiced welcome.

"All our rooms take on a distinct style. The decor and

theme of this room is based on the copper-colored Lox-ura butterfly. As you can see it compliments a wonderful view of the garden. This room features a B&O sound system with Bluetooth connection and an Illy espresso maker. If you need any other libations or nibbles, please ring room service. In the bathroom you will find Aesop bath amenities, a spacious–"

"Thank you so much," Shep interjected, handing the porter some euros. "We have an urgent matter we need to attend to. We'll call the concierge if we have any questions."

The porter took the money with the corners of his lips pulled tight and he left briskly without a backward glance.

"Wow, I never thought he was going to leave," Mariana said as she sat on the bed. "Tell me what you learned."

"Well, I didn't have that much time to search, but I did see several pads of paper with the same letterhead naming a lawyer and his firm," Shep said as he pulled the piece of paper out of his pocket and handed it to Mariana.

Sywert Van den Berg, Managing Partner
Deacon Brown Andrews LLP

"Let's hope that's their lawyer," Mariana said. "What else did you find?"

"Just a stack of envelopes all addressed to the same bank in London," Shep replied as he handed his phone displaying the image of the address to Mariana. "Perhaps they have a personal banker? It says, *Attention: Allen Walker.*"

With a sigh of disappointment that Shep didn't find anything more concrete, Mariana asked, "Well where do we go from here?"

"Let's look up the name of that law firm. Maybe they're located here in Amsterdam. If so, I think we should try to meet with this Sywert Ven den Berg and see if we can get any useful information out of him."

Mariana nodded and pulled out her laptop to research the location of Deacon Brown Andrews LLP, a global environmental law firm. "Looks like they have a local office here in the city center on a street named Herengracht. It's only a ten-minute walk from our hotel."

"Okay, it's too late in the day now. I'm sure they're closed. Let's try tomorrow morning. Hopefully he'll be in."

"Should we set up an appointment?" Mariana asked.

"No. I doubt he'd see us so quickly. Let's just walk in tomorrow and come up with a reason for why we need to see him so urgently."

"Sounds good. And what about this banker in London? Should I try calling him?"

"Let's call him in the morning. I think we're at a standstill for now. It's been a long day anyway and I'm starving. We forgot to eat lunch," Shep replied.

Flopping back on the bed, Mariana felt her stomach rumble as if it heard Shep mention food. Mariana laughed. "Clearly, I'm hungry, too! Can we just order room service? I really don't feel like watching our backs all during dinner at some restaurant."

Shep nodded and searched for the in-room dining

menu. After they selected their meals and placed the order, Shep checked his work emails while Mariana closed her eyes for a few minutes before dinner. When Shep opened his email, he was overwhelmed with the number of people asking him where he was and work staff complaining that things had become a bit chaotic. Frustrated that he hadn't been better at delegating to folks at work, he made a mental note to change this when he got back. After thirty minutes of answering emails, he closed his laptop and tried to compartmentalize the stress of his work so he could continue to focus on supporting Mariana.

A couple hours later, belly full and tired of talking about CellSpot and how to clear her name, Mariana announced that she would love to shower, get ready for bed and watch a movie to take her mind off everything. She grabbed her toiletries and headed to the bathroom.

The shower was a large walk-in with white Italian marble and a built-in bench seat. Mariana found the Aesop bath amenities the porter had raved about as sumptuous as he described and a luxurious treat. The Geranium Leaf Body Cleanser smelled amazing, and she made a mental note to buy some in the future. After she lathered up, Mariana stood under the water with her eyes closed allowing the high pressure to rinse her body and relax her neck and shoulders. The steam of the hot shower created a fog in the confined quarters so she couldn't see that well, but she heard the door opening as Shep stepped in to join her.

"Sorry to interrupt you, but I couldn't resist," he said as he wrapped his arms around her slick body. Mariana leaned back against him, relishing the embrace. Shep grabbed the shampoo bottle, squeezed some in her hair and massaged it into her scalp. Mariana moaned in pleasure, appreciating the special attention he was giving her. His soapy fingers traveled slowly down to her neck and back, then around to her belly and up to her breasts. He caressed her softly and kissed the back of her neck. Mariana spun around and pulled his face down so their lips could join in a deep, sensual kiss. Reaching behind him, Mariana grabbed the soap bar and rubbed it across his broad chest enjoying the feel of the silky suds against his hard body. She proceeded to lather him up all over, taking her time to cleanse every surface area. Overstimulated, Shep grabbed her hands and backed her against the shower wall kissing her until her lips felt swollen. The steam from the hot shower and their passionate connection made her feel dizzy. She sat down on the shower bench to catch her breath then reached out and pulled him toward her.

They didn't end up watching a movie. They both felt spent after the long shower, so they crawled in bed and fell into a deep sleep.

THIRTY-SEVEN

BACK ON THE GRID

Amsterdam, Netherlands

"Cleaning service," a maid called out as she lightly knocked on the door.

Startled and disoriented, Shep hopped out of bed and announced from behind the closed door, "No thank you, we're fine." Then he turned to look at the clock. Shocked that they slept in so late, Shep decided to brush his teeth and get ready for the day. When he emerged from the bathroom, Mariana was standing by the window in her hotel robe, looking down on the garden.

"Good morning," Shep greeted as he approached her to kiss her on the forehead.

Mariana looked up at him and smiled, then headed

into the bathroom to get ready as well. When she walked out Shep was wearing his workout clothes.

"I need a good workout. I saw that they have a fitness center. Do you want to join me?" Shep asked.

"That sounds great. I'd love to go for a run on the treadmill." As Mariana collected her workout clothes she saw Tess's AirPods in her suitcase. Plugging them into the wall socket she asked, "Do you mind if we wait a few minutes? I'd like to charge these a little bit first."

"No problem," Shep replied, undoing her belt, allowing her robe to fall to the floor. "I can think of something we can do in the meantime." Then he pushed her onto the bed to show her what he had in mind.

An hour later they were in the crowded gym. Several other hotel guests appeared to have had the same idea, seeking a good workout before the weekend festivities. The King's Day Festival technically started on Saturday, but many of the businesses planned to shut down early in preparation for the fun celebration. Shep went over to the free weight section while Mariana found an open treadmill. Mariana opened up the AirPod case, connecting it to the treadmill so she could stream music during her run. After a solid hour of burning calories, Shep and Mariana retreated to their room to prepare for their visit to the law firm.

THIRTY-EIGHT

GREEN LIGHT

Mountain View, California

Raj had assembled several members of the product and marketing teams to discuss the status of the upcoming CellSpot press event. He had also invited Tess to sit in for Mariana since she was still out on personal leave. The group sat around the conference table waiting for the meeting to begin.

Raj set his phone down and started the meeting by asking for updates from each team regarding *Project Hover*.

The head of marketing began, "We're a green light at this point. All invites are out, and we've received most RSVPs. We are currently at a 90% acceptance rate. Our teaser campaign to journalists has been well received.

We chose the Computer History Museum off Shoreline Boulevard here in Mountain View for the venue. It's the perfect spot to showcase our new charging station technology with actual cars on stage, and it's also easy access for the media across the Bay Area. We have the CellSpot video completed, and it will run first. Then, various CellSpot executives will provide short presentations discussing how the company is doing and the state of the industry. Raj, you'll then drive on stage in a demo car and drive over to the mocked-up charging station on the other side of the stage. When the music changes, you should get out of the car and make your way to the podium where you will deliver the keynote. Then, after you are done, a video will play for the audience providing more details. This will give you time to assemble outside with three journalists where you will do a live demonstration in an autonomous vehicle and we'll livestream it to the audience. We're actively marketing the live event across social media and relevant blogs and podcasts. We think it'll be a major hit."

Raj sat back in his chair with a broad grin on his face. "It sounds terrific. We'll make a huge splash at a perfect time in the industry when scaling electric vehicle charging is about to accelerate." Raj then scanned the group with a serious look and asked, "What about the technology? Are we ready with the latest hardware and software release? This demo must be flawless."

The head of advanced R&D looked at Raj confidently and replied, "Yes, everything looks good. We're in final testing for the software release, and we already have the final hardware devices assembled on our prototype cars. One of the self-driving vehicles will be for you to take three journalists on a driving demo to one of our new charging stations. We've installed mics and cameras throughout the car to capture the journalist's reactions throughout the demo."

Raj slowly nodded, indicating he liked what he heard, then directed his attention towards Tess. "And how are you feeling about the software release? Are things still on track with Mariana absent?"

Tess cleared her throat, took a deep breath, then said, "Everything is coming in hot. We have a complete build, but we fully expect to find numerous bugs that we'll need to fix. Given we still have a week, I believe we'll be fine and should have time for automated and manual testing to ensure we're ready. The team is really excited about showing the new features to the world."

Raj scanned the room and asked for any other comments or questions. No one spoke up, signaling that they were all aligned, so Raj closed the meeting. "I want to thank all of you and your teams for working so hard to get this done on time. I deeply appreciate that we've managed to keep this confidential and haven't had a leak. This will be a gamechanger for the industry and society in general. You should all be very proud of what we're about to announce. However, if any issues or concerns come up, I want you to immediately raise them to me so I'm aware. We only have a week to pull this together, so all hands on deck and keep the communication flowing."

THIRTY-NINE

THE KNOTS

Amsterdam, Netherlands

The Dutchman was in his office meeting with clients. He noticed that his encrypted phone was lighting up with a new message–extremely rare. He quickly wrapped up the meeting and hustled the clients out of his office, then retrieved the phone and opened the message. It was from the Spaniard.

CellSpot targets are in Amsterdam. Staying at The Dylan Hotel. Somehow they got the address to the antique shop. One of our agents tracked them coming out of the store. They may have found clues that point them to you. Be on the lookout.

The Dutchman processed the information and then typed:

```
Send me a picture of the subjects.
I will check with my wife who runs
the antique shop to see if she has
seen them.
```

FORTY

CONFRONTATION

Amsterdam, Netherlands

When Mariana and Shep walked into the lobby of the Deacon Brown Andrews LLP law firm they noticed that the ultra-modern interior was in stark contrast to the traditional brick exterior. The chic lobby featured sculptural, blue chenille armchairs arranged around petite side tables, ideal for setting down a cup of coffee or laptop. There were several monitors affixed to the walls showing video loops of environmental causes. An oval reception space took up the middle of the lobby with two women behind the counter. One of the women looked up and smiled in greeting while the other continued to work on her computer. On the counter were cameras and screens to sign in and identify yourself. Behind the oval reception desk was a glass encased elevator. Mariana and Shep walked up to the reception counter and introduced themselves as Mike and Lisa Roberts.

Mariana continued, "We are here to see Sywert Van den Berg. We don't have an appointment, but he was referred to us by a close mutual friend. We're only in the area today and hoping to meet with him as it's an urgent matter."

Unconvinced by their story, the receptionist's smile turned flat. "Well, Mr. Van den Berg is quite busy and doesn't have the time for drop in visits. I can write down your names and let him know you stopped by. I'm sure he'll reach out to you if you do have a mutual friend." She continued to stare at them intently as though she was calling their bluff.

While this was happening, the other woman noticed the resemblance of the couple to the picture Mr. Van den Berg had given them a couple hours ago, asking them to alert him if they arrived. She messaged Mr. Van den Berg, and he responded immediately, telling her to keep them there and that he would come down.

The woman then cleared her throat and spoke up. "Actually, Mr. Van den Berg may have an opening. Please wait in the reception area, and we will see if he can come and talk with you."

Shep and Mariana looked at each other and shrugged and then went to sit in the blue chairs. Mariana leaned over to Shep and whispered, "What was that about? All a sudden he's free?"

Shep thought for a minute then responded, "I'm not sure. Hopefully we haven't been spotted."

Mariana was about to whisper something else when the elevator chimed and a man stepped out and started walking towards them. If they had been spotted, it was too late to do anything about it now.

The tall man appeared to be in his fifties, thin with a regal appearance. He had wavy brown hair–slightly disheveled–and strong blue eyes. He walked with a purpose. As he approached, he held out his hand and said in a confident voice, "Hello, my name is Sywert Van den Berg. I understand we have a mutual friend, and you are looking to meet with me?"

Mariana stood up and shook his hand. "Yes, I'm Lisa Roberts and this is my husband, Mike."

Shep stood up as well and shook his hand.

Mariana continued, "We have an urgent matter to discuss with you, but could we do it in private?"

"Of course, follow me," said Sywert. He led them back to the elevator, and they rode up in silence to the top floor.

When they got to his office, Sywert beckoned them to sit in the two chairs across from his desk. Sywert filled two glasses of ice water and placed them in front of Shep and Mariana, then walked around to the other side of the desk and sat down.

"Well, how can I be of service to you?" Sywert asked.

There was an awkward silence until Mariana spoke up, "Thank you for seeing us on such short notice. We don't actually have a mutual friend, but we believe you may have important information you can share with us on a very urgent matter."

Sywert leaned forward, put his hands together on his lap, and scrutinized them. "This must be *very* important for you to fabricate a story to get me to meet with you. I have a full schedule, and I'm trying to be polite. Tell me what you're looking for, and I'll see if I can be of any help. Then I must ask you to leave."

Mariana's face flushed and she looked at Shep. Shep stepped in and said, "We need to track down the perpetrator of a cyberattack that occurred in Prague. We discovered that the IP address that initiated the attack went through Moscow but originated in an antique shop here in Amsterdam. We visited the shop and found a wall of servers in the back. We also found some documents with your name and law firm on them. We were hoping you could tell us who owns the building and why they might be involved in a cyberattack in another country."

Sywert sat back in his chair and clasped his hands behind his head. "Do you mean the antique shop in the Nieuwe Spiegelstraat with all the antique clocks for sale?"

"Yes, that's the one," replied Shep.

Mariana was transfixed staring at Sywert's left wrist. He was wearing a classic watch with the band in the shape of a square knot. She was so focused on the watch that she wasn't listening to any of the conversation. It looked just like Tess's watch. Her mind raced a million miles a minute.

Sywert continued, "Yes, we do represent them, but

I'm not at liberty to tell you the name of the company that owns the building. It's confidential and I really can't provide any information to you without their consent. I know the shop quite well. How did you get into the backroom to see the servers and look through private documents?"

Shep didn't blink. "We were looking for whoever runs the place. The door was open, so we walked in. No one was there so while we waited, we looked around."

Sywert nodded and dismissed the answer not wanting to get into an unnecessary argument.

Mariana tried to refocus and grabbed her water glass. Condensation had dripped down the glass and onto the coaster, so the coaster stuck to the bottom when she tried to take a drink. Clumsily, she grabbed the coaster and looked at it while she was taking a sip. There was a picture of a man standing in a field with a fire behind him. He seemed to be encouraging groups of people to follow him forward. Mariana turned the coaster over and on the bottom was another image of a square knot. *What the heck is going on with these square knots?* Bewildered, she quietly brought the coaster to her lap and then slipped it in her pocket.

As she regained her composure, she focused on the conversation again.

Sywert was saying, "I can tell you that the company would have nothing to do with a cyberattack. They have a global e-commerce business and that is the reason for the servers. We support them with global duties, taxes, and any environmental issues. They are an upstanding company, and you must have been given incorrect information about the address. I'm sorry I cannot be of more help to you."

Mariana deceptively asked, "I noticed your watch. The watch band in particular is quite unique. Does it signify anything?"

Sywert gave a smooth smile. "The band is a square knot which I have been told represents the ongoing struggle and connection between two forces. I got it in England."

Mariana shrugged and stood up, announcing, "Well, I'm sorry we wasted your time. And that we tricked you to get the meeting. We appreciate you giving us as much information as you can. We won't take any more of your time."

Both Shep and Sywert glanced up at Mariana in bewilderment, confused as to why she was ending the meeting so abruptly. The men followed suit and stood up as well then proceeded to shake hands in closing.

"Good luck with your investigation," said Sywert in a clipped voice. "I hope you get to the bottom of it."

With that, one of the receptionists magically appeared behind Mariana and Shep and ushered them back to the elevator and down through the lobby.

As they walked out the front entrance, Shep turned to Mariana. "What was that? Why'd you end the meeting so quickly? I was still trying to get more information out of him."

Mariana raised her hands open wide and gave an expressive shrug. "Because he wasn't going to tell us anything helpful. I could tell he was lying and just feeding us what we wanted to hear. Plus, I found some clues while we were talking, and I think they could be important."

"Really? What did you find?"

Mariana grabbed his arm and guided him down the street. "Hold on. Let's get out of here and find a quiet place to talk."

The Dutchman opened his desk drawer and pulled out his encrypted phone. He typed in a message to the Spaniard.

Targets came to my office just now. They know about the Prague cyberattack test and that the IP address originated from Amsterdam at the antique shop. They don't know much else. I was polite with them but made it clear that the antique shop has nothing to do with Prague. I don't think they know what else to do at this point. Will advise if I hear more.

FORTY-ONE

A NEW LEAD

Mountain View, California

Tess woke up and followed her daily routine. She went to the gym, grabbed coffee on the drive into the office, and once at work went through all the emails and slack messages that had piled up overnight. Around 10:00AM her mind started to wander, and she began to worry about Mariana again. She picked up her phone and opened the *Find My* app. She clicked on Devices and pulled up her AirPods. She sat straight up in her chair as she realized there was an update. It said, *Keizersgracht 384, 1016 GB Amsterdam, Netherlands, 6 hours ago*. She quickly checked the address on her phone. *Mariana was in Amsterdam?* She immediately pulled up Booker's contact and placed a call.

Booker answered after a few rings. "Hello, this is Agent Booker."

"Booker! This is Tess Givens. I have another update on the location of my AirPods. But it doesn't make sense because it says they're out of the country."

"Interesting. Can you text me the exact address and time it was updated?"

"Yes, it looks like they're in Amsterdam. I'm texting you the location now. Please keep me posted and let me know if you find her."

"Will do," Booker promised and then clicked off the phone.

Booker and Pat had already landed in London. They had been trying to figure out how to locate Mariana after Prague, so Tess's call was timely. They were eating in their hotel restaurant when the call came through.

Booker turned to Pat after ending the call. "That was Tess. We have a lead for Mariana's location based on tracking the AirPods. She must've charged them and got close enough to other iPhones. Here's the address." He handed the phone over to Pat who put it in her phone.

Pat looked up. "Okay, it's the address for a boutique hotel in downtown Amsterdam called The Dylan. I could call the front desk and ask to be transferred to Mariana Morales, but I'm sure they're not using their real names. We know they had fake documents they used in Prague and for all we know they are now using a different alias. We don't want to spook them either. I say we get on a plane and stake out the lobby to see if they show up."

Booker responded, "Agreed. Will you look for the

next available flight to Amsterdam? I'm not going to inform our CIA friends until we know more."

After a few minutes of working on her phone Pat looked up. "It looks like most flights are booked, but there's one flight at 7:00AM that's available that gets us in at 9:15AM."

"Book it. Let's hope they're still there."

FORTY-TWO

MAKE IT WORK

Mountain View, California

Raj slammed his fist on the desk. "We're running out of time. The press event is less than a week away!" he barked to the head of advanced R&D.

"I'm sorry. We're moving as fast as we can. As Tess mentioned, there are a lot of technical bugs we need to work through. It's taking longer than we expected to fix them. At this time, I'm nervous we won't be ready to meet the deadline."

"We made commitments! Our funding is dependent on this launch date. I don't care what it takes–just make it work!" Raj said, then he stood up and stormed out of the office.

Everyone on the floor, who clearly overheard

everything, cringed as Raj marched down the hall back toward the executive offices. Heads down, the tech team scrambled to get back to work, praying that Raj didn't yell at them too.

With a deep sigh, the head of advanced R&D stood up. "Well, you heard him. The timeline is not budging, and we need to make this work. Clear your calendars everyone. Looks like we're in for a long stretch of late nights! So, who wants pizza for dinner?"

FORTY-THREE

SQUARE KNOTS

Amsterdam, Netherlands

When Mariana and Shep left the lawyer's office, they crossed a couple bridges over the canals and found a street lined with restaurants. They decided to grab a bite to eat at The Black Dog Gastro Pub. The place had a relaxed feel with various groups playing card games and drinking pints. The walls were covered with paintings of enormous black dogs, some looked friendly yet others a bit menacing. Mariana found a quiet table towards the back of the room while Shep ordered them two draft beers to calm their nerves.

Mariana started the conversation. "I'm sorry you had to take over the questions with the lawyer, but I saw something that really shook me up. He was wearing almost the exact same watch that Tess wears. I've never seen anyone else with a watch band in the shape of a square knot. It's quite unusual."

Shep put his glass down and his jaw dropped open. "I just remembered. The guy that I fought on the train had a tattoo on his forearm that looked just like a square knot. That's weird."

Mariana pulled out the coaster from her pocket and held it up for Shep to see.

"Did it look just like this?" she asked, pointing to the square knot symbol on the back of the coaster.

"Yes, that's it," remarked Shep. "Where did you get that coaster?"

Mariana explained, "The lawyer placed my drink on it. When I grabbed my glass for a sip of water it fell onto my lap. I saw the square knot on the back and wondered if this could be a connection, so I took it when he wasn't looking. Sywert must be part of whatever group is behind this. There's no way this can be a coincidence."

Mariana and Shep were quiet for a moment, thinking through all possibilities. Finally, Shep said, "Do you think this is their covert insignia?"

Mariana's eyes grew large as the implications hit her. "But wouldn't that mean Tess is involved too? Could she seriously have been the one who set me up at CellSpot?" Shaking her head Mariana added, "I don't want to believe it."

Shep responded, "I don't know about Tess. You guys are best friends. I can't imagine she would do something like that. I do think it's likely that this symbol represents some type of secret group. I remember Sywert saying it represented the ongoing struggle and connection between two forces, or something like that. I wonder what two forces he was referring to?"

"I don't know," Mariana responded. "I remember Tess told me that the man who gave her the watch hoped it would remind her to slow down and not let life progress too fast."

Taking a big sip of her beer, Mariana thought through Tess's potential involvement. "Tess knows my laptop password. It's the name of my cat and the year I got him. She could have easily gotten access to my laptop when I wasn't around and loaded a virus. I would never know."

Shep steered her back to the other clues. "Let's worry about Tess later. What's on the other side of the coaster?"

Mariana turned over the coaster and examined it closer this time. "It looks like an image from an old drawing. Let me check something."

She picked up her phone and loaded the Google app. She clicked on Google Image Search and held her camera up to the coaster and clicked. Google's AI thought for a second and then spit out the following information.

This image depicts Ned Ludd, the mythical leader of the Luddites, an early 19th-century English protest movement against industrialization[...]

Shep said, "There's got to be a reason why they picked this image for their coasters. Does it say where the illustration is located?"

Mariana did some more searching and then said, "It says it's on display at the British Museum in London."

"Interesting," Shep said. "If you recall, the name and address we found at the antique shop was for a bank in London. Maybe we should go to London to follow these leads? I don't see much else for us to investigate here. The antique shop was a dead end, and the lawyer isn't going to tell us anything else."

Mariana took another sip of her beer, wishing everything would magically turn to normal. "I don't know. I'm exhausted from all this travel, and I'm not sure we're getting any closer to the truth. Maybe we should just go back to California, work with the FBI, and deal with the consequences."

Shep's face softened. "I understand. This has been a crazy trip. But we don't have enough concrete evidence to go home yet. They'll assume you're guilty. It's easier for us to go through London anyway to get a direct flight home, so how about we fly there tomorrow and try one more time to get some real evidence? Then we'll go home and figure this out."

Mariana shrugged. "Okay, I'm up for that. I think I should call Tess and get some answers from her, too. I'll wait for a time when I know I can reach her. I'm still concerned she may be involved in this, and I know that if I press her hard enough, she'll open up." But Mariana wasn't sure she wanted the answers.

FORTY-FOUR

KING'S DAY

Amsterdam, Netherlands

The next morning, Shep could tell that Mariana was not herself. She seemed indifferent and beaten down.

"We have some time this morning before we need to go to the airport," Shep said as they were getting ready. "How about we grab some food and check out the King's Day Festival."

Mariana looked up. "Actually, that sounds good. But what if that man sees us and starts following us again? We still don't know what he wants or what he might do to us."

"I think he's just watching us and reporting back. Clearly, he didn't want to hurt us, or he would've caught up with us the other day before we ditched him. But we should stay alert just in case."

Looking out the hotel window, Mariana saw a massive crowd of orange and said, "Well maybe it won't be an issue at all. Come look at the crowd of people getting set up for the festival."

Shep walked over to Mariana and looked down at the street. "Great. Let's bring our backpacks so we can buy orange shirts and change our clothes. Also, we can bring the laptop to search for anything new that comes up. I'll throw in our passports just in case we need them."

When they stepped out of the hotel lobby, they were engulfed in a sea of orange. Shep looked around, mesmerized by the crowds, and told Mariana, "Time to go shopping."

Five minutes later, Shep spotted a place selling orange clothing. They bought orange shirts and hats, then blending in with the throng of people, they strolled down the alleys enjoying the camaraderie and excitement of the crowd. They found a cafe and got some pastries and coffee to go, then continued to meander by the canal as the parade floated by on boats. For an hour, they just walked around, not really talking, distracted from their own internal concerns and doing their best to enjoy the festival atmosphere.

Meanwhile, Booker and Pat had landed from London into Schiphol Airport in Amsterdam. The moment they entered the terminal; they were swallowed by a flood of orange-clad people. The sheer volume and shared purpose of the crowd created a palpable hum of excitement throughout the airport.

Booker said to Pat in jest, "Now I know the national color of the Netherlands. Wow, this airport is packed. I hope we can find transportation to The Dylan."

Pat had been typing away on her phone and looked up, "Most public transportation is shut down this weekend going into the city center. But it looks like we can take the train and then walk to the hotel."

Like everything else, the train station was packed. Thirty minutes later, they finally squeezed onto a train. Booker and Pat, in their dark suits, looked conspicuously out of place.

When the train stopped at their destination, they could barely navigate through the immense crowd. Pat opened Google Maps and found a walking route to The Dylan. It was another twenty minutes later when they finally approached the hotel. Not wanting to be too obvious, they decided to hang out on the street adjacent to the front entrance of the hotel and wait to see if Mariana and Shep walked out.

Shep noticed Mariana was finally starting to relax. They were holding hands and engaged in fun conversations talking about the various landmarks they saw and all the crazy people running around. They found themselves walking through the alleys of the Red-Light District and made lots of jokes as they looked through the windows of the sex shops and live sex shows that were advertised along the way. Shep was happy to see Mariana having fun and forgetting about all her struggles, even if just for a short amount of time. As they were walking along, Shep realized it would be almost impossible for them to get to the airport. He went online and figured out they could take a train to the airport. Trains ran eight times an hour to the airport from the city center and it was about a fifteen-minute trip. He calculated how much time they would need and let Mariana know they should probably start making their way back to The Dylan.

A short time later, Mariana and Shep rounded a corner and saw their hotel down the street. They had finally made it back through the throng of festivalgoers. As they crossed the street to enter the hotel, Mariana's smile dropped to a frown. She tensed up but forced herself to keep walking. She pulled on Shep's arm, leaned in, and said with a serious voice, "Don't stop walking and keep looking forward. We have a problem. I just saw two people in dark suits who look like the FBI agents I met in San Francisco. I don't know how Booker and Pat found us, but I swear it's them. What should we do?"

Shep couldn't help himself. He glanced over his shoulder and saw them standing out like dark shadows against the crowd's orange glow. His pace faltered. It was enough motion that Booker glanced over and recognized Mariana.

Booker yelled out, "Mariana! Stop! I just want to talk

with you."

Shep and Mariana stopped in their tracks in the middle of the street and looked at each other. Instinctively, Shep grabbed Mariana's arm and said, "Run!"

Shep led Mariana away from where Booker and Pat stood on the canal bridge. They moved as fast as they could, weaving through the mass of people. They made it to the next canal bridge and turned right toward the city center. Then they backtracked along the canal's other side, moving slowly to blend in, gambling that Booker and Pat would not expect them to retrace their steps. They turned left at the next street which was full of pubs.

Shep and Mariana found a huge group of revelers in orange standing outside. They quickly worked their way into the middle and pretended to mingle with everyone. Meanwhile, Booker and Pat ran around the corner and came to a hard stop. All they could see were people in orange and no sign of Mariana and Shep. They decided to split up and keep looking, but they knew they had probably lost them.

Shep turned to Mariana. "We can't go back to the hotel. We'll have to leave our suitcases and clothes behind. We can buy new stuff in London. We need to get to the train station asap if we have any chance of catching our flight. Let's try to stick with other groups of people in orange along the way so they don't spot us."

Mariana nodded, too stunned to speak. They started to make their way to the train station, scanning along the way, looking for the dark suits in the sea of orange. They made it to the train station, got tickets and finally relaxed on the train when it headed out to the airport.

Mariana looked over at Shep. "How the hell does everyone keep finding us? I don't understand."

Shep just shrugged and stayed quiet, lost in his own thoughts as they traveled to the airport.

FORTY-FIVE

THE KNOTS

Undisclosed Location

The Spaniard had called another meeting to assemble a select few of the KNOTs to discuss next steps on the autonomous vehicle program. They had made the trip to the same location and had gone through the same security procedures. They were now gathered around the table in the conference room.

The Spaniard started speaking. "The time has come. We are now in final preparations for the main event. Our contacts in the media are prepped and will influence the initial news articles in mainstream press as well as social media. Similarly, our investments in related companies and industries should be able to take advantage of the market's upcoming volatility. The next CellSpot software release will go live in a couple days. Our updated virus has been uploaded into their new software."

The American interrupted with a question. "I thought the programmer we were using to access their software is on the run from the FBI. How are we able to still infiltrate their software?"

"Because we have access to two software programmers at the company. Since our initial virus only operated in low probabilities for a short time, CellSpot believed whatever happened was over. Our second contact is still accessing their software builds almost daily through her compromised laptop," said the Spaniard.

"What is different about this latest release?" asked the woman from Brazil.

"It is in essence the same virus, just with different settings on a couple variables," the Spaniard responded. "The first virus was made to only provide incorrect sensor data in a very limited number of occurrences. In addition, the virus was designed to stop operating after a couple weeks. Its purpose was to make sure our approach worked and to start the cycle of fear and concern around autonomous vehicles. The second version of the virus is made to create a crisis and force the industry to acknowledge the risks of having computers and AI control our cars. Incorrect sensor data should occur in almost one hundred percent of driving situations, and the virus will continue to operate until folks figure out how to remove it."

The American asked a follow up question. "If we're trying to scare the world about AI, why aren't we targeting a virus in the AI models?"

The Spaniard gazed around the table with a smug smile. "Because the AI models are very robust and continue to get better. It's difficult to directly impact the models. However, any brain, whether human or artificial, is only as good as the inputs it receives. That is the fundamental weakness of the AI model. It assumes the incoming data is correct. We're attacking the easy part by changing the sensor data. The rest of the action is done by the AI models which are operating correctly but having harmful effects. Just like with human brains, if it perceives a new signal, it will react accordingly. A good example of this is allergies. When someone with allergies breathes in pollen, the brain mistakenly identifies it as a threat, releasing histamines and triggering an overreaction, causing symptoms like sneezing, runny nose, and skin rashes, all unnecessary. Moreover, if the brain or AI model starts to lose confidence in the input signals, then their ability to make decisions comes to a halt, and we create even more chaos."

The Brit spoke up, "When can we expect to see this play out?"

"CellSpot has a big press event in a few days where they're showcasing new charging technology," replied the Spaniard. "As part of this event, they're releasing the new software. At that point forward, it should be in the system and start to affect all kinds of self-driving cars that use CellSpot charging stations."

The Dutchman cleared his throat. "What is the latest on the first CellSpot programmer that has been trying to locate us?"

The Spaniard frowned. "After they met with you in Amsterdam, our agents lost them the next day at the King's Day Festival. We're currently trying to locate them. They are a liability and need to be taken out at this point when they resurface. I will let all of you know when this occurs."

A movement on the ground caught the Spaniard's eye. He glanced down and swiftly squished the spider crawling across the tapestry rug with the sole of his shoe. The spider never had a chance.

FORTY-SIX

MOVING ON

Amsterdam, Netherlands

Booker and Pat searched all over Amsterdam for Mariana and Shep. They showed pictures of them at various restaurants and hotels, but no one recognized them. Booker kept trying to call Tess at home, but it went straight to voicemail. He realized it was still early in California. They eventually headed back to The Dylan to scope it out in case Mariana and Shep came back. A few minutes after 3:00PM, Booker's phone rang. It was Tess.

Booker quickly picked up. "Tess. Thanks for calling back."

"Sorry, I just woke up. I saw that you called several times. Is everything okay? I had my phone on sleep mode."

"Yes, we're in Amsterdam, and we thought we were close to connecting with Mariana, but she isn't at the hotel anymore. Can you check the *Find My* app again and see if there's an update?"

Tess switched to speakerphone, "Hmmm, let me pull it up. Well, this is weird, it shows that she's in the London Heathrow Airport right now!"

Booker shook his head in disgust and motioned to Pat. "Okay, we just keep missing her. Please keep checking. We'll fly to London and see if we can connect there. Keep your phone close by in case I need to call again for an update."

Tess responded, "Will do."

An hour later Tess sent Booker a text to inform him that Mariana's location was tracked at the Haymarket Hotel in London's theater district. Then she hopped in her car to head into the office. En route her phone, connected to Apple CarPlay, announced, "Call from Unknown Caller."

Thinking it might be someone from Booker's office, Tess clicked accept and said hello.

"Tess, I need to speak with you," Mariana announced in a clipped voice.

"Oh my God! Finally! I've been so worried about you. Why didn't you call sooner? What is happening?" asked Tess.

"There's just a lot going on right now, but I need to

ask you something."

"What about? Where are you?" Tess responded with a tentative tone.

Why's she so short with me? Is she mad at me? Should I not have given Booker her location? Tess questioned silently.

"Listen, I don't have a lot of time," said Mariana. "But I want to ask you something...about the watch you always wear. Where did you get it?"

"My watch?" Tess replied, sounding puzzled. "I told you. I got it from my professor who ended up hiring me to intern at his environmental engineering firm. He sent it to me when Addie was in the hospital after being hit by the car. Remember?"

Mariana did remember, but she was trying to catch Tess off guard. She responded, "Oh yeah, that's right. Do you know where he got it by chance?"

"I have no idea. Why are you asking me about my watch? Where are you?"

"I just met someone who has the exact same watch, and I find it pretty odd because it's quite unique," Mariana replied, keeping her tone even.

"Mariana, I don't understand what's going on. First you just leave without telling me anything. Everyone is asking about you at work. And now you're calling me to ask me about a watch someone gave me?"

"I'm sorry. Things got crazy. I had to leave. It looked like I was the one who started a virus at CellSpot, and I felt like the FBI was about to arrest me. I had to get away and try to figure out who was behind setting me up," said

Mariana.

"Well, you should have kept me in the loop. I could have helped you! I was worried you were taken by someone or something even worse." Then, pretending like she didn't know, Tess asked again, "Where are you?"

Mariana, still on guard as to whether Tess was involved, decided to respond vaguely and tell her that she was in Europe then proceeded to give Tess a high-level overview of what she had discovered. Tess remained quiet while she listened and processed this information. *Now it makes sense why Booker was searching for Mariana.*

Tess didn't want to make Mariana mad, so she decided not to disclose that she was tracking her on the *Find My* app. Instead, she told her, "I can try calling the professor and ask him where he got the watch if you think that would help. I don't know if I'll be able to reach him though, he left that firm right after we graduated. He's in charge of some big company now, so it's hard to get in touch with him."

"Would you please try to get it?" Mariana responded. "I don't know if it will help or not, but we keep running into dead ends. I'm so tired and scared."

Tess's ears perked up. "You said *we*. Who are you with?"

"Shep. And before you go all crazy on me, let me just say this was *not* intended and I feel horrible that I got him involved. I can't even begin to tell you what a huge help he has been," said Mariana. Then she quickly added before Tess commented further, "Listen, I really need to get going, but please let me know if you find out where the watch was purchased. You can text me at this number but *don't* give it to anyone! I don't know who I can trust right now."

Feeling guilty that she had already been sharing her location with Booker, Tess promised to keep Mariana's cell number a secret.

"Oh, by the way," Mariana interjected before hanging up. "I saw the strangest thing on the airplane. I was looking through their Leisure and Travel Magazine, and it has a whole spread on visiting Iceland. It was weird because one of the pictures has the exact same backdrop as the picture Keith sent you. At first, I thought it was a coincidence, but then I noticed the clouds even had the same shape. They were unique because they were clustered together in the shape of a dinosaur. When you showed me the picture of Keith, I remember thinking it looked like he had a white dinosaur sitting on top of his head."

"Wow," responded Tess. "That is strange. I haven't connected with him in a while. He told me he's out-of-pocket for some work assignment."

"It was so bizarre I took a picture of it. I'll text it to you. Anyway, gotta go. Give Drake a big hug for me." The line went dead.

Tess disconnected the call on her end. Feeling guilty and stressed that Mariana will figure out that she was the one who had been informing Booker of their location, Tess shot Booker a text after she pulled into the parking lot at CellSpot.

Tess: Please don't tell Mariana how you learned that she's in London! I don't want her to know I got involved

Booker: No worries. Pat and I will be careful. We don't want her to run again anyway. Plan to just follow her and see what she's up to

Tess thought for a minute about whether she should try to contact the professor about the watch before she headed into the office. Before she could search for his number, another text came through. This time it was the picture Mariana promised to send. Tess opened it up then compared it to the picture of Keith that she had saved. Mariana was right. The two backdrops did look the same.

Oh my God, Tess thought to herself. *Did Keith send me a deepfake? Have I been catfished?* She couldn't believe that was the case. She thought about all the texts back and forth where she thought they were connecting on joint passions around environmental issues. *Was it all just a lie?* She quickly texted Keith a simple *hello*.

Tess forgot all about trying to reach her old professor to find out about the watch. She was more concerned that Keith wasn't responding.

FORTY-SEVEN

NIGHT OUT & NIGHTMARE

London, England

When Mariana hung up the phone with Tess, Shep could tell she was struggling again. Mariana seemed melancholy and defeated. He walked over to her and gave her a comforting hug.

"How was your call with Tess?" he asked.

"Well, I didn't learn much, but she confirmed her initial story about the watch. She's going to reach out to the man who gave it to her to see if he recalls where he got it. I don't know...I feel like we have all these pieces to a puzzle but none of them fit together properly. It's just so frustrating and I'm scared we'll never figure this out."

Shep felt her shaking in his arms. He felt awful. He wished he could just make this all go away. He hated to see Mariana upset like this.

"I think we continue to pursue the leads we do have. While you were on the phone with Tess, I looked up the location of the bank, and it's pretty close. But, tomorrow is Sunday, so we need to wait another day. We've been running around so much in different time zones I forgot what day of the week it is. Museums are open though, so we can go check out that illustration."

"Ugh," Mariana replied in frustration, looking even more dejected.

Shep hugged her tighter then pulled back and gently wiped the tears from her cheeks. "Listen, no one knows we're in London. Let's try to set this all aside for a bit. There's nothing we can do right now anyway. It's only 5:00PM. How about we make the most of Saturday night in London?"

With a slight smile, Mariana nodded then went into the bathroom to take a quick shower and get ready. By the time she emerged, dinner was set up in the room and Shep handed her a glass of wine.

"Wow–that was fast," Mariana exclaimed.

"Yes, I asked them to bring us a quick dinner because we only have an hour," Shep said, pulling out the chair for her to sit and lifting the lid off her plate.

"Ummm, this smells delicious. But what are we rushing off to?"

Shep smiled, "I bought us tickets to *The Phantom of the Opera*. I figured you could use a nice distraction for a couple hours to get your mind off everything. It's playing at the theatre right across the street."

"Really? I've always wanted to see that play! But I don't have anything else to wear," she said looking down at her clothing.

"Don't worry. There isn't any specific dress code."

The play ended up being the perfect escape for them. Within moments they found themselves getting lost in the music and storyline. By the time they got back to the hotel they were both wiped out physically and emotionally, so they crawled into bed with *The Music of the Night* playing in their heads.

In the middle of the night, Mariana dreamt that she and Shep were being chased. They kept getting away, but then other people found them. They were finally caught and Shep was beaten up badly. Right as someone was about to shoot him in the head, Mariana woke up and jolted upright in bed. Her heart was racing. Her sudden movement and gasp alarmed Shep.

"Are you okay?" Shep asked groggily. "Bad dream?"

"Yes, it was awful. I don't want to talk about it."

Shep reached out to comfort Mariana. Eventually she stopped shaking and fell back asleep in his arms. The next morning Shep convinced her to head to the gym with him for a hard workout, knowing it would help ease the tension from her bad night's sleep.

The two of them had a grueling workout. After they cleaned up, they headed to breakfast to plan their day. Assuming neither the FBI nor the mysterious *square knot* secret group were able to track them from Amsterdam to London, they decided to walk to the British Museum to take a closer look at the Ned Ludd illustration they saw on the coasters in Amsterdam. While they were waiting for their omelets, Mariana grabbed her phone and started to research more about Ned Ludd.

"This is fascinating," Mariana said after a few moments. "Apparently, Ned Ludd started a worker revolt against the Industrial Revolution in the early 1800s. The first industry that was affected by the Industrial Revolution was textiles. Before the rise of machines and cheap products, clothes were made by hand by families in their homes. They controlled their lifestyle and were able to make a living selling either high-end or low-end clothing. With machines, they were forced to leave their homes and work in dangerous factories. Many people lost their ability to earn a living. Ned Ludd encouraged the workers to maintain their lifestyle by breaking the machines and revolting against the factories. The British government ended the revolt by capturing many of the workers and hanging them."

Shep interjected, "I vaguely remember studying about the Luddites in school during history class. Now it makes more sense."

Mariana laughed. "Yeah, until something is relevant for you, it doesn't really sink in. I barely remember anything I was taught in history class."

"What happened to Ned Ludd and this group?"

"It appears Ned Ludd wasn't even a real person according to several articles I am reading. The revolt was

squashed but the legend of Ned Ludd and what the Luddites were fighting for continues. Any time there is a pe-
riod in our history when modern technology threatens
the current lifestyle for people, there are calls for similar
action and *Luddite* revolts. It says here that labor unions
came out of the Luddite movement to defend workers'
rights and job security."

"Interesting. Do you think this means you were set
up by a bunch of Luddites fighting a new battle with
computers and AI?" asked Shep.

Mariana frowned, "I have no idea. It doesn't sound
very feasible. Maybe it's just another symbol for them
like the square knot. Hold on, let me search the meaning
behind square knots."

Shep dove into his breakfast while Mariana continued to refine her search. Finally, he asked her, "Well,
what did you find out?"

Mariana looked up, "Not much. I guess the square
knot originated in myths around Hercules, the son of
Zeus, as a symbol of strength. It then became a popu-
lar symbol used in marriage ceremonies to represent
the strong lasting bond between two people. It was also
used by sailors to join two lines together without creating a lot of stress on the lines. That doesn't seem very
relevant to this situation. The Boy Scouts use square
knots for award recognition, and I guess it was picked as
the symbol because it relates to first aid and is supposed
to remind boys to help others. Beyond that, I don't see
much else."

"You said the square knot on the watch band was

unique. Didn't you say one side of the knot looked like it was made of braided leather and the other looked like it was made of braided steel?"

"Yes," said Mariana. "I searched for those materials too but didn't see anything."

Shep said in a reassuring voice, "Oh well. I'm sure we'll figure it out. Let's walk to the museum and check out this illustration. I looked it up and it's only a mile walk to the museum."

As the pair walked out of the hotel focused on figuring out which direction to start heading to the British Museum, they didn't see Booker and Pat watching from around the corner.

FORTY-EIGHT

A LITTLE BREAKTHROUGH

London, England

As Shep and Mariana got to the museum, they were shocked to see a long line of people wrapped around the building. They got in line then noticed that everyone had entrance tickets. Mariana tapped on the shoulder of the women in front of them.

"Excuse me," Mariana said. "Do you need a ticket to enter? I thought I read that it was free admission."

"Yes, you do if you are in this line," the woman responded. "You can walk around the building to the other entrance if you do not have a timeslot reserved."

"Thank you," Mariana said, then grabbed Shep's arm and pulled them out of line, directing them around the building.

When they got to the back entrance on Montague Place, Shep looked at the line of people and said, "Hopefully this won't take too long. It seems to be moving at a pretty good pace."

When they finally stepped through the doors 15 minutes later, they were overwhelmed by how massive the building was. Mariana grabbed a map from the kiosk and said, "Let's see if we can figure out where this illustration is."

Still outside, Booker said to Pat, "I don't think we should follow them inside. I have no idea why they are here, but it's extremely crowded. We'll either lose them or bump into them by mistake."

Pat pulled up The British Museum website on Google and determined there were two exits: one on Great Russell Street and one on Montague Place. They agreed to split up. Pat headed to Montague Place to find a secure hiding place to watch the exit from that side. Booker spotted a Starbucks directly across the street from the main entrance on Great Russell Street. He grabbed a seat right by the window with a perfect view of anyone exiting through a narrow gateway since the courtyard was completely enclosed by a large fence.

Mariana and Shep spent at least thirty minutes navigating their way from room to room through the crowd. They kept getting stuck in the wrong galleries and had to backtrack up and down various staircases. Frustrated that they felt lost in the maze of the museum, Mariana saw that there were guards sitting in chairs in each gallery room wearing yellow construction-like vests. She proceeded to ask directions and eventually they found the gallery room where the Ned Ludd illustration was located. They positioned themselves in front of the glass case exhibit where several works of art were displayed highlighting the worker revolts during the Industrial Revolution. They both stood there for a few minutes without saying anything, absorbing the exhibit and the museum commentary.

Finally, Shep said, "The illustration is a lot smaller than I expected, but I can see the detail here versus on the coaster. And another thing–Ned Ludd looks weird. Not much of a folk hero. Why do you think he is pictured in a woman's dress and wearing only one shoe?"

Mariana was thinking the same thing. "Maybe they're showing how poor and beat down he was compared to the factory owners? Maybe those are the clothes that he made at his house without the use of machines? I really don't know. I know this is an old illustration, but it's not really what I expected either."

Shep continued to look at it from various angles. "Spot anything interesting about it?"

"Not yet. I keep looking at all the symbols and the various people in the background waving and cheering Ned on, but nothing stands out."

"Can you read what is written at the very bottom? The print is so small I can't read it."

"Hold on," said Mariana as she leaned in to get a better look at the writing. "I still can't make it out. Let me take a picture and we can then enlarge it on my phone." She snapped a photo then enlarged it to read the script. "There is a date *May 1812* and then there are several people's names. It also says *Sweetings Alley Royal Exchange*. I don't know what that means."

Shep pulled out his phone and started searching.

"Okay, it says it's now called Exchange Alley or Change Alley. It's a narrow alleyway connecting shops and coffeehouses in an old neighborhood in the city of London."

Shep kept reading and summarizing for Mariana, "The Royal Exchange was started in the 1500s and was the center of commerce in London for a very long time. It's also where stocks were traded which then became the inspiration for the London Stock Exchange. It says it burnt down twice. It's now a high-end shopping area and full of restaurants. I guess this Sweetings Alley doesn't exist anymore after the fires. There seems to be disagreement of where it used to be located. I see some consensus that it was located on the East side of the Royal Exchange between Cornhill and Threadneedle Street. There is a lane called the Royal Exchange. Does that help?"

"I'm not sure," said Mariana. "Should we go check it out and see if there is anything interesting that points us in a new direction?"

"Why not? We have the time today and we don't have other clues." Shep then opened the navigation app on his phone and plugged in the name of the alleyway. "Looks like it's about two miles away. Let's head outside and figure out how best to get there."

Shep and Mariana made their way slowly back out to the main exit. As they approached the street, filled with people trying to get into the museum, Booker was still sitting in Starbucks and saw them come out the exit door.

Booker quickly texted Pat, "I've got them. They're coming out of the exit now. I'll follow them and let you know where they go and we can figure out how to meet up."

Pat responded with a thumbs up.

Shep looked at his map on the phone again as they were standing on the sidewalk of Great Russell Street. "It's not that far. Maybe we should walk and get some exercise?"

Mariana responded. "Agreed. Let's walk. I need the fresh air after being cooped up in the museum with so many people."

Shep plugged in the directions for walking, and they headed off through the crowds of people milling around.

Booker contacted Pat. "Looks like they are walking. Why don't you meet up with me and we can follow them, but we need to be careful they don't spot us. I'm sending you my position right now so you can see where I am."

"Holy Cow, where are they going? This is becoming a very long walk," Pat commented to Booker as they carefully trailed far behind Shep and Mariana.

"Who knows," replied Booker. "Gotta love this part of the job. The mystery keeps you motivated."

"Is that what attracted you to the FBI?" asked Pat, sidestepping around a homeless person asleep on the sidewalk. "Why did you join the Bureau?"

"That's a long story," said Booker. "Let's just say I had a colorful upbringing that eventually led me here."

"Well, now I'm intrigued. Spill the beans, Boss."

Booker chuckled. "I was raised in multiple foster care homes. Bouncing from one home to another was not easy, but life became even more difficult when I aged out of the foster care system. I quickly found myself scrambling to get by and even ended up living on the streets like that homeless guy you just stepped over."

Pat looked up at Booker with wide eyes as they

continued to keep up the brisk walking pace.

"It all escalated when I got caught stealing food and clothes for some of my peers," Booker continued. "I was lucky though. The judge who oversaw my case had a big heart. He knew I was one of many who became a victim of the system. I guess he saw some potential in me because instead of closing the door on me, he opened more doors."

"What did he do?"

"He agreed to reduce my sentence to petty theft as long as I met certain conditions."

"Wow. What were those?"

"I had to do six months of community service, enroll in community college, and assist Alameda County Social Services in designing a more effective emerging adult foster program. The judge took me under his wing as a paid intern and advised me through the process."

"That's incredible," said Pat.

"Yeah, he became an amazing mentor in my life and really helped me find a new path. I ended up joining the military and eventually was recruited into the FBI."

"That's quite a background, Booker. Now I understand your motivation."

Around forty-five minutes later, Shep and Mariana arrived at Threadneedle Street and the location of the Royal Exchange. The area had been renovated into an upscale shopping gallery. They looked around and walked through the corridor. Right in front of them was a statue of a man sitting in a chair.

Shep read the placard below the monument. "It's a statue of George Peabody. Do you know who that is?"

Mariana shook her head side to side and pulled up her phone to search. "Looks like he was an American that lived here and became a big philanthropist for developing low-income housing in London. I don't see any connection to the Luddites."

Shep walked around the statue and then responded, "Let's keep looking."

Meanwhile, Booker and Pat arrived at the same location and went into one of the many shops lining the street to watch them through the window.

Booker said, "Let's take pictures of what they're looking at and then we can analyze more closely later and figure out what they're searching for."

Shep and Mariana walked the full length of the short passageway to take it all in. On the other end of the lane, they found what looked like an ornate statue with four Romanesque columns. Mariana used Google image search again on her phone, and it turned out to be an old-fashioned drinking fountain from 1911 called the Cornhill Fountain. They decided it had nothing to do with Ned Ludd either and they started walking back through the lane again. In the middle of the walkway, they found another statue of a man with a long inscription down the front. It was a bust of Paul Reuter, the founder of Reuters news organization. They walked around the bust looking for clues but didn't find anything. Frustrated and tired from walking all the way from The British Museum, they looked around at anything else that could be related. On the side of the Royal Exchange alley and tucked away by itself, they saw another statue of a woman breastfeeding a baby with a toddler at her feet. It appeared to be another fountain with built-in benches around it. Mariana looked it up on her phone. It was called La Maternité.

Mariana turned to Shep and read some of the details. "This fountain was built in 1878. It was originally located where the George Peabody Statue is now that we were just looking at. I guess you can tell it was located there because the water drains are still in the ground surrounding the Peabody Statue."

Shep glanced over toward the Peabody Statue. "Does it say anything else that would connect it with the Ned Ludd illustration?"

Mariana was silent while she continued to read. "Actually, this is pretty interesting. It was commissioned by two medieval guilds from the clothing industry. The Merchant Taylors and the Drapers. Given that the Luddite Revolts were based on textile workers, maybe these guilds were related and somehow this fountain is a clue?"

They both walked around the fountain examining the various viewpoints and engravings. When they circled the entire fountain, they both looked at each other, shook their heads and sighed, realizing they had come to another dead end.

They decided to sit on the bench to give their aching feet a break. Before Mariana sat down, she noticed a small bronze plaque on the back of the bench. She leaned down to read it. She couldn't believe what she was reading.

IN MEMORY OF KING LUDD
THIS BENCH WAS PRESENTED TO THE CITY OF LONDON FOR
THE FREE EXCHANGE OF IDEAS, CORPORATE TAKEOVERS
AND SUBVERSIVE PLOTS

At the bottom of the plaque was a series of strange numbers.

Mariana stared at it in amazement and then nudged Shep to turn around and read it. "Do you think they're referring to Ned Ludd?" exclaimed Mariana pointing at the plaque.

Shep also read it for several seconds then said incredulously, "Holy shit. This is crazy. Maybe this whole thing is real."

Contemplating the meaning behind the inscription, Shep then asked, "What does it mean by subversive plots?"

Mariana started searching on her phone again and responded, "I can't find anything on this specific plaque wording, but it does say that there's a whole underground movement in London where people buy plaques for park benches to write creative phrases and dedications. I guess there are some famous ones. I don't know if this is part of that or not."

Mariana looked up at Shep and said, "Let me see on-line if King Ludd is related to Ned Ludd." Sick of typing, she hit the voice search button on her phone and asked, "Who is King Ludd?" She read the response and then looked up disappointingly at Shep. "Darn, it says King Ludd was a pre-Roman British King that supposedly founded London. It's unclear if he was a real person or just folklore. There's a 14th century statue of him in the St Dunstan-in-the-West Church on Fleet Street. Here, take a look."

Mariana handed her phone to Shep. Shep started reading the background but suddenly stopped. He looked up at Mariana with a huge grin and handed the phone back to her. "Mariana, it gave you the answer for King Lud, with one *d,* not two." He quickly typed, *Who is King Ludd?* on his phone and read the response.

"Mariana, King Ludd is the same person as Ned Ludd. That's the name people called him. We were right. This plaque is referring to Ned Ludd."

Mariana laughed at the mix-up and then hugged Shep in excitement while he continued to examine the plaque. "What do you think those numbers and symbols stand for at the bottom?"

Mariana leaned in closer, "I'm not sure. They're hard to read. It looks like a random series of numbers. Let me take a picture."

Mariana took the picture and zoomed in. She read the series of numbers to Shep.

52.9515563, -1.1479456

"Any idea what these could stand for?"

Shep thought for a second, "Not really. They don't look like an address or a date."

They were both silent for a minute trying to brainstorm on what the numbers could represent. Mariana stated, "One number has nine digits and the other has eight. Maybe they are phone numbers?"

"I don't think so," Shep responded. "I don't understand how the negative symbol would work. What about a bank account? We're going to that bank tomorrow. Maybe it refers to a bank account there?"

"We should keep that in mind when we visit the bank, but it doesn't look like account numbers to me," said Mariana. "They both have seven decimal places. I wonder what numbers require seven decimal places."

"Interesting," Shep said. "Let me type it into my phone and see what comes up." Then he added, "No way! I think they're GPS coordinates. I haven't seen coordinates written like this before. The first number relates to latitude whether it's North or South of the equator. In this case, it's positive so it's North of the equator. The second number relates to longitude, whether it's East or West of the Prime Meridian. In this case, it would be West because it is a negative number."

Mariana interjected, "As I recall, the Prime Meridian runs right through London, so negative one would be pretty close, right?"

Shep typed more information and then said, "The coordinates match to a place in Nottingham, England."

Mariana quickly pulled up her phone. "Hold on. I

remember something when I was looking up the history around Ned Ludd." She typed for a while and then exclaimed, "Yes, Ned Ludd was from Nottingham. That's where the Luddite revolts took place. Maybe these coordinates tell us where to go in Nottingham. Keep zooming in on the map to get a closer look."

Shep zoomed in and announced, "It looks like the coordinates point to the Old Market Square and a specific building, but I can't see the name of it."

"This is great. We may have finally made a breakthrough. Let's head back to the hotel and figure out how we can go there tomorrow after we meet with the banker."

Shep and Mariana hailed a taxi given they were tired from all the walking.

Meanwhile, Booker turned to Pat, "Damn, I wish we could hear what they're saying. They look animated and excited. I wonder what they found. You stay here and take pictures of all the places and things they were examining. I'll jump in a taxi and follow them."

Once again, Shep and Mariana had renewed energy based on this new lead. Back at the hotel, they bought swimsuits and goggles at the gift shop then headed down to the hotel pool to swim laps. Shep had a pool workout ready to go and they spent the next hour doing various combinations of strokes and intervals. When they passed each other in the lane, it was hard for Shep to not focus on Mariana's long, toned legs kicking away in the water. After they finished the workout, they put on hotel robes over their swimsuits and went back up to the room.

Shep couldn't hold back when they entered the room and the door closed behind them. He reached forward and grabbed Mariana, pulling her into him. While kissing the back of her neck, Shep untied her robe and let it fall to her feet. He turned her around slowly and gently removed her bikini top and then slid her bottoms down to her ankles letting her kick them off her feet. Mariana then reciprocated by pulling off his robe and sliding down his swimsuit, letting her hands come back up his legs and settle in his mid-section. Shep took a few moments to enjoy the arousal then guided Mariana over to the bed and they fell on the mattress together. After their previous times of unbridled, passionate sex, this time they took it slow, and both enjoyed the intimacy of caressing each other and exploring a more thoughtful and prolonged pace. Looking into each other's eyes for positive feedback, they moved as one and felt a sense of connectedness that only happened by being selfless and vulnerable.

The rest of the night was equally peaceful for Shep and Mariana. They showered, ate a light dinner, and planned the next day. As they fell asleep, they had no idea Booker and Pat were continuing to take turns staking out the hotel and analyzing the places they had visited today.

FORTY-NINE

BANKING ON THE BANK

London, England

The bank didn't open until 10:00AM so Shep and Mariana woke up with enough time to eat breakfast in the hotel restaurant before they had to head out. While they were feasting on the expansive breakfast buffet, Mariana leaned forward with a huge smile on her face. Her eyes lit up in excitement.

"I feel good about this Shep. I think we finally have a solid lead."

"I hope so," Shep replied, keeping his emotions a bit more reserved. "We definitely need to figure this out quickly."

Mariana sighed and her shoulders slumped. She understood they could be caught any moment, but this was the first time she felt a glimmer of hope.

Shep looked up from eating and said, "By the way, I was thinking about when we introduce ourselves at the bank. Let's use fake names so we don't burn our names associated with our passports."

Mariana said, "Good point. Let's agree on the names now." She paused for a moment and then said, "How about Jack and Kate Johnson? Those names seem pretty generic."

Shep responded, "Perfect. I think we should get ready to go."

The two of them finished eating then grabbed the hotel's loaner umbrellas and headed out to the bank. It was a typical grey, rainy day in London, but Shep and Mariana opted to walk the short distance to the bank. Booker and Pat, following not that far behind them, had their own umbrellas shielding them from the rain as well as from Shep and Mariana's view.

Shep and Mariana entered the bank soon after the doors opened for the day. They walked up to the nearest teller to inquire if there was a person by the name of Allen Walker working at the bank today. The teller nodded and asked if they had an appointment with him.

"No," responded Mariana, then she fabricated a story. "A mutual friend of ours recommended we contact Mr. Walker the next time we were in town. We recently came into a large sum of money, and we were hoping he could help us out."

The teller's smile widened. "Let me see if Mr. Walker is available. And whom shall I say is interested in meeting with him?"

"Jack and Kate Johnson," Mariana said quickly before Shep potentially blurted out their other fake names.

Mariana glanced over at Shep with a mischievous smile.

"One moment please," the teller responded then she motioned for them to sit in the reception chairs.

When they went to sit down Mariana noticed the teller tap on the door of the large corner office to announce their presence to the man sitting behind a big mahogany desk. Mr. Walker looked up from his paperwork, took off his glasses and glanced at the reception area to view his unexpected guests. Mariana couldn't make out what he said to the teller, but she nodded and quickly left the office as he picked up the phone and closed his office door. The teller walked over to Shep and Mariana and informed them that Mr. Walker would be with them shortly.

"We have a situation," Mr. Walker, the Brit, spoke on the phone to the Spaniard. "It looks like the two Americans made their way to London. They are here at the bank sitting in the reception area and requested to meet with me. How would you like me to proceed?"

"Interesting," the Spaniard replied slowly. He hesitated for a moment then said, "Buy a little time, but keep them inside the bank. I will call some of our agents to head over and take care of them once and for all."

"What should I say if they ask about the Amsterdam office inside the antique shop? They must know something if they made the connection to my bank."

"Just make something up," replied the Spaniard, sounding angry and impatient. "At the end of the day it won't make a difference." Then he slammed down the phone, cutting the Brit off to do his job.

Several minutes later the corner office door opened, and a bald, portly man walked over to Shep and Mariana.

"Good morning, I am Allen Walker," he announced, holding his hand out to Shep in greeting. Mariana quickly stood up and shook his hand as well. "Nice to meet you Mr. and Mrs. Johnson. I heard you need my assistance. Would you like to come into my office so we can speak in private?"

Shep and Mariana both nodded and followed him into his office.

"What can I do for the two of you?" Mr. Walker asked them after they sat down.

Shep launched right in. "Well, we are hoping you could help us track down the perpetrator of a cyberattack that occurred in Prague. We discovered that the IP address that initiated the attack went through Moscow but originated in an antique store in Amsterdam. We visited the shop and found a wall of servers in the back. We also found some envelopes all addressed to your attention at this bank. We're hoping you can tell us who owns this shop and why they might be involved in a cyberattack in another country."

Like the response Shep and Mariana received from the lawyer in Amsterdam, Mr. Walker told them that he was not at liberty to divulge that information. "We keep all our clients confidential. I am sorry. I cannot help you." But wanting to engage with them longer to allow time for the KNOTs agents to arrive, he continued to ask them why they were so interested in this cyberattack.

Mariana let out a breath of frustration. "I work for a company that appears to be the recipient of similar malicious malware. Unfortunately, this was somehow infiltrated through my computer, and I am being targeted as the villain, but I was set up. I have no idea why I'm being targeted, and I'm trying to clear my name."

Mr. Walker stared at her with concern in his eyes. He sat back in his office chair, propped one arm over the other and placed his index finger over his mouth in thought, exposing his wristwatch–with a square knot band. Hoping to buy more time he said, "Hold on a minute. Let me check on something that might help you out." Mr. Walker proceeded to get up and leave the office.

"Oh my God," whispered Mariana to Shep. "Did you see his watch? It's the exact same watch both Tess and the lawyer wear!"

"Yes," Shep whispered back. "We're definitely onto something. This must be a secret group–I just wonder what their mission is. I highly doubt he will give us any useful information. He's just going to try to throw us off track. Let's see what he comes back with then let's get out of here. We need to come up with a new strategy."

They decided to quit talking about it in case they were being recorded or someone was listening. Time ticked by and they wondered what was taking so long. Eventually Mr. Walker returned and handed them a piece of paper with a name and number written on it. "This is an investigator I have used in the past. Maybe she can be of assistance. My apologies, but that's all I can do for you."

Shep grabbed the paper and they both stood up. "Thank you so much for your time," Shep said. "We're sorry to have bothered you."

"Best of luck to you both," Mr. Walker responded as they walked out of his office.

Once they stepped outside, they didn't get far. Within seconds they were flanked by two men in trench coats with guns hidden in their coats pointing at them. One of them demanded, "Come with us and do not make a scene or we will kill you." The men escorted Shep and Mariana to a black van parked in front of the bank, opened the door and shoved them inside. The van drove off quickly.

Meanwhile, Booker and Pat, hiding across the street, witnessed the two of them being taken away. Booker quickly hailed a taxi and told the driver to follow the black van. The van navigated several blocks to Westminster Bridge. They crossed the bridge to Borough Road and continued to Crosby Row until they entered Southwark. Multiple times during the drive Booker instructed the taxi driver to keep his distance so the people in the van did not catch on that they were being followed. Eventually the van pulled into what appeared to be an abandoned building. The taxi pulled over around the corner and Booker handed him a wad of money. Booker told the taxi driver to wait a couple blocks down and that he would give him more money if he waited. Then he and Pat hurried out to investigate.

As Booker and Pat scrambled over to get a closer look, they saw four people get out of the van and then pull out Shep and Mariana. Both had hoods over their heads, and their hands were tied behind their backs. Booker and Pat drew their guns, prepared to act. They conferred for a few seconds and then split up. Pat crossed to the other side of the street so they could have two angles to approach the situation. The four men were starting to push Shep and Mariana over to the warehouse door. Booker didn't want them to get inside so as soon as they got to around fifty feet from the van, he yelled out, "Freeze! This is the FBI. We have you surrounded. Drop your guns and let them go."

Pat quickly dropped behind a car so she wouldn't be seen and prepared to aim her gun.

All four captors stopped in their tracks. One of them turned, and said to the others, "Spread out and watch your backs." Then he responded to Booker, "Fuck you! You have no jurisdiction here. Leave now or we'll start firing."

Booker kept moving forward, ducked behind a car about thirty feet away, and aimed his gun at the man talking. "Last chance. Let them go and walk away."

The man turned in Booker's direction, then aimed his gun at him and fired. The other men started firing at Booker also and kept moving towards the warehouse door, pulling Shep and Mariana.

While Booker got lower to the ground shielding himself from the bullets, Pat moved to the right, behind a closer car, then stood up and fired at one of the men, hitting him in the stomach. He dropped. The other three panicked as they realized there was a second shooter. They all started firing in the direction where the shot came from. At the same time, Booker stood up, took time to aim, and fired a shot at one of the men, hitting him in the chest. The other two men looked at each other and let go of Shep and Mariana. They bolted to the warehouse door, leaving their colleagues lying on the ground moaning.

Booker ran up to Shep and Mariana while Pat stayed behind the car, prepared to shoot anyone who came out of the warehouse. Booker kicked the guns away from the two men lying on the ground. He then went over to Shep and Mariana, pulled off their hoods, and with a knife, cut the rope free from their hands.

With a sense of urgency, he said, "Come with us. We'll explain later. We need to get you out of here now!"

With no delay, Shep and Mariana followed Booker away from the warehouse. Pat trailed after, protecting them from behind.

Fortunately, the taxi driver was still waiting. He said, "What the hell was that? Were those gun shots I heard?"

Flashing his badge, Booker responded, "It's okay. We're the FBI. Take us to the Haymarket Hotel immediately."

The taxi driver gave them a quick look, then hit the accelerator, and the taxi took off.

No one talked during the drive back. When they got to the hotel, Booker handed the driver enough cash to keep him happy. As they hurried to the hotel entrance,

Booker said, "We know you're staying here. Let's go to your room and talk."

Riding up the elevator, Pat turned to Booker and quietly said, "What should we do about the two people we shot?"

Booker considered the question, then said, "I'll make a call to my CIA contacts and let them know what happened. We can't do anything more, and our authority here is questionable."

They got to their room, and Shep unlocked the door. They all walked in and found places to sit.

Booker spoke up. "Are you guys okay? That was quite the abduction."

Shep responded, "Yes, we're fine. They didn't hurt us. Just tied us up. How did you know this was happening?"

Booker said, "We found out you were in London, and we've been following you for the past day. When we saw them take you in the van, we knew we had to intervene. Do you know who they were?"

Mariana jumped in, "We think we do, but it's a long story. I know you want to arrest me, but you need to believe I'm innocent, and we're close to proving it."

Booker said thoughtfully, "I'm beginning to agree with you, especially after what we just witnessed. Why don't you tell us the whole story and then we can figure out how to move forward?"

Mariana proceeded to tell Booker and Pat the entire story from leaving Santa Cruz and going to Las Vegas, to their journeys through Europe and uncovering the *square knot* mysterious group. She wrapped up with what they learned at the Royal Exchange and their plan to go to Nottingham tomorrow to investigate.

Pat and Booker asked a ton of questions that both Shep and Mariana tried to answer. Eventually, the questions subsided, and Booker said, "Okay. Your story makes sense in a weird way. We don't want to lose you again, and we probably need to protect you now that there seems to be people out to hurt you. We can go with you to Nottingham and check out this lead. If it turns out to be nothing though, you need to come back with us to California, and we can continue the investigation over there."

Shep and Mariana agreed.

Booker continued, "I doubt the people that tried to take you today know where you're staying or they would have grabbed you here. Just to be safe though, let's have you check out now and we can get on a train to Nottingham this afternoon and find a new hotel there."

Nervous Mariana and Shep would try to make a run for it again, Booker turned to Pat, "I can stay here with them as they get ready. Why don't you go back to our hotel and check both of us out and grab our stuff. Meet us at the train station. I'll investigate buying tickets."

Mariana took a deep breath and finally registered the enormity of what just transpired. They could have easily been killed if it weren't for Booker and Pat. As Pat was getting ready to leave Mariana blurted out, "Thank you both for rescuing us. I thought I could figure this out on my own and just wanted to clear my name. But I'm glad you're here."

Shep leaned over and squeezed her hand to show he agreed.

"Just doing our job," Pat replied. "We're here to get to the truth, and you should know that you can trust us to find out who is behind this."

FIFTY

THEY GOT AWAY

London, England

The lead agent for the KNOTs was stunned. Two of his men were badly injured while he and his partner barely escaped. *How did the FBI find us?* Angry, frustrated, but most of all, nervous and embarrassed to have to admit that they failed, he tried to summon the courage to inform the Spaniard. Finally, he knew too much time had gone by already, so he carefully crafted the message and sent it off.

```
Regret to inform you that the subjects
got away. Two FBI agents must have
followed our van leaving the bank and
ambushed us at the scene to protect
```

```
the subjects. Two of our men are down.
Taking them to a safe medical facility.
Current location of subjects unknown.
```

The Spaniard couldn't believe this disappointing news. This should have been an easy abduction. The two suspects were naive amateurs, and his professionals should have had no problem with this assignment. *When and how did the FBI track their location and start following them?* He started typing a response.

```
This is unacceptable. Continue to scan
the area. Contact taxi dispatch to
identify if they can track the driver.
Monitor all public transportation. It
is critical we locate them right away.
```

Once sent, he threw the phone across the room.

FIFTY-ONE

ANOTHER TRAIN

The Midlands, England

Shep, Mariana and Booker made it to the train station and bought four first class tickets from London's Pancras International Station to Nottingham on the East Midlands Railway. The travel time was only one hour and thirty minutes. Pat arrived at the station with their luggage and met up with the three of them at the platform for the departing train. They had a reserved table with four seats so they could have more privacy to discuss the next steps on the way to Nottingham. Shep pulled out his phone to research hotels in Nottingham near where the GPS coordinates corresponded. He then made reservations at the Lace Market Hotel in the city center. Although the four of them believed they hadn't been followed onto the train, they kept glancing around at the other passengers, looking for anyone suspicious.

After the train started moving, Booker finally said, "Okay, what do we hope to find in Nottingham again?"

Mariana filled them in again on the plaque they'd found on the park bench. "We believe this could be this group's headquarters, and we're hoping we can uncover evidence that they were behind the cyberattack."

Pat interjected, "Will you give me those GPS coordinates again?"

Mariana read off the coordinates and Pat plugged them into her phone to see if she could discern an actual image of the location.

"It looks like it is a watch shop," Pat announced.

Shep immediately turned to Mariana and her wide eyes revealed that she noticed the same connection.

"This must be the watch store the lawyer in Amsterdam mentioned," said Shep. "I bet this is where they make the square knot watches."

Booker pulled his notebook and pen out of his pocket and jotted a few notes down. Then he picked up his phone and started dialing. "I'm going to ask my contacts to see if they can find out the owner of the building."

While Booker was communicating with the FBI office, Pat, Shep and Mariana devised a plan for checking out the watch shop. She recommended that she and Booker stay back while the two of them go into the store to try to learn more.

"I have tracking devices I can plant on you," said Pat. "This way we can track your location and make sure you don't get in trouble again. I will also position a wire on you, Mariana, so Booker and I can hear your conversation."

Booker got off the phone and relayed the information. "Not much luck on identifying the owner. Initial search looks like a shell organization. They're going to dig deeper, but they doubt it will give us much insight."

Pat brought Booker up to speed on their plan. They worked on the details some more and agreed on a phrase Mariana should use to warn Booker and Pat if they felt they were in trouble and needed help. They decided on the phrase; *do you have a bathroom I can use?*

The train was almost to Nottingham. Lost in thought, Mariana stared out the window at the countryside rushing by. Shep reached over and held her hand to silently show his support.

"It feels like such a long time ago that I was looking out the window on our drive to Vegas," Mariana said. "That drive felt so slow. Now everything is moving so fast."

Shep squeezed her hand. "I just hope time is on our side."

FIFTY-TWO

END OF THE ROAD

Nottingham, England

The next morning Mariana, Shep, Pat and Booker met for breakfast at the hotel pub called Cock & Hoop. They sat in the corner of the pub in four velvet armchairs with a short circular table in the middle where they placed their food. After they reviewed the plan again and got coaching from Pat and Booker on potential questions to ask, the four of them went back up to the hotel room to outfit Mariana and Shep with the tracking devices and wire. Pat tested the devices and confirmed they were ready to go.

The shop was about a quarter mile away from the hotel. As Shep and Mariana walked towards the storefront, they noticed in one of the windows by the door a small sign with the symbol of the square knot. They had come to the right place.

Mariana grabbed the door handle and pulled it up. A small bell attached to the door announced their presence. As they walked in, they both looked around. There were wooden worktables interspersed around the room with wooden chairs and a smorgasbord of equipment on each table, presumably for assembling or repairing watches. All along the walls were paintings of people making watches or detailed views of the inside machinery of watches. Along the back of the room were several modern cabinets full of watches for sale. They saw several other rooms connected to the main showroom that also looked full of watch equipment and other watches for sale. There were a couple people working at the wooden tables and a clerk behind a desk in the corner typing on a computer. The clerk looked up, smiled and walked over.

"Welcome to our shop," said the clerk in a strong British accent. "How may I be of service?"

Mariana smiled back and said, "Hello. We are looking for a very specific watch and were told you made it here."

The clerk was eager to engage in the conversation and started to explain about the store, "Yes, we have many custom watches made here that are all hand assembled, preserving the craftsmanship of watchmaking. We've been in business for over a hundred years. As you can see, we like to emphasize the skill and knowledge of watchmaking. My name is Edward, and I'm what's known as a Horologist. That is a fancy name for a watch-maker, but it requires a lot of education beyond watches and watch repair. We are artisans and focus on the study of time and the art of measuring it. It is both artistic and technical. Along with selling watches, the top floors of this building are also an educational institution teaching students in the field of Horology. Will you describe the watch design so I can see if we make it here?"

Mariana took a deep breath and then said, "It has a beautiful ivory colored dial with black hands. However, the part that is most distinctive is the watch band. It resembles a square knot. One side of the band appears to be made of a black braided leather, and the other side of the band is made of braided silver. Does this ring a bell at all?"

Edward's big smile evaporated to a neutral expression. He looked at them quizzically for a moment and then regained his composure. "Hmmm, interesting. Not off the top of my head. Let me check our catalog on my computer and see if I can find something similar. Why don't you peruse around the shop while I do some searching?"

Edward gave a short bow to both, walked back to his desk and started typing on the computer.

Shep and Mariana couldn't tell if their watch description had rattled the clerk or if he genuinely wasn't aware of the design. They retreated to the far end of the store and pretended to look at the various new watches for sale in the cabinet cases.

Meanwhile, Edward messaged one of the owners

who worked in a different section of the building about his two customers and their inquiry. The owner messaged back that he would check the camera monitors. A couple minutes later, the owner responded and told Edward to keep the customers in the store, and he would personally come in and talk to them.

The owner, also known as the Spaniard, opened his encrypted laptop and sent a message to a few key partners.

```
Subjects have arrived at our location
in Nottingham. No idea how they found
it. I will deal with them now that they
are here. The PR event at CellSpot is
still scheduled for later today. All
signs are green for a positive outcome.
Will keep everyone informed.
```

With that, the Spaniard told a few of the guards on duty what to do, then made his way to the showroom.

Meanwhile Edward walked over to Mariana and Shep and said, "I'm sorry that took so long. I was searching for your specific watch design. So far, I haven't been able to find anything that resembles your description from our store and several others I checked. I mentioned it to one of our owners, who happens to be here today. He would like to personally meet you and discuss the watch that you are looking for. He said he would be around shortly if you don't mind waiting a few more minutes?"

Shep and Mariana played along with the charade. "That would be great," Shep replied.

Edward nodded, then disappeared into another side room, seemingly busy with another task.

Shortly after, a distinctive man walked into the showroom from another entrance. He made eye contact with Mariana and Shep, smiled broadly, and started to make his way across the room towards them. He appeared to be in his late fifties, about six feet tall, with dark curly hair, a short beard, and a mustache. Stylishly dressed in a fitted suit, he seemed strong and fit, but not overly bulky. He carried himself with confidence and emanated a good-natured personality.

Shep and Mariana waited for him to walk up and then said hello and shook hands.

"Hello. My name is Carlos," said the Spaniard.

Shep and Mariana introduced themselves as Mike and Lisa Roberts.

Carlos smiled and said, "Yes, yes of course. I am glad you have come to visit us. I am eager to talk with you about many things including the watch you described. Will you accompany me to my office?"

Shep and Mariana hesitated and exchanged looks. Deciding they had nothing to fear with the wire and tracking devices attached to them, Shep said, "Yes. That would be fine. We too have many questions for you."

Carlos nodded courteously and said, "Please follow me. It's a little bit of a walk, but we can talk in private there."

The three of them walked through several smaller rooms and then opened a door that went down a set of stairs. As they descended way more stairs than a typical staircase, the air got musty. The stairs were formed from raw stone and became more rugged and slippery the further they went. The walls were also made of stone, and as Mariana touched the wall to maintain her balance, she noticed that the surface was rough and gritty. When she removed her hand, she felt the grains sticking to her fingers. There were lights on the walls along the way, but they flickered and only provided a small amount of light. Finally, they arrived at a landing and walked to a metal door. Shep and Mariana glanced at each other again questioning their decision, as Carlos used his fingerprint and an eye scanner to open the door. The door slid open, and they entered another hallway. They continued down the hall and noticed several tunnels going off in different directions. Carlos guided them along one such tunnel for a little while and into an office of sorts with a desk. It also had several couches. Carlos gestured for them to sit on the couches. As he sat down across from them, two large men built like professional body builders entered the room from behind Shep and Mariana and stood at attention.

Carlos began, "Okay, we are here. Please don't mind my bodyguards. They are only here as a precaution. Now, let's be done with the pretenses. I know who you really are, Mariana, and this must be Shep. I congratulate you on your journey to find us. You have been quite determined and persistent. I'm impressed. I'm sure you have lots of questions. I'm here to answer them."

Realizing they were out of their league, Mariana asked, "Do you have a bathroom I can use before we start the discussion?"

Carlos smiled again and said, "Of course. One of my men will escort you to the bathroom. Shep and I will stay here and wait for you."

Mariana got up, glanced at Shep, and then followed one of the guards to the bathroom hoping that Booker and Pat had received the distress message.

Booker and Pat had set up their surveillance post across the street in a cafe. They were pretending to be in deep conversation at a table to disguise the fact they were listening to their earpieces providing them audio from inside the watch shop. They heard the whole exchange with Edward and the introductions with Carlos including the invitation to talk in his private office. But then, as Shep and Mariana appeared to be walking to Carlos' office, the connection for the wire and the tracking devices suddenly went dead.

Booker leaned over to Pat, "What do you think happened? There must be some kind of interference. I didn't hear any struggle or either of them calling out for help."

Pat nodded in agreement. "It's almost as if they went into a faraday cage and lost the signal. What do you want to do?"

"Let's give them some time. We know they're in the shop. If they leave the building and try to take them somewhere else, the trackers should start working again and we'll know. If we don't hear anything in a while, we'll need to go in after them, but let's see if the signals come back."

Mariana came back from her artificial need to go to the bathroom with confidence that the FBI were on their way. She knew she needed to buy time because it would take Booker and Pat a while to find them. She walked in the room and saw Shep holding one of the square knot watches in his hand, looking it over. It was the perfect opportunity for her to get Carlos talking. She figured if she could play into his ego, then Booker and Pat could sneak in and locate them. With a pretend gasp, she pointed at the watch and asked Carlos, "So you have the same watch as well?"

Carlos responded, "Yes, of course. It's a symbolic watch for our group. Do you know what it stands for?"

Mariana sat down next to Shep and held the watch. "Not really. We researched square knots, but it didn't give us any kind of answer. What does it mean?"

Carlos, seeing no reason to not share freely, stood up, emanating with pride. "Our group has been around for over two hundred years. It started with Ned Ludd and his revolt over the automation of the textile indus-try right here in Nottingham. The Luddite Revolts in the early 1800s were the foundation for our society. Greedy factory owners created textile machines that could rep-licate the work that trained lace workers had spent at least seven years perfecting as apprentices and forced them to work in factories in horrible conditions with extremely low pay. Our purpose and mission have evolved over time, and we've taken on a new name. We call ourselves the KNOTs, short for the Knights of Nottingham. Like other knights, we have a code. We dedicate ourselves to the protection of the weak. Nottingham is also where the famous Robinhood took place. Like him, we don't seek glory or fame. We stay in the shadows. We exert influence and investment indirectly to further our cause. We believe that the pace of technological advances must be regulated and that humanity must have more of a say in how technology changes our lifestyles. We aren't against technology per se. We are against the greed and ambition that drives the pace of technological advances faster than humanity can absorb it. Governments, labor unions, world bodies have all failed in this role, and it is left to us to be the invisible hand to strike the right balance. We have representatives all over the world in key positions and we have vast amounts of resources to apply as needed. The Luddites were just the first group to be exploited. Every time there is a technology innovation, the story repeats itself. The square knot, our symbol, represents the unbreakable connection between technology and humanity. Constantly pulling against each other. Humanity is represented by leather and technology is represented by steel. They are inextricably interconnected. We strive to maintain the equilibrium."

Mariana processed his lengthy oration then said, "In a weird way, that sounds somewhat admirable. But your methods are dangerous and hurt the same people you say you are defending. Also, you're only focusing on the potential negative impacts of AI. There are many reasons to be optimistic. For self-driving cars, think of the increased safety on the roads. Think of the increased human productivity from not having to drive that will be created. Transportation could become free. After all, there'll be no more labor costs without drivers. Think of what that will enable for society. All these things will spur new value creation and lead to new jobs.

The Spaniard sat back. "Everything you say is true, but it's happening too quickly. This transition should happen over decades, not a couple years. Society will collapse. We are sacrificing a few to save the many."

Unfazed, Mariana continued, "Tell us about the cyberattack on CellSpot. Why did you do it, and why target me?"

Carlos sat down again, then leaned in close, his wicked smile tightening as his cold eyes locked on hers. He continued, "Sometimes our actions must be lethal to get attention and make people change. It's unfortunate but necessary. The cyberattack was necessary to get people to realize the danger of AI and the impact on society. The pace of autonomous vehicles is accelerating exponentially. At this rate, before we know it, millions of working-class jobs will be gone and the gap to retrain these people and create new jobs is years away at best. The wealth divide will grow even worse, and social unrest will overflow. We believe it's necessary to slow it down until everyone is better prepared for the change. AI in general will become a massive issue for society, and we decided self-driving cars would be a good industry to highlight. You weren't a target. Just an opportunity, but now you've become a liability. I realize that won't make you feel better, but it's the truth."

As his words settled in, Mariana felt a cold dread spread throughout her body. A heavy throb began to pulse incessantly behind her eyes as the intention behind his words rang clear. Shep sensed her anguish. He felt it too.

"Why are you telling us all of this?" Shep blurted out. "What are you going to do with us?" His normally calm voice became panicked. "We just want to clear our names. We don't want trouble with you."

Unemotionally, Carlos responded, "I understand, but unfortunately your persistence to find us has left us in a tough spot. As you can imagine, we can't let you tell the world about our organization. Right now, I plan to hold you here. I have some pressing activities I need to attend to today, so you will stay with my guards in another room, and we'll continue this discussion later."

Before Shep and Mariana could react, the two guards grabbed them aggressively and attached plastic zip ties to their hands behind their backs. They removed their phones, and then they led them out of the room, back into the cave, down a hallway, and into a room that appeared to be an old jail cell with an iron gate and stone walls. They were instructed to sit and wait.

Mariana leaned over to Shep and whispered, "Where the hell are Booker and Pat? What's taking them so long?

I sent our distress code a long time ago."

Shep said, "I know. I've been thinking the same thing. They should've been here by now. Do you think they were caught trying to get into the building? Do you think they are being held also?"

Mariana groaned. "Or, even worse, do you think they were killed?"

FIFTY-THREE

THE BIG EVENT

Mountain View, California

CellSpot's PR event had just started. Executives were giving various presentations to the audience about the current state of the industry and CellSpot's tremendous growth. Raj was in the back room pacing back and forth focusing on his upcoming announcement and pumping himself up. The demo car was next to him and all set to go. Tess was going over her checklist one more time and leaning into the car to look at how the touch screen was responding to her controls. Raj saw her and walked over.

"Tess," he said. "Here we are, finally! I'm so excited to make this announcement and do the test drive. Is everything looking good on your end?"

"Yes. We're all ready for you," replied Tess. "We'll be watching from the back room monitors so we can adjust anything that doesn't respond correctly in real time."

"Awesome. This is going to be historic. You've done an incredible job filling in for Mariana. Thank you so much."

Tess glanced up at Raj with a bashful expression. "Thanks, Raj. I'm just happy to help get this over the finish line." Tess grabbed her stuff and hurried out of the room. She had so many conflicting thoughts. While she was happy to receive the praise from Raj, she was becoming increasingly concerned about Mariana's absence and what it could mean.

One of the marketing leads signaled to Raj that he was up in a couple minutes. The last presenter was just finishing up. Raj checked his outfit and looked in the mirror to make sure his make-up and hair still looked right. He also fidgeted with the wireless mic strapped to his head even though he knew it was completely controlled by one of the production crew remotely sitting in the operations room.

With his winning smile in place, he climbed into the car and turned it on. After about thirty seconds, the lights went dark, the screen opened wide revealing the car to the audience, and music started to blare out of the speakers. The famous beat of *We Will Rock You* by Queen focused the attention of the audience. The spotlights turned on and circled around the stage, eventually coming together as one on the car. A huge monitor on the back wall of the stage came to life and the audience saw a live image of Raj behind the wheel. The audience erupted in a loud cheer as Raj pumped his fist and started slowly driving the car out onto the stage. The music continued to draw the crowd's growing excitement.

Raj drove across the stage and came to a stop at a pretend parking spot. Suddenly, the parking spot lit up with multi-colored LED lights and the monitor image changed from a camera looking at Raj to a camera focused on the car's touch screen. An image of the charging system appeared on the touch screen. A notification started blinking saying "Car is Charging." On the top portion of the huge monitor a big message was displayed saying, "Wireless EV Charging is Here." At the same time, the music changed to *We are the Champions*, also from Queen, and Raj stepped out of the car. The audience went crazy. Everyone's phone was out snapping pictures and videos. Raj walked across the stage casually taking in the moment, while the music pumped out the tremendous energy of the song.

As Raj got to the podium, the music died down and eventually the audience became quiet.

Raj shouted, "Well, how about that!"

The crowd erupted in applause. Pausing for effect, Raj began again, "Wireless charging for EV's is here. Just think about it. Wherever you stop your car, it can now be charging in the background. No more concerns around range. No more concerns about finding a charging station that is available. No more worries about installing charging cables in your garage or in your front yard. We all expect this from our iPhones, why not with our cars too? The future has arrived."

The audience started cheering again and a video started playing on the big screen explaining the technology and how it could work with new EV cars as well as with legacy EV cars with an accessory that fit under the car built by CellSpot.

Tess watched the whole event from the back operations room. While she knew this was just a canned demonstration, she realized how nervous she had been the entire time. She forced herself to take a deep breath and noticed that she had been clenching her hands since the music started so she shook out her arms to get her circulation going again. Everyone was cheering and high fiving each other in the backroom. Tess tried to relax and enjoy the moment, but she knew the real test was coming next and didn't participate in the celebration around her.

As the video ended fifteen minutes later, a spokesperson announced to the audience that on the big screen they would see Raj and three selected journalists as they took a ride in a self-driving car. The entire drive would be captured over a livestream and broadcast for everyone to follow. They would navigate the car to a real-life wireless charging station that had been set up several miles away.

The big screen bedazzled with light again, and then the livestream of Raj and the journalists began as they walked towards the car and piled in. There were various camera angles that had been set up in the car and the livestream switched between these cameras in regular intervals to show all angles. There was no steering wheel as it was not needed. Instead, there were four captain's chairs, two in the front and two in the rear. They swiveled around so all passengers could turn to each other and talk as a group. There was a huge touchscreen on the front panel for the front passengers and a touchscreen on each of the side doors for the passengers in the back.

After a few minutes of chatter and playing with the various options on the touch screens, Raj addressed the journalists. "One of the cool things about this specific car is that you can personalize the AI voice service with whatever name and tone you want. I have named him *Spot*, short for CellSpot." Raj then addressed the car, "Spot, drive to a nearby wireless charging station so we can charge the battery."

The car responded, "Hello, Raj. Setting a course for the nearest wireless charging station. It will be a five-minute drive with current traffic. I will start moving as soon as all four passengers have their seat belts connected."

One of the journalists looked down and realized she hadn't fastened her seat belt. Her face turned red as she scrambled to secure it. This got a big laugh from the audience watching in the auditorium. The car turned on and started navigating out of the parking lot.

Raj swiveled his chair around to face the journalists as the car started driving through the streets. "We have been working on wireless charging as a top-secret project for several years now. As you can imagine, there are numerous technical challenges that needed to be solved. As an example, all cars are made differently and the distance between the bottom of the car and the wireless charging pad is very important for efficiency.

We struggled with this for some time until we developed a dynamic part that gets installed underneath the car. When the car is parked, this part will sense the charging pad and will move down automatically until it is at the optimum distance. By creating an industry standard for this approach, we can solve the charging efficiency problem for all cars at the same time versus each car maker designing their own model that won't work across the industry. The AI software in the car ensures that the car has aligned itself correctly with the pad and the receiver under the car. We also designed a cover that slides over the receiver when the car is in motion and only opens when the car is parked and aligned with the charging pad, so it stays clean. This dramatically helps with charging efficiency as well. Any questions so far?"

The journalists immediately started peppering Raj with technical and business questions related to this innovation. Everything was going exactly as planned, and the audience was captivated by the question-and-answer session that was occurring while the journalists were enroute to the wireless charging station.

Suddenly, one of the journalists in the back row looked up and said, "Hey, we're heading towards a red light. Why isn't our car slowing down?" As the other passengers in the car processed what the journalist had said, they turned around to look and see that the car was heading into the intersection at a fast speed.

The journalist in the front yelled out frantically, "Watch out for the bus on the right! It's coming directly at us!"

There was a huge crashing sound, and the cameras and livestream went dark. Everyone in the audience was eerily quiet, waiting to see what happened. Nothing happened. The livestream remained dark with no audio for at least a minute.

Finally, the lights came on in the auditorium. A spokesperson approached the microphone, cleared his throat, then announced in a high-pitched voice, "I'm sorry to announce but there has been an accident. Emergency vehicles are enroute, and we will provide updates as soon as we hear from the authorities. Currently, we haven't been able to communicate with Raj or the other passengers. Please be patient as we determine what has occurred and if people are injured."

FIFTY-FOUR

REVELATIONS

Nottingham, England

Sitting in the cafe, Pat and Booker tried to stay relaxed but couldn't stop fidgeting. It had been well over a half hour and still no audio on the wire nor pings on the tracking devices. They talked it over and finally decided they needed to act. They agreed that they would both go in together through the front door. There hadn't been too many customers walking in the store since Shep and Mariana went in so they knew it would be quiet in the showroom. Their plan was to pretend to be shoppers.

"I'll grab the attention of the store clerk to distract him while you scope out the inside and look for other parts of the building and clues to where they might have gone," directed Booker.

Pat nodded tersely. "Just make sure he can't see me snooping around. It's hard to tell how big the shop is."

"Well, if need be, I'll hold him hostage and force him to take us to the boss's office."

While they were finalizing their plans, Booker's phone rang. He glanced at the number. "It's headquarters," Booker said. "I'm sure they're wanting a status update. I'm going to step outside for a minute."

Pat started taking notes when she overheard the couple at the table next to her talk about going on the *City of Caves* tour. Pat's ears perked up as the man described the caves to his wife. She quickly pulled out her phone and searched Nottingham and caves. She read for a while, and then sat back in her seat, stunned. Seeing that Booker was still on the call, she grabbed her blue sticky notes and wrote down *City of Caves*, then bolted outside and handed Booker the note. He looked at her quizzically, then quickly completed the call and followed her back inside.

Pat began packing her items up and said in a rushed voice, "You won't believe this. This town is built on a special type of sandstone and there's an extensive network of manmade caves under the city that were developed over centuries. They've discovered over nine hundred caves so far and are still finding new ones. The caves have been used since medieval times for all kinds of purposes. Some of the caves were used as bomb shelters during World War II. I wonder if this building is on top of a cave. If they took Mariana and Shep there..."

"That would explain the sudden loss of communication with the electronic devices," Booker completed her sentence with concern in his eyes. "This is worse than I thought. If they went into a network of caves, we would have no idea where they've taken them by now."

Thinking through the logistics Pat asked Booker, "Should you call Headquarters back and ask for local back-up? We don't know what we're walking into."

"No. We don't have time and we can handle this. I don't want local authorities to slow us down."

Pat looked at him with concern in her eyes and reluctantly responded, "Right. Let's go. We promised them we'd look after them. I feel sick to my stomach."

As they crossed the street to the store Pat explained more about what she had learned. "The type of sandstone found here happens to be perfect for caves, soft enough for tunneling but durable enough not to collapse. They call it the *goldilocks of sandstone*. I wonder how extensive the network is."

"Let's hope we can find the entrance," Booker responded, then opened the storefront door. The clerk was in the back of the store at his computer sitting behind the desk. Booker and Pat split up.

Booker approached the clerk and said, "Hello. Can I get some help looking for a watch?"

"I would be glad to help you. My name is Edward. Is there something specific you are looking for?"

Booker said, "I'm not sure. Can you show me some of the watches in these cases here?" He positioned himself away from any of the other customers and got behind

Edward. Edward pointed to several watches and started explaining the differences between several of them. Booker couldn't see Pat anywhere, so he decided to pull his gun covertly from his jacket and gently placed it on Edward's back.

Booker said in a quiet yet aggressive tone, "Don't make any sudden movements. I have a gun aimed at your back. This is not a robbery. I need to ask you some questions, but I need you to not overreact. Very casually, walk into the back room here so we can have more privacy."

Edward stiffened and then nodded. "Please don't shoot. I will do what you want. There's no reason for you to use the gun."

After they walked into the back room, Booker said, "Edward, two people came in here earlier. You spoke with them about a watch that has a unique square knot band. You introduced these people to your boss named Carlos. I need to know where Carlos took them. You need to show me now."

Edward started fidgeting. "I don't know what you are talking about. I don't know these two people you are describing. I can't help you."

Just then, Pat came into the room and said, "I found a door in the back leading downstairs to what might be a cave entrance. Let's bring him and check it out."

In defiance Edward said, "You can't go in there. It's not allowed." He started to break away from Booker and tried to escape. Booker pulled back and punched him hard with his knuckles right in his windpipe so Edward couldn't scream or call for help. Edward bent over in agony, coughing. Booker took his right arm and pinned it behind him, almost breaking his elbow. Edward grimaced hard but was still trying to recover from the blow to his neck so his resistance was futile. They moved towards the entrance, forcing Edward to start walking. They descended the stairs slowly, guns out, listening for any strange noises. When they finally got to the bottom and walked through the hallway, they came to a steel door blocking their path. Pat examined the keypad and laser fixture on the side.

"It looks like we need fingerprint and eye scan detection to open it," Pat said as she looked over at Edward who was trying to free himself from Booker's arm hold. "Let's try him. Maybe he has access."

Booker pulled Edward's arm even higher behind his back to the breaking point and pushed him forward toward the door. Pat grabbed his left index finger and placed it on the pad. The pad scanned the finger and within a couple of seconds, the pad turned green, indicating that he passed. Next, Pat took a hold of Edward's head and forced his face in front of the eye scan. Edward closed his eyes in defiance, so she took both of her hands and pulled apart his eyelids. The scan proceeded and then another green light blinked. Immediately, the steel door started to slide open. Booker could hear voices down the hallway. He was afraid Edward would give up their stealth, so he pulled out his gun and hit Edward on the side of his head, knocking him out cold. Booker dragged Edward over to the side of the hallway and tried to hide him as best he could in an alcove in the rock wall. Satisfied that Edward would be out for a while, Pat and Booker drew their guns and crept down the hallway through the steel door.

There were numerous cave pathways to take, all spreading out in various directions. Booker and Pat turned to each other, and Pat said, "How do you want to work this? Should we separate or stick together?"

Booker responded, "Let's stick together. It may take longer to search, but we don't know the territory at all, and we need to watch each other's backs."

They cleared several cave passages without finding anybody nor any sign of Mariana and Shep, just empty conference rooms or offices.

At the same time Booker and Pat were searching the cave network, Carlos was in his office on a teleconference with several of his partners via a secure line.

Carlos announced, "Our contacts just informed me that the CellSpot press event occurred, and our virus appears to have worked right on time. The car that Raj and some journalists were in went through a red light and was hit by a bus coming the other way. Unclear what the injuries are but regardless, this incident will get national or even global coverage and draw attention to the concerns around AI controlling our cars. Our folks are in place to drive the media coverage and influence the messaging. Congratulations! This is a big step in the right direction. I will let you know as I find out more. The virus should be starting to make its way into Cell-Spot's network of charging stations so we should see additional accidents happen soon. Panic will set in, and all autonomous vehicles will be put on hold until they figure out what's happening. This will be our opportunity to influence more regulation and oversight in the industry. I'll keep you informed as I learn more."

Carlos hung up the line and sat back in his chair contemplating what to do with Mariana and Shep. They were liabilities and needed to be handled as such. Still, he felt the need to tell Mariana that his plan had worked prior to killing them. He wanted to see her face when she realized what she had inadvertently caused. He walked down the hall to the jail cell, entered and sat on a bench by the door.

"Well, I'm happy to inform you that the second virus has successfully penetrated the CellSpot network. This one is much more damaging than the first. Any autonomous vehicle that encounters the virus will be presented with erroneous sensor data and create havoc. Your arrogant CEO was our test pilot, and he was just involved in a crash while showing off your new charging feature to a team of journalists. The best part was this was livestreamed, so now, the whole world will know that these vehicles are dangerous." He watched to see the reaction from Mariana and Shep. They both gasped and their bodies stiffened like stone.

Mariana pleaded to him, "You can't do this. So many innocent people will get hurt. There must be another way to make your point and impact the pace of change. Please call it off!"

Carlos smiled disparagingly. "It's already done. I can't stop it now. I'll come back to talk with both of you later."

Shep yelled, "You're a monster! What you're doing is worse than any impact from technology. You won't get away with this!"

Carlos gave them a cold, menacing look then stood up, kicking the wooden bench aside. He slammed the door closed and locked it, then walked back to his office. He picked up the phone and told his guards what to do with the prisoners, then poured himself a glass of fine scotch to relish the moment.

Booker and Pat were about to give up on the third cave passage when they saw shadows in the distance. They fell back around the corner and hid on both sides of the cave where it was dark. They saw two guards walking towards them about one hundred yards away when they stopped at a gated door and used keys to open it. The guards went inside and closed the door. Booker and Pat glanced at each other and nodded, both sensing that this could be where they were holding Shep and Mariana. As quickly and quietly as they could, Booker and Pat moved toward the gated door. Through the opening they saw the two guards standing over Shep and Mariana who were seated in chairs with their hands tied behind their backs. The guards stood behind them with knives out. Booker stormed into the room and fired his gun at both guards, killing them instantly. The noise from the gunshots was deafening in the caves. Booker knew that whoever else was down here surely must have heard the shots. Pat grabbed one of the knives on the ground and cut the bindings around Shep and Mariana's hands, then gave each of them a hug. Booker checked the guards and found Shep and Mariana's phones and handed the devices back to them.

Booker directed, "We need to get out of here now!"

"Booker, you have to stop Carlos," Mariana said desperately. "Find him. He's started another cyberattack in the US and it's going to cause much more destruction. We need to know how to stop it! I'll try to reach Tess and see if she can abort it on her end."

Booker thought for a second and then said, "Okay. Pat, you take them out of here. I'll go search for Carlos and see what I can do to stop this. We'll meet back at the cafe."

Pat considered the risk of this plan but nodded in agreement. "I got them. Don't worry. You be safe though."

Booker turned and raced down the cave passage where the guards had come from. Pat, Mariana, and Shep headed out the opposite direction.

Meanwhile Carlos heard the gunshots and immediately started reviewing the various security cameras installed throughout the cave network. His eyes widened as he saw two people with guns walking down the main cave passage on an earlier feed. He turned on the live camera feed and saw one of them now hurrying down the passage with Mariana and Shep.

His face flushed and sweat began to bead on his forehead as he pounded his fist on the table in anger. "I can't let this happen," he yelled. "They cannot escape and tell people what they've seen and heard here!"

Maniacally, he went over to another control panel and typed in some commands. Immediately, a soft alarm started buzzing. His control panel showed that he had initiated the self-destruct option for the cave network. He then sent a message to the remaining guards in the operations center and told them to stop the prisoners from making it out of the caves. He gathered some materials and then headed out himself. He knew he only had a short amount of time before the cave network imploded.

As Pat was trying to remember how to navigate out of the caves, Mariana stopped for a second and pulled out her phone to call Tess. She realized there was no signal. Frustrated, she shoved the phone in her pocket.

Right then, two guards rounded a corner and saw the three of them. Pat quickly directed Shep and Mariana behind a curve in the passageway. She took cover as well when the guards started shooting at them but wasn't fast enough. One of the bullets went into Pat's left shoulder pushing her into the wall. Instinctively, Pat fired a couple shots in return with her right arm but wanted to preserve her ammunition. They were trapped from going forward.

Mariana looked horrified at Pat. "Are you okay?" There was a lot of blood on the FBI agent's shirt.

Pat's face was ashen and her expression couldn't hide the fact she was clearly in extreme pain. "I think I'll be alright. It doesn't seem to have hit an artery. I can still use my right hand to shoot if needed. Let's go back the other way and find another exit."

Shep helped Pat regain her balance. To buy time, Pat fired more rounds at the guards. The guards took cover while the three of them jogged in the opposite direction.

At the same time, Booker had been running down various cave passageways searching for Carlos. He turned a corner, and up ahead saw a man walking briskly the other way. He yelled out, "Carlos!"

Carlos turned around to see who was calling his name. Immediately, he realized he should have ignored it. He saw the man running towards him with a gun, so he turned and started dashing down the hall. He had a long way to the secret exit at the other end of the underground network. Eventually, Booker made up the space between them. As he got close, Booker yelled, "Carlos, stop or I *will* shoot!"

Carlos stopped and turned around to face him.

With a sinister smile Carlos said, "You are out of time. This place is going to implode any minute. Without me, you won't be able to find the exit, and you don't have time to go back the way you came. You won't shoot. You're not that stupid."

Carlos turned and started walking briskly again.

Booker said, "Stop! I mean it. I'm sure I can find my way out of here. And your bluff about this place blowing up is probably not true."

Carlos let out a deep sigh and stopped.

Booker said, "You're done. We know about your secret organization. Mariana and Shep are safe. Tell me about the new cyberattack. How do we stop it?"

Carlos laughed maniacally. "Mariana and Shep are not safe," he said. "In the event that they and your partner haven't already been shot by my guards, they won't make it out of the caves before the explosions."

Blood drained from Booker's face, but he stood firm and alert with his gun pointing forward.

Carlos continued, "You can't stop the cyberattack. It's already started. There is no turning back. And you won't get out of here alive either."

BOOM! An explosion somewhere in the cave system rocked the earth. The cave shuddered and debris fell all around them. The ground shook and Booker lost his balance momentarily. Carlos had been expecting it and quickly closed the space between them, knocking Booker's gun away. They started to struggle. As they were exchanging blows, another explosion occurred, this time much closer. A part of the ceiling fell and landed on

Carlos. He collapsed to the ground unconscious. Booker collected himself and realized Carlos had been knocked out. Knowing his time was limited, Booker decided to leave him and raced ahead down the passageway in the direction that Carlos was heading, hoping he would find another exit.

Meanwhile, Pat, Shep, and Mariana kept looking for the exit. Once they sensed that they were not being followed anymore, they stopped to address Pat's wound. Blood was soaking her shirt, and she was starting to feel dizzy. Shep ripped off the bottom section of his shirt and wrapped it tightly around Pat's shoulder, carefully applying enough pressure to make the bleeding slow down. Mariana scoped out the area and motioned for them to circle back in the direction she believed the exit was located. They were walking down the passageway when they heard the series of explosions, and the caves shook, causing debris to fall all around them. The cave network was coming down. They rounded a corner and came face-to-face with a guard. Pat and the guard reacted at the same time, pulling their guns up to shoot. Pat was a split second faster and shot the guard in the chest, dropping him. As another explosion detonated, they stepped over the dead man and kept moving. A few moments later, they came around a corner and saw the staircase leading up to the shop. They burst through the steel door and saw Edward still passed out in the hallway. They ran up the stairs, through the shop, and bolted outside, running down the street. A large crowd of pedestrians had gathered, trying to figure out what the noises were.

"Take cover," Pat shouted to the crowd as the three of them sprinted away.

While Pat, Shep and Mariana managed to escape, Booker, still down in the caves, was getting concerned. He had been running in what felt like circles, but he believed it was still the right direction. Booker's anxiety built with the anticipation of another imminent explosion, and his surging adrenaline kept him moving. When he spotted a large door, he unlocked the deadbolts that prevented outsiders from entering and then opened it. In front of him were more stairs, which he quickly climbed, only to find another locked door that he had to open. Fresh air blasted his face as he stepped into an alleyway several blocks down from the main entrance to the store. With a sigh of relief, he gathered himself and checked the tracking device on his phone to calculate how to get back to the cafe. Another series of explosions boomed from below him; he felt the ground tremor.

Once Pat, Mariana, and Shep found a quiet place that felt secure, they stopped running.

Shep helped Pat sit on the ground and put added

pressure on the gunshot wound. "How are you doing Pat?"

Pat shrugged off the question and asked Shep to grab her phone out of her pocket.

"What do you think happened to Booker?" Mariana asked.

Pat shook her head and said, "I don't know. I hope he isn't caught in the caves. I'll try to text him."

Pat texted Booker but got no response.

Now clear of interference, Mariana pulled out her phone and dialed Tess. The call went through, and Tess picked up.

"Tess! We need to talk."

Tess interrupted, "Mariana! I know. Isn't it horrible? Raj was in an accident during the press event and died. We're all mortified."

Raj was dead? A lead ball formed in Mariana's stomach.

"Listen to me," Mariana said anxiously. "We found the people responsible for the cyberattack. They initiated a new, deadlier attack with the latest software release. You need to stop the release from going broader immediately!"

"Oh my God!" Tess exclaimed. "I figured it was just a fluke accident. Are you sure? As part of the press event, we released the new software to all our existing network."

Mariana gasped. "Yes! You need to trust me. Roll it back and shut down the charging stations! Now!"

"Okay. Crap. I need to go! I'll call you when it's done."

Mariana hung up and turned to Pat. "Anything from

Booker?"

Pat's somber expression conveyed all she needed to know. "No. Nothing yet."

Just then Pat's phone pinged announcing a text message. She looked down and said, "Thank God, it's from Booker. He said he made it out. Carlos did not. He's on his way to meet us."

BREAKING NEWS

Fatal Crash Involving CellSpot CEO and 3 Journalists During Livestreamed Press Event

Autonomous Vehicle Ignoring Traffic Signal Struck by Oncoming Traffic

By Joline Michaels

MOUNTAIN VIEW, CA — During a livestreamed press event, CellSpot CEO, Raj Anand, accompanied by 3 journalists (names not to be disclosed until family members notified) were fatally struck by oncoming traffic when the autonomous vehicle they were in failed to recognize the red traffic signal and entered the intersection. The driver of the oncoming vehicle was transported to Stanford Medical Center and is currently in critical condition. An investigation is underway to determine why the autonomous vehicle malfunctioned causing this tragedy. According to sources at CellSpot, the accident occurred during a broadcast event to highlight the company's newest charging feature...

BREAKING NEWS

Global Extremist Group Behind Cyberattack Responsible for Deaths of CellSpot CEO and 3 Journalists

By Joline Michaels

MOUNTAIN VIEW, CA — According to sources at the FBI, a global extremist group, known to be called The KNOTs, is responsible for the fatal crash last week involving an autonomous vehicle carrying CellSpot CEO, Raj Anand, and 3 journalists respectively named Nancy Blakely, Michelle Johnstone, and Tom Stevens. The KNOTs appear to be a society that believes the pace of technological advances must be regulated and that humanity must have more of a say in how technology changes our lifestyles. They claim to be against the greed and ambition that drives the pace of technological advances faster than humanity can absorb it. Specific members of The KNOTS have not been identified, but sources say their headquarters in Nottingham, England was destroyed recently. No bodies have been recovered from the site...

BREAKING NEWS

U.S. Department of Transportation Announces New Administration to Set Oversight and Regulations Related to Autonomous Vehicles

New Administration to take lead role on emergence of autonomous vehicles

By Juliet Harrison

Washington, D.C. — Due to public outcry and recent crashes related to autonomous vehicles (AV), the U.S. Department of Transportation has created a new Administration to govern the safety of the commercialization of autonomous vehicles nationwide. Congress demanded this move given the lack of one governing body setting safety and testing regulations for autonomous vehicles. This Administration is widely expected to halt new AV launches until standards and testing procedures have been put in place. Other countries are quickly setting up similar governing bodies to manage and control the pace of this new highly disruptive technology...

EPILOGUE

A Few Months Later

It was a beautiful Sunday on the coast. Mariana and Shep were back in Shep's Gym finishing their CrossFit workout. Exhausted and sweaty, they both showered and got changed at the gym.

When she walked out of the women's locker room, Mariana found Shep in his office. "Let's go buy some fresh fish on the pier, and we can barbecue tonight out on the porch."

"That sounds great. And we can get some bread and vegetables at the farmer's market. Let me just shut down my computer."

Shep closed his office, then the two of them jumped on his Vespa and headed out.

Two weeks prior, Shep took Mariana on a hike in Big Sur. At the top of the cliff overlooking the Pacific Ocean, he knelt and proposed to her. After all they had been through, it seemed a natural progression of their blossoming relationship. Mariana had moved into Shep's condo, and life had somewhat returned to normal.

After the dust settled from the disastrous press event and subsequent acknowledgement of a cyberattack, Tess received a promotion from the interim CEO at CellSpot to recognize all the work she had done while Mariana was out. The entire leadership team was impressed with Tess's ability to react quickly and thwart the second, more deadly cyberattack. While she was grateful for the recognition, it didn't feel right. She decided she needed to get back to her passion and find her true balance. She quit her job at CellSpot, reconnected with her CEO contact from the engineering environmental firm, and took a role in the company. The pay was less than she made at CellSpot, but she was excited to focus on what really mattered to her, and the pay was enough to continue to help support her sister. Tess took over Mariana's apartment lease, although Drake moved out with Mariana, much to the disappointment of Tess. Tess got her nerve up to try dating again, but no more dating apps or remote, online relationships. Tess and Mariana still managed to find time to work out in the mornings together.

One morning, while Mariana was deep in thought working at her desk at CellSpot, she got a phone call.

"Hello, this is Mariana," she said.

"Hi Mariana, this is Booker Stevens. How are you? I heard about your engagement. Congratulations!"

"Thanks! Great to hear from you, Booker. All is well here. I was sorry to hear that you didn't get the promotion to Section Chief. I thought for sure you'd get it."

Booker responded, "Thanks for the vote of confidence. It's okay though. I finally learned a big lesson about the importance of following protocols. I hate that I was responsible for Pat getting shot, and I should never have dragged any of you into that situation without clearance and back-up. My superiors at the FBI made it clear that they appreciated what I accomplished, but they couldn't in good conscience promote me since I got the results by ignoring rules and procedures." After a brief pause, he continued, "I understand their position. I know I can get to the next level. It's just going to take more time, and I need to be more patient."

"That's great to hear," Mariana said, then added with a snicker, "Having been on the other side of your investigative powers, I know you'll succeed."

"All the credit goes to you and Shep for deconstructing the complexity of what the KNOTs were doing." He paused and then continued, "And that's actually why I'm calling."

"What do you mean?"

"Well, Pat and I were discussing how effective you and Shep were at following up leads and connecting disparate pieces of data. If you'd ever like to get more in-volved with the FBI, we think you'd both be able to pro-vide amazing feedback working as a team. What do you think?"

Mariana laughed in bewilderment, "Booker, you must be joking! We're done playing detective. That was the most stressful thing I've ever done."

Booker chuckled. "Yes, I realize that, but both of you were persistent and had great instincts. I think you could be very valuable assets for us. Will you at least think about it?"

Mariana was quiet for a moment and then respond-ed, "I highly, highly doubt it, but I will talk it over with Shep and get back to you. Goodbye, Booker."

That same morning Tess ran into her old professor, the CEO of the environmental firm she was now working at. She hadn't seen him since she started with the compa-ny, but she was working primarily remote. She had gone into the office for some follow-up meetings and hap-pened to enter the building the same time he arrived.

"Good morning, Tess! How are you?" he asked while placing his hand on her shoulder in greeting.

Tess responded with a big smile and told him she was enjoying the company and thanked him again for the job.

"It's my pleasure, Tess, and you earned this job. Just like you earned the right to wear that watch," he said, gesturing to her left wrist. "We've been watching you for a long time and have big plans for you."

Tess looked down at her watch, unsure how to respond. When she looked back up, he was gone–stepping into the elevator while answering a call on his phone.

On the other side of the globe along the Riviera, the Italian sat in his veranda that overlooked the Mediterranean while watching the news. He poured himself another drink and then walked across the room and poured a new drink for his companion. They toasted each other and smiled.

The Spaniard raised his glass and said, "Felicidades, buen trabajo!" Then he switched from his native Spanish language to English. "Well, it didn't go as planned, but once again, the ends justify the means. We achieved our goals with just a few setbacks. We've implemented our back-up plans and successfully relocated our headquarters, so let's discuss our next target..."

ABOUT THE AUTHORS

This is the debut novel by Pete and Sheila Thompson. Married for over thirty years, with three children, they decided to follow their passion and write a story together after becoming empty nesters. Taking a break from their primary careers, they have enjoyed developing a process for co-writing and traveling to locations for hands-on research. Pete has an extensive background in the technology space working at companies including Microsoft, Amazon, and eBay, and Sheila has been involved in various not-for-profit organizations including President for the national Boys Team Charity (btc, Inc.). Pete and Sheila grew up together on the same block in San Diego. As they enter a new chapter in life, they plan to transition to this new stage working together versus working independently. Storytelling has become the perfect new adventure.